Whispers of Change

Book Five in the Whispers of New England Series

Sue Mills

Choose The Front Row Media

Whispers of Change

Published by Choose The Front Row Media

Contact: choosethefrontrow@gmail.com

This book is a work of fiction. Names, characters, places and incidents are products of the author's imagination or are used fictitiously. Any similarity to actual persons, living or dead, is coincidental and not intended by the author.

All products/brand names/ Trademarks mentioned are registered trademarks of their respective holder/companies.

Cover Design by Emily Hensley of smallfrymarketing.com

Editing and Proofreading by Red Adept Editing Services

Paperback ISBN: 979-8-9986795-1-3

E Book ISBN: 979-8-9986795-0-6

Blurbs

"After a destitute childhood and tragic early adulthood, Sophie moves into a house owned by Sam, a friendly single father with an unsatisfying romantic history. What will happen once their tenant/landlord relationship becomes something more? Fans of contemporary romance will be greatly pleased with this dramatic, tense, and heartwarming book." Virge B., Proofreader, Red Adept Editing

Author's Note

THANK YOU FOR PICKING up Whispers of Change.

This is the fifth book in the Whispers of New England series and with the fourth book, Whispers of Healing, forms a duet that tells Sam's story.

Healing began where Whispers of Forgiveness ended with Sam returning to an empty house. He did the heavy work with Archie, his therapist and in Change, he's finally ready for a serious relationship.

These books came about because I love Sam, and when Quinn ended up with Caden, I couldn't leave Sam with nothing. I hope you enjoy reading Sam and Sophie's story as much as I enjoyed writing it.

Playlist

Forever – rei brown

vulnerable – Dhruv

Outside – Fiji Blue

It Takes Two – Figi Blue

Day 1 – HONNE

Like Crazy – Jimin

Please Don't Change – Jung Kook, DJ Snake

Falling – Harry Styles

Late Night Talking – Harry Styles

a thousand years – Christine Perri

I Will Follow You into the Dark – Death Cab for Cutie

The Only Exception – Paramore

Contents

Chapter One

Moving In

Sophie

SOPHIE PALMER SEARCHED HER phone for the address Sam Carpenter had given her and tried unsuccessfully to tamp down the nerves making her stomach jump. Sam seemed nice. He'd bought her that coffee before Christmas, and her colleagues at school spoke highly of the family. Now that her contract had been extended through the end of the year, she was eager to move out of the run-down hotel she'd been staying in. But the thought of sharing living space with other people still brought forth butterflies. Blowing out a breath, she pulled up to the house precisely at ten in her white Subaru Outback. When Sam came out to greet her, she said, "Hi! Is Piper here?" Having Piper there might make this a little less awkward.

Sam shook his head. "This is her weekend with her mother." They entered through a mudroom. "There will be room for you to hang a jacket here, and you'll be able to put your car in the garage."

That was more than she expected. "I'd love not having to scrape the window every morning."

Sam started the tour of the house in the kitchen. "Will two cupboards be enough with one shelf and one side of the door in the fridge?" He pulled out the freezer drawer at the bottom. "I have a small freezer in the basement, so you can use this."

"I think that will work. It's a big fridge." *Space for my food is the most important thing to me. Is he going to find it strange if he sees how full I keep my cupboard?*

Sam led her to the bedroom. "The bed is a double because anything bigger would overwhelm the space, and the closet is kind of small." He was apologetic. "This was our study."

Sophie opened the closet door. *I'm embarrassed to admit my clothes will only fill about half this space, but Sam doesn't need to know that.* "I think it's fine." She looked toward the other door in the room and cocked her head at Sam.

"That's what I consider the room's biggest selling point." His smile was wide as he opened the door. "You'll have your own bathroom."

2

"Nice," Sophie murmured. She took in the fluffy white towels nestled in a basket in the corner. "I've never had a roommate provide me with towels."

Sam's cheeks flushed. "My mom kind of dressed the place up when I told her I was going to rent the extra bedroom. She was trying to help me sell people on the space."

With the tour done, they sat in the living room to discuss details. She started with the good points. "You didn't need to do anything extra to sell me on the house. It's stunning," she said. "That fireplace is something."

Sam's cheeks reddened again. "Thanks. I built it. I'm as proud of that as I am about being able to French braid Piper's hair." A smile crossed his face but faded quickly. "I hate to ask, but you said you're single. Is there a boyfriend in the picture? I'd prefer that my daughter not see men coming and going." He looked away for a moment then back at her. "Sorry, I don't mean that the way it sounded."

Oh. We're going right into the nitty-gritty. "I understand what you're asking, and I don't have a boyfriend, nor am I looking for one. Working out at a gym in White River is my social life." She smiled a little. "I spoke with Mr. Donovan last night about the propriety of me living with a student, and he doesn't have any issues with it. What about your wife? Will it bother her? If you reconcile, will you want me to move out?" She looked down at the floor. "I'm trying to get an idea if this will be a long-term solution for me." She snorted, meeting his gaze again. "Well, long-term until June."

"Norah and I aren't married. And we're not working on reconciliation. We get together for a meal once a week, so she'll be here for dinner on Sundays when I have Piper. We're trying to figure out the co-parenting thing and decided it would be healthy for Pip to see us being good to each other." His tone was matter-of-fact.

Sophie ran her hands through her hair. "I seem to have a talent for putting my foot in my mouth as far as you and Piper's mom are concerned. I will never say another word about the two of you."

"Don't worry about it." He leaned forward a little. "Do you want to try the room for a month? We can evaluate if it's working at the end of February."

"I like that idea. When I said 'roommates' earlier... I realize we're going to be tenant and landlord—sorry if it sounded like I was making some kind of assumption." Her embarrassment eased when Sam shook his head and waved his hand, obviously dismissing her concerns. She gave him a small smile. "Does it work for you if I go now to pick up my clothes and check out of the hotel? I'll be back in a couple of hours."

Sam nodded. "Feel free."

When she returned, Sam met her in the driveway and helped move everything into the room. He first grabbed two boxes and flinched at the weight. "Whoa, what do you have in here?"

"Books and journals."

After he deposited them in her room, he said, "I think there was one more box. Let me go get it."

"That one can go to the kitchen." She met him there and began putting dishes and cooking utensils in the cupboard Sam had told her she could use.

As he helped, he looked at her curiously. "I thought you said you were from Rhode Island?"

She smiled. "I grew up there. Why?"

"Your car. Real Vermonters drive Subarus." Sam smirked. "But it's registered in Maryland."

"I've learned you can't be a real Vermonter unless you were born here, even if you drive the unofficial car of the state."

They both laughed.

"Do you have a permanent home in Maryland?" he asked. "Where you keep the rest of your stuff?"

"This is all I have. I've adopted a minimalist lifestyle. Try to keep it light." She turned to the bag of groceries she'd brought in. "I'm a nomad." She began placing cans of soup on the shelf. "Maryland was the last place I stayed long enough to register a car. Maybe Vermont will change that for me."

"When Norah moved out, she took almost everything in the house. I beat myself up over having so little that was mine." He chuckled. "I should have called myself a minimalist, huh?"

"It's nice to be unencumbered."

"I guess." He looked around. "I didn't even have beds for Piper and me. We slept on air mattresses for a few weeks. My parents surprised me with some of their old stuff. It's made things a lot easier."

"Adding kids into the equation probably makes it harder to be a minimalist."

"For sure." He paused. "Piper is with me on Monday and Tuesday night and every other weekend. I won't be able to tell her you've moved in until Monday."

Sam had built a fire in the enormous stone fireplace while Sophie was gone. When she finished in the kitchen, she paused in the living room to look at it longingly.

Sam noticed. "You're welcome to sit out here anytime you want," he said. "I build a fire almost every night in the winter."

"Thanks." Sophie continued to her room, sat on the bed, and looked around. Dark-stained bookshelves lined one wall. *They match the kitchen cabinets. Cherry, maybe?* She smiled. *I'll be able to unpack my books. It's been over three years.*

The remaining walls were a warm caramel color, and the bed was a pencil-post style, covered in a patchwork quilt in warm fall colors.

Sophie walked into the bathroom, which coordinated with the bedroom, and noticed the towels again. *I feel like I'm at a luxury hotel.* She returned to the bedroom and unpacked her clothes. And as she had suspected, they took up only half the closet space. *I should go shopping. Maybe this will be the end of feeling like I must make sure all my possessions fit in my car.*

Almost a year ago, Sophie had realized that for the sake of her mental health, she needed to leave Maryland. She'd started searching for jobs in New England. When she was offered a ten-week position in southern New Hampshire, she took it, hoping another job would follow. Her desire to flee the site of her biggest mistake far outweighed the extreme nervousness caused by the insecurity of a temporary position.

However, housing was more expensive than she expected, and camping had been her solution until the weather grew too cold. She closed her eyes, pictured the campground where she had lived the prior summer and early fall, then opened them and looked around the room. *This is a far cry from my little tent or the budget hotel I've been in since I came to Vermont.* Her body flushed with heat, the same way it always did whenever she thought about money, whether she considered the lack of it or the funds she refused to touch.

Taking a deep breath, she opened the first box of books, placed them lovingly on the shelves, and stood back to admire them before diving into the second box. As she finished unpacking those, Sophie chuckled. The shelves would not be full. *I'll have to buy more books too.*

The third box held her journals, and she placed them on the bottom shelves. When she removed the last one from the box, what she saw beneath it made her gasp. "Oh!"

She backed away from the box, her hand going to her mouth. *I forgot about that.* She kneeled, removed the framed photograph, and sank to the floor. "Oh, Corey." Her voice broke as she said his name. Her fingers ran over the glass covering the picture of her with Corey, handsome and sporting a military haircut. His arm was around her waist, and their smiles were glowing.

Sophie slowly rose from the floor and placed the photo next to her favorite books. "This is the kind of place we should have been living in. We deserved it." She sat down on the bed. "Will you ever forgive me? Or will..." She trailed off and shook her head. "So many people I hurt. But you're the one I truly want forgiveness from, and that absolution can never come."

On Monday night, Sophie walked in as Sam was finishing in the kitchen after dinner. Piper was sitting on the couch with a book, and she jumped up when she saw Sophie. "Hi!"

"Hi, Piper. Do you remember me from school?" Sophie asked.

Piper nodded enthusiastically.

"Did your dad tell you I was going to live in the extra room?"

"Yes. And he showed me which c-cupboards are for you."

Sophie smiled at her. "Yes, I'll need a place to keep my food."

"C-Can I read to you?" Piper waved her book at Sophie, who said she would like that.

As Piper read aloud, the stutter impeding her, Sophie considered strategies to try. Her heart hurt listening to Piper struggle, but she felt more relaxed with the little girl in the house. She hadn't talked to Sam much since she moved in, unsure exactly how she was supposed to interact with him.

Sophie sensed him watching them, and when she looked up, he smiled and flashed a thumbs-up. His eyes were icy blue, but whenever he smiled at her, warmth emanated from them. Shyly, Sophie returned his smile.

Chapter Two
Snow Angels

Sophie

SOPHIE LOOKED OUT THE window as she came out of her room. "Still snowing, huh? I was hoping to make it to the gym this afternoon."

Sam was reading on the couch. "It's not supposed to let up until late afternoon. The biggest storm of the winter."

"I guess the gym is out, then. What are you reading?"

"A book on codependency that my therapist recommended."

A fire was roaring in the fireplace, and the living room was warm and welcoming. Sophie longed to sit down and enjoy it. "The fire is nice. It makes it cozy in here."

Sam smiled at her. "Join me."

She'd been renting the room for three weeks, and he'd offered her a glass of wine a couple of times, but she always declined, feeling like sharing a drink with her landlord might be inappropriate.

"We should talk about how things are going," Sam added. "It's almost been a month."

Sophie sat down in the recliner, nervous that Sam was going to say he wanted her to leave. She waited for him to speak first.

When he did, he smiled, and Sophie felt the warmth there. "I hope you'll want to stay. Pip loves having you here, and she's always my first concern. I was a little nervous about how things would work in the kitchen, but there's been no conflict."

Sophie blew out her breath, still too on edge to smile, but relieved all the same. "This is working out well for me. I'm closer to the school than I was before, so mornings are easier, and you're right about the kitchen. I want to stay, but..." She had met Norah when she came for dinner on Sunday night. "How does Norah feel about me being here?"

"She doesn't have a problem with it." Sam shook his head with a rueful smile on his face. "She was afraid I'd rent to some whack job, so she was pleased to find out I'd rented the room to you. And she's grateful that Piper is getting extra help for the stutter. We both are."

"Can we keep our arrangement open-ended?" Sophie asked. "My contract only goes until the end of the school year."

"Of course."

Sophie nodded. "I'm going to get my book." She stood. "It's not as mind-expanding as yours. I lean toward romance and cozy mysteries." Sophie went back to her room and sat on the edge of the bed for a moment, happy and relieved she was going to remain in Sam's house. It had been years since she'd felt this comfortable.

Still, doubts plagued her about sitting in the living room with him—and she could no longer deny it was because of a growing attraction she'd been unable to quell. Sam had given her no sign that he thought of her as anything other than a tenant, which she hoped meant she'd managed to hide her feelings. On evenings when she worked at the dining room table, she often snuck glances at Sam, hoping to see another of his smiles. He was gentle and loving but firm with Piper, who liked to push the envelope on bedtime and putting away her toys. Watching him as a father only amplified his attractiveness.

Sophie laughed at herself. She hadn't had a crush like this since she was in high school.

When she came back with her book, Sam had fallen asleep on the couch, snoring softly. She curled up in the recliner and watched him for a few minutes before beginning to read. A sense of calm washed over her.

After a while, she heard noises from Sam.

"Oh God, I fell asleep, didn't I?" Sam stretched as he sat up.

Sophie nodded at him, smiling.

"Hope my snoring didn't disturb you," he said. "It looks like the snow has stopped, so now comes the shoveling."

"You don't have it plowed? Or use a snowblower?"

"No. My brothers and I grew up doing physical chores—shoveling, mowing the grass, chopping wood. You name it, we did it. These days, I sit at a desk and don't do much of that stuff. So I shovel for exercise and to keep me humble." He grinned at her.

"Do you want some help?"

"Sure." He looked at her, and his eyes narrowed a little. "Do you have a coat other than that green one? That won't work very well for shoveling."

"I don't." Sophie tittered nervously.

Sam raised a finger before walking to his bedroom. When he returned, he tossed her a heavy sweatshirt. "This should work. It's not that cold out, and we'll probably work up a sweat."

Sophie pulled it over her head, drinking in the scent that she knew must be Sam's. "Thanks."

Sam started her shoveling near the house while he went to the end of the drive, where the town plow had packed the snow high. He was nearing the middle of the drive when he lobbed a snowball at her back.

She whirled around. "Hey, what was that?"

"You can't shovel without a few snowballs being thrown."

Sophie packed snow into a ball and threw it back at him. It hit him square in the chest, and he staggered from the impact, then flashed a smile.

Oh God, that smile. It does me in.

When the driveway was clear, Sam dropped onto the lawn and lay on his back in the snow.

"What are you doing?" Sophie asked.

"Second rule of snowstorms—make a snow angel." He spread his arms and legs to make the angel.

"I haven't done that in ages." Her mind traveled back to the winter storms that used to hit the coast where she lived as a child, ones that brought as much wind and rain as they did snow. Lying in that wet snow was not appealing when you had no proper winter coat and no way to dry your clothes. "We didn't get a lot of snow where I grew up."

"You're living in a snow belt now. It's your chance to make up for lost time."

Sophie lay hesitantly in the snow and mimicked his movements, then she grasped the hand he extended to help her up.

He put his hands on her shoulders and turned her to face the angel she'd made. "Congratulations! The first of many. She's beautiful."

As they walked inside, he said, "I have beef tips in the slow cooker. Do you want to join me for dinner?"

She paused then said, "That sounds delicious." She pulled the sweatshirt off and hung it to dry on a hook in the mudroom.

"It'll be about an hour before they're ready." Sam peeled off his shirt, and Sophie's heart skipped a beat. He turned to toss the shirt into the basket on top of the washer, giving her a view of his well-muscled abdomen, and her stomach twisted.

Does he know that he's torturing me?

Sam walked to his bedroom and came back buttoning a flannel shirt. "I'm going to have a beer. Would you like a glass of wine to warm up, or something else?" He put more wood on the fire as he was talking to her.

Sophie squeaked out, "Sure. I need to change into dry clothes."

She went to her bedroom, peeled off her jeans, and replaced them with sweatpants. She took a couple of deep breaths, hesitant to rejoin Sam before she got herself under control. Because when he came back, wearing that partially buttoned flannel shirt, her lady parts had started throbbing, and they didn't seem remotely done yet.

When Sophie returned to the living room, there was a glass of wine waiting for her, near the recliner. "How did you learn to cook?"

Sam shrugged. "My mom taught us the basics, and Norah was big on splitting the household duties. I sucked at house-keeping, so I took on the cooking."

"I've seen the meals you make for you and Piper. They always look appealing." When they went to the table, Sam refilled her wineglass and put a glass of water at his place. "You're not having another beer? Making me drink alone?" Sophie joked with him.

Sam shook his head, and when Sophie offered to clean up after dinner, he turned her down with a smile.

Before she went to her room, she paused to look at him. "This was fun today, and dinner was great. Thanks."

"Thank you for the shoveling. You were a big help."

Chapter Three

Sam to the Rescue

Sam

ALMOST A WEEK LATER, Sam stretched out on the couch, glad that it was Friday. Piper had been with him all week before a trip to Florida with Norah, but they had left for the airport, and he was looking forward to having the house to himself. Well, except for Sophie. Her standoffishness during the first few weeks had lessened since the snowstorm. She'd become more friendly and had even joined him for a glass of wine one night during the week.

He was thinking about heading north in the morning if Joe had something that needed to be done at the cabin. As he picked up his phone to call his brother, it dinged with a text from a number he didn't recognize.

> *Caden: Hey, Sam, this is Caden. I just ended things with Quinn, and I think she could really use a friend.*

> *Sam: WTF, how did you get my number?*

> *Caden: From Quinn's phone. Please be a friend to her.*

> *Sam: Anything for Quinn, man. What happened?*

> *Caden: She can tell you if she wants to. She can tell you all of it. Thanks.*

Sam sat up and read the exchange again. "What the hell?"

He scrolled through the texts he and Quinn had exchanged over the last couple of months. She hadn't indicated anything was wrong. If anything, his impression was that everything was great. She had even admitted Caden had initially been jealous because of him, but that after their lunch on the mountain, Caden had realized they were now simply friends.

What happened? Sam called Quinn, but it went to voicemail. He texted but got no reply. *Dammit.* Finally, he got up to grab his car keys.

From the parking lot for Quinn's townhouse, he could see the lights were on in her living room. *Should I have come or waited to hear from her?* He drummed his fingers on the steering wheel, then got out of the car. *I need to know she's okay. If she doesn't want me here, she'll tell me.*

He approached her door with a sense of dread and knocked.

After a second, Quinn opened the door and seemed startled to see him. "Sam, what are you doing here?"

"Caden sent me a text saying that you could use a friend because he had ended things with you. What's going on, Quinn?"

Her face crumbled, and she began sobbing.

He reached out and caught her as her knees buckled. After scooping her up, he carried her to the couch and settled her on his lap. He rubbed her back and murmured that she would be okay, the same way he did to comfort Piper. She buried her face in his shoulder, and her tears soaked his shirt. She cried for a long time without saying a word.

After a while, he asked, "What happened?"

With her face still buried in his shoulder, Quinn tried to answer through the sobs. "Late... condoms... Sam... abusive..." The words jumbled together and made no sense to him.

"Sweetheart, what are you saying?" Then he gently asked again, "What happened?"

The sobbing intensified as she tried to talk, but the only word he could make out was "abusive." Did Caden abuse her somehow? Sam never would have expected something like that, but he was aware that the least likely people could be abusers.

"Quinn, honey, did he hurt you? Did Caden hurt you?"

Quinn vigorously shook her head in response.

As the sobs quieted, he lifted her in his arms. "I'm going to put you to bed. I'll stay in your guest room."

Sam carried her to her bedroom and laid her on the bed. He ran back downstairs to turn out the lights and returned to find her on her side with her eyes open, staring at nothing. After a moment, he turned out the bedroom light, pulled a blanket up, and sat down beside her. Rolling toward him, Quinn put her head in his lap.

Sam stroked her hair, hoping she'd fall asleep. When her breathing evened out, he eased her head onto the pillow. She didn't stir, so he moved to the chair and watched her for a long time until he couldn't stay awake any longer.

Sam walked to the guest room, thinking about the night he'd spent there in December. So much had changed since then. He lay on the bed and tried to make sense of the words Quinn had said through her tears. The idea of Quinn being abused enraged him. He hadn't seen bruises, but he hadn't been looking for any either. If Caden had hurt her, Sam would kill him.

Sam tried to remember the other words. *Late. Condom. Sam. Did late mean she was pregnant? Condoms? We used condoms every time we had sex. Why mention me? If Quinn is pregnant, is it my baby? Or does Caden think it's mine? We were only together a few times, and it was over three months ago. If she's pregnant, isn't it more likely to be Caden's?* He fell asleep with these thoughts swirling.

In the morning, after checking on Quinn, Sam went to the kitchen for coffee and found a grocery list on her counter. As he drank his coffee, still trying to figure out what had happened the night before, he decided he would go home to get his laptop because he had assignments to submit, then he would shop for food.

Before leaving, he climbed the stairs to Quinn's room and found her still asleep or pretending to be. "Quinn," he whispered.

"What?" Her voice was flat.

"I'm going out. I'll be back as soon as I can."

"You don't have to come back."

"I'm coming back. Try to rest."

His house was empty when he arrived. *Sophie must be at the gym.* He sent her a text telling her something had come up, and he didn't know when he would be home. Sophie had started that habit when she went away overnight with her friend Ali from the gym, and Sam had continued it, letting her know when he went up north. He was usually less cryptic in his texts, telling her he was going skiing or would be working with Joe, but mentioning Quinn to Sophie felt odd to him.

Quinn was asleep when he returned, so he put away the groceries and finished some assignments for his online master's class. After he had some lunch, he checked on Quinn again and found her awake, once again staring at nothing. "Do you want some lunch?"

"No."

He sat down on the bed, and she leaned against him.

"Thank you for being here," she said, her voice breaking on the last word.

Sam rubbed her back and stroked her hair as she wept. He fell asleep, not waking until the sky was dark and he was hungry.

He stretched and could tell Quinn was awake. "Do you want a burger?"

"No."

"You need to eat something."

"I'm not hungry. But I'd like a glass of wine."

Sam cooked two burgers, poured a glass of wine, opened a can of beer, and took them all to her bedroom, hoping she would eat the burger.

Quinn reached for the wine but refused the food. Then she looked at his beer. "I bought that for Cade."

"Do you want to talk about it?"

Quinn looked away. "I can't."

Sam ate and refilled her glass.

After drinking the second glass, she said, "I need to sleep. How can I be this tired when all I've done is lie in bed all day?" She looked down at her T-shirt and then up at Sam. "Did you undress me? Put me in this?"

"No. You must have changed during the night." *I've accepted that all we are and will ever be is friends, but seeing her naked would have pushed the envelope.* He smiled to himself. *Should I tell her that? Will she find it funny? No. She will not see humor in anything tonight.*

"I can't remember anything about last night except, except Caden walking out." Tears streamed down her face, and she burrowed into the blankets.

On Sunday afternoon, Sam was sitting on the couch, watching a basketball game, when Quinn came downstairs. "You're up."

"Yeah, I needed to shower and get ready to go to work tomorrow. Thank you for being here. I feel like I owe you an awful lot."

"You don't owe me anything. It's what friends do."

"You can go home. I'll be okay. What'd you do with your daughter?"

"She's in Florida with Norah. I'll leave tomorrow. I bought food for dinner tonight. Will you eat?"

Quinn sighed and twisted her hair into a messy bun. "I'll try. I'm not sure if I'm hungry or what I'm feeling."

"Come keep me company while I get it ready."

"I can cook. You've done enough."

"Let me take care of you one more night." He poured her a glass of wine and opened a beer. "Will you tell me what happened?"

She sighed. "I can't. If I talk about it, I'll start crying, and I can't cry anymore."

"He gave his permission." Sam watched Quinn's face contort in confusion. "Caden's text said, 'She can tell you all of it.' That seemed kind of mysterious to me."

"I will tell you, but I need a little more time. You came to my rescue. You deserve to know the entire story."

"Okay, when you're ready."

Chapter Four

Did He Get Lucky

Sophie

SAM WAS AT THE table on Monday night when Sophie got home. The empty house surprised her on Saturday morning until she received his text. She appreciated the way he had followed her lead and let her know when he was going to be gone. Sophie had been totally independent and alone for a long time—knowing someone cared where she was and cared enough to let her know where they were, felt good.

"Hi there," Sophie called from the kitchen. She had wondered all weekend if he was with a woman. "Did you get lucky this weekend?"

"What?" He sounded irritated. "Why would you say that?"

"You're never gone unexpectedly. If you go to work on the cabin, you tell me that. I figured maybe you met someone. Piper's gone. It's the perfect time."

"No, nothing like that."

Sophie had been putting groceries away as she talked and finally turned to look at him. The grim frown on Sam's face was more serious than anything Sophie had seen from him. "My God, what happened?" she asked. "You look terrible. I was teasing."

"A friend of mine was in rough shape because her boyfriend ended their relationship. I let her cry on my shoulder, then hung around in case she needed something."

"You look rough. She must be a close friend."

"Her name's Quinn. She's a former girlfriend. We dated when I was in college."

"And you successfully transitioned to friendship? Congrats on that. It's not an easy feat."

"It's recent. We hadn't seen each other in a long time."

"Is she okay now?"

"She pulled herself together enough to go to work, so yeah, she's in better shape." Sam rubbed his jaw. "Let me ask you something. Quinn was out of it when I arrived. She cried for well over an hour. I asked what had happened, and she tried to talk through the tears, but it was incomprehensible. I could only make out stuff like 'abuse' and 'abusive.' I asked if Caden had hurt her, and she vehemently said he hadn't. But I can't help wondering what her words meant. What do you think?"

Sophie pulled out a chair and sat across from him. "Do you know the guy? How did you find out about the breakup, anyway?"

"Caden texted me and said she could use a friend. I've met him twice. He's a doctor, for Christ's sake!"

"Anyone can be an abuser, but isn't telling you he broke up with her a little weird?" Sophie frowned and put her hand on top of his. "You're genuinely upset by this, aren't you?"

"Yeah. I mean, if he hurt her, I don't know what I'll do. On Friday night, I was ready to kill him."

Sam

That afternoon, remembering Archie's words about exercise, Sam had taken advantage of Piper being gone, to go for a run. And then he kept it up throughout the week. He spent some time online looking at half marathons and 5Ks. After not racing for several years, he wanted to get back into it.

He texted Quinn every day, making sure she was okay, and late Friday afternoon, he bought dinner to share with her.

Sam: I bought us a pizza for dinner. Will be there shortly.

Quinn: Okay.

When he arrived, Quinn greeted him with a hug.

Sam smiled. "I'm surprised you didn't tell me not to come."

"It's Friday night. I don't want to be alone. You wouldn't have listened, anyway."

"Nope." Sam walked into the kitchen to get a beer. Quinn was already working on a glass of wine. "How'd your week go?"

"Caden's sister Claire was here when I got home on Monday. She brought her son Rory. He's eleven weeks old. Something about holding a baby takes all the stress away in the moment." Tears filled her eyes. "I thought I'd be holding Caden's baby at some point."

"Are you—are you pregnant?"

"No," Quinn said, wiping her eyes. "Why do you ask that?"

"Friday night, you said something about being late. I thought you were talking about your period."

Quinn hesitated. "I probably was, but no, I'm not pregnant. When does Piper get back?"

"They fly in tomorrow afternoon. She and Norah are coming for dinner tomorrow night."

"So I don't get to have you all weekend, huh?" She smiled at him.

Stricken by guilt, Sam leaned forward. "Will you be okay?"

"I'll be fine. I'm giving you a hard time." Quinn shook her head. "You must have missed her."

"Piper? Yeah, I have, but we've talked every night."

"Not missing Norah?"

"Nope, not at all. I've learned to enjoy my own company, and I've also been spending some weekends up north." He told her about reconnecting with his family and the work at the cabin. At the top of the stairs, she hugged him again before going into her room.

In the morning, Sam found Quinn sitting on the couch with two mugs of coffee.

She patted the cushion beside her. "Sit."

After Sam sat down, Quinn took a deep breath. "Caden was supposed to get married right after New Year's three years ago. He went home early on New Year's Eve and found his fiancée naked, wrapped in white Christmas lights, riding some random guy. He told him to get the fuck out of his house and went into the bathroom, where he lost his lunch. When Caden came out, they were both gone, and he's never seen her again."

"Jesus, Quinn!"

"I know. He'd been with her for nine years and discovered she'd been screwing around most of that time. It messed him up. I'm the first woman he let himself care about since that happened. Back in December, when I told him you stayed in my guest room, he had a flashback to that day. His therapist told him it was a panic response to trauma. It happened again on New Year's Eve when one of his friends asked me to dance.

"Two weeks ago, my period was late. I wasn't pregnant—I took two tests—but I felt like he should know. When I told him, he lost his mind. He stumbled outside, barefoot, in the snow, to catch his breath and..." Quinn's voice broke. "Honestly, he wanted to get away from me because he was convinced I'd been screwing around, probably with you. For three or four minutes, he was not the man I'm in love with. When he calmed down, he apologized, and we talked it out. Then last week, he came back only to tell me we can't be together. That what he did verged on abuse, and he wouldn't be an abuser. Nothing I said made any difference."

Sam blinked. "I don't know what to say."

"Yeah, it's a lot. We'd been together about six weeks when he told me about the broken engagement. He told me how he fell apart, and his friends stayed with him. That's why he texted you and why Claire stayed with me. He arranged it. Does that sound like an abuser?"

Sam shook his head.

"I miss him. I miss his good-morning texts. I miss his calls at ten thirty every night." Quinn had remained composed as she told him Caden's story, but now tears were streaming down her cheeks.

Sam took her in his arms. "I'm so sorry you're going through this." He held her for several minutes until she pulled away from him.

"Do you remember the discussion we had about me not waiting for you to get over Norah?" she asked.

He nodded.

"I am going to wait for Caden to come back to me. I was single and content before he came into my life, and I'll be single and content until he gets himself together. I truly love him, and I will not let go of that."

Sam got ready to go home around noon. "I'm sorry I have to leave."

"I know. I'll be fine." When he looked skeptical, Quinn said, "I will not get drunk. I will not go out and score some drugs, and I'm not suicidal. I'll be fine."

"You'll call me if you're tempted to do any of those things?"

"Absolutely! Now go home and get ready to love on your daughter."

Chapter Five

Missing Cookies

Sophie

SOPHIE PAWED THROUGH HER cupboard, murmuring to herself, "Where the hell are my cookies? I know I left them in the front." After she removed two cans of soup and a box of crackers, she finally saw the package jammed in the back. It felt much lighter than it had when she stored it the night before.

She unfolded the top and saw only two cookies. "What the f..." Sam was in the living room reading with Piper, and Sophie reminded herself not to swear in front of the little girl. "Sam, did you eat my cookies?"

He looked surprised. "No, I don't get into your cupboard."

Sophie's irritation increased as she heard the laughter in his voice. "It's not funny! The bag was almost full. Now I have two left. And it was stuffed way in the back, not where I left it."

"You must have eaten more than you remember."

"*No*, I didn't."

Sam went into the kitchen, with Piper trailing behind him.

Sophie crossed her arms, looking at them both. "Someone has been in my food. I just bought those cookies yesterday." She took a breath. "Piper, did you eat my cookies?"

Piper shrank behind Sam and didn't answer.

He turned to her. "Pip, did you get into Sophie's cupboard?"

She nodded and kept her eyes on the floor.

"I thought you told her the cupboard was *my* space." Sophie could feel herself spiraling out of control. "What else has she done? Has she gone into my room?" *Get a grip on yourself. She's a child.*

Sam held up his hands. He leaned down toward Piper, who had begun to cry silently. "Honey, go to your room, please. I'll be in to talk to you in a minute."

"I'm s-s-sorry." Piper walked to her room, crying all the way.

"What's going on, Sophie? It's cookies. You look like you're about to lose it."

"They were *mine!* The first thing I asked you was if I'd have my own kitchen space. When I buy something and put it in *my* space, I expect no one is going to touch it. I expect it to be there when I need it." Sophie had her hands clasped together, and she was rubbing her thumb against her palm. Her breath was coming in brief gasps.

"Okay, I get it." Sam sighed. "How much did they cost? I'll pay for them."

"You don't get it." She shook her head. "What they cost isn't the point. I... don't know if I can stay here."

"Over cookies?" Sam looked shocked. "I thought things were going well. We enjoy having you here."

"I thought so too." Sophie angrily brushed away the tears threatening to leak from her eyes. "I need to clear my head. I'm going for a drive."

The village was dark as Sophie parked in front of Cara's Coffee Shop, but it was closed. Nothing stayed open past five on a Friday night. She leaned her head against the steering wheel. *I'm being irrational. Sam's right. It's just cookies. I made a little girl cry.*

Sitting back, she took several deep breaths and squeezed her eyes tightly shut, trying to block out the vision of an empty cupboard.

Drawing a shaky breath, she pulled her phone out of her pocket and quickly tapped a message to the therapist who had been her lifeline for the last year and a half.

> Sophie: *Sorry to bother you on a Friday night. Do you have a minute to talk?*

Her phone rang almost immediately, and Sophie began to relax as she and her therapist talked.

When Sophie came back to the house an hour later, Sam was sitting in the living room.

She stopped in the kitchen for a glass of wine, took a deep breath, and walked in to face him. "You didn't need to wait for me. I'm a big girl."

Sam raised his eyebrows. "I was concerned."

She studied the wineglass, then raised her eyes to face Sam. "I overreacted."

"You think?"

Sophie raised her wineglass to her lips. "Are you familiar with the term 'food insecurity'?"

"Yes, I'm aware of that."

"I've had times in my life where I was food insecure, so I'm obsessive." She took a sip of her wine. "I could keep my food in my room. I've done that in other spots I've rented. But..." She put her glass on the coffee table. "I'm trying to act like an adult who lives in a house, instead of a transient who keeps all her stuff within arm's reach."

"You mean like a homeless person with a shopping cart?"

Sophie's eyes widened, and a wave of nausea roiled her stomach. Her hand went to her mouth as she took a few deep breaths.

Sam flinched. "Jesus, I'm sorry. That's what came to mind when you mentioned a transient."

Sophie forced a small laugh. *He has no idea how close he is to the truth.* "Similar. Would you mind if I talked to Piper about it? I didn't mean to come at her like that." Sophie hoped Sam wouldn't ask a lot of questions. *But if he does, I'll answer them. It's nothing to be ashamed of.*

"That's a good idea. I talked to her after you left, and she knows she was wrong to get into your space. I'll be surprised if she does it again." His eyes bored into Sophie. "Are we good? You don't still feel like you need to leave?"

Her heart fluttered as she absorbed his stare. "I'm not leaving. We're good."

Piper was on the couch, watching television, when Sophie entered the living room the next morning.

"Is it okay if I sit with you, Pip?"

When the girl nodded, Sophie sat down. "I want to talk to you about last night."

Sam moved into the dining room, and Sophie felt him watching them. She couldn't blame him for being protective—she could see the nervousness on Piper's face. "I'm sorry I lost my temper. I shouldn't have reacted like that. Can I explain why I did?"

Piper nodded slowly.

"When I was growing up, about the same age that you are now, sometimes I didn't have enough food, so when I'm sure I have something to eat and then it's not there, I get upset."

"Like the c-c-cookies?"

"Yes, like the cookies."

"A c-couple of kids never bring snacks. Is that what you mean? D-Did you not have snacks?"

"Sometimes I didn't."

"Did your teacher give you snacks? That's what happens with the kids in my class."

"That's good."

"I haven't been in your room." Piper looked at Sophie with big, expressive blue eyes. "*Really.*"

Sophie wanted to reach out and hug her. "I know. I was angry and lashing out, and I shouldn't have said that. Would you like to see my room?"

Piper shrugged.

Sophie stood. "Come on." She led the girl down the hall and opened her door.

"You have a lot of books," Piper said as she looked around.

"I do." Sophie chuckled. "I have some chapter books on the shelves that I use with my students. Would you like to pick one out? We could read it together."

Piper clapped her hands. "Yes! I love b-books!"

They selected a book together, then Sophie said, "It's a pretty boring room, huh?"

"It's okay."

When they walked back to the living room, Sophie asked, "So, are things okay between us? Still buddies?"

Piper nodded.

"If you ever want something from my cupboard, please ask me," Sophie said. "I'll share with you."

That night, Sophie lay on her bed, still beating herself up over her actions the night before. She journaled about it and was trying to decide which book she wanted to read when there was a knock on her door. When she opened it, Piper was standing there with a nervous smile on her face.

"We're having movie night. D-d-do you want to watch with us? We'll share our p-popcorn with you."

"I'd like that." Sophie was pleased to see Piper's smile blossom from tentative to confident. She followed Piper to the living room and sat in the recliner.

Piper filled a bowl with popcorn and handed it to her.

"What are we watching?"

"*Lady and the Tramp*," Sam said. "We usually have some kind of animal theme going on."

Sophie smiled, and they settled in to watch the movie. When it finished, Piper was nearly asleep, and Sam carried her to bed.

A vision from long ago flitted through Sophie's mind. A man who had carried her the same way Sam carried Piper. She shook her head then closed her eyes, hoping to see that picture from her childhood again. *Was it a memory?*

Sam returned. "Sophie, I'm going to have a beer. Would you like a glass of wine?"

Her eyes fluttered open. "That sounds good."

Sam handed her the wine before settling back on the couch.

"This was fun." She tucked the vision away. "Thanks for inviting me to join you."

"It was Piper's idea."

"That touches my heart." She smiled. "I'm surprised you don't have a dog, considering how much Pip likes animals."

"Shhh, don't say that too loudly. I don't want her getting any ideas." Sam laughed. "We'll get a dog at some point, but I need to get squared away with what I'm doing about the house." Sam fiddled with the label on his beer bottle, then raised his eyes to look at Sophie. "You were good with her this morning."

"Thanks. I'm sorry that I lost it last night."

"She was wrong to get into your stuff. Lessons learned all around."

Sophie nodded. "What do you mean about the house?"

"I need to buy out Norah's share by June. I wasn't sure initially if I'd be able to keep it or not. But I finally paid off the last of my student loans this month, and I've gotten a promotion at work, so I should be okay, financially speaking." He took a sip of his beer. "I started the process at the bank this week. I'm going to refinance in my name, get her name off the deed."

"It's a nice place. I'd want to keep it." She took a swallow of her wine. "Congrats on the promotion. How's your friend doing?" She knew he'd had dinner with Quinn on Thursday night.

"Quinn's okay. It's been a few weeks, and the time passing seems to make it easier."

"Did you find out about why she was talking about abuse that first night?"

"Yeah, her boyfriend. Well, I guess he's her ex-boyfriend at this point. He has some stuff in his past that he's dealing with." Sam described the issues, and Sophie listened, sympathetic to Quinn and Caden both.

After they finished their drinks, Sophie returned to her room. She closed the door and leaned against it. *This is what a family looks like. Even though it's just Sam and Piper, they're family.* She picked up the picture of her with Corey. *We should have had this, Cor.*

Sam

Sam awoke on Sunday morning, thinking about the conversation with Sophie. He picked up his phone and sent a text.

> Sam: Hey, Caden, it's Sam. Wondered how you are?

> Caden: Is Quinn okay? Has something happened to her?

Sam: She's okay, missing you, but that's not why I texted. She told me what happened. The entire story. You arranged support for Quinn. Is someone supporting you?

Caden: I've got friends, but honestly, I want to be left alone. And those friends think I'm crazy for walking away from the best thing that ever happened to me. That I'm seeing a therapist twice a week and have a prescription for anti-anxiety drugs probably confirms it.

Sam: My anti-anxiety drug was beer. Yours are better.

Caden: I hope so. I'm not the most pleasant person to be around right now.

Sam: I hope you can get on top of it.

Caden: I've been dealing with it for three years. I'm not feeling hopeful.

Sam: Hang in there, man. I'm a no-judgment zone if you need a friendly voice.

Caden: Thanks, good to know.

Sam: One more thing, in case you're wondering. Quinn and I aren't planning to rekindle anything. We both agree we're better off as friends. And her heart belongs to you.

Caden: I recognized that when we had lunch at the mountain. I don't want her waiting for me, though. I feel like I'm going to be fucked up forever.

Sam: She's very loyal and stubborn. She will not move on easily.

Caden: She texts me every few days. I'm ignoring them. I'm not good for her.

Chapter Six

Can I Run With You

Sophie

A COUPLE OF WEEKS after her *cookie meltdown*, as Sophie thought of it, Sam was working at the table when she came home. "Okay if I join you?"

"Sure." Sam closed his laptop. "You're later than usual."

Sophie filled a glass with water before sitting down. "Yeah. Long meeting after school, which meant I was late getting to the gym. And when I finished later than usual, I didn't want to cook, so I went to a restaurant with Ali. What are you working on?"

"I just submitted my final project. I have a couple of courses left that I can take in the fall. My plan is to enjoy the spring and summer."

Sophie took a deep breath. "Can I ask you for a favor?"

"What's that?"

She took a swallow of water and drummed her fingers on the table before starting to talk. "You can say no. It won't hurt my feelings."

He smiled. "Okay, but what do you need?"

Her heart thumped at his grin. "You've been going out running. Have you ever run in a race?"

"Yeah, I raced in college and a few times after I graduated."

"I run at the gym. I do five miles a few times a week."

"That's great."

Sophie fiddled with her hands. "I started because..." She hesitated. Did she want to tell Sam that her therapist had urged her to work out? "Well, never mind that—it's not important why I started. The school is putting on an end-of-the-year carnival as a fundraiser, and there's going to be a 10K race."

"Six miles. I like that distance."

"I signed up for it." Sophie ducked her head self-consciously. She wanted to challenge herself, but she'd realized she knew nothing about running in a race.

Sam's smile widened. "Outstanding! Have you raced before?"

"I've never even run outside!" She sighed. "That's the favor I need. Could I run with you? Can you, like, maybe train me?" She took another long swallow of her water.

Sophie watched, wondering what Sam was thinking, as he considered her request.

Finally, he nodded. "Yeah, I could do that. Let's look at the calendar and figure out a schedule." As he opened the calendar app on his phone, he said, "Let's try to avoid nights that Pip is here."

Sophie nodded.

They marked days on the calendar. Then Sam looked at her. "Are you okay with skipping the gym on days we run?"

"Yeah, I expected to." After they agreed on a schedule, Sophie considered her shoes. *If I'm going to get serious about this...* "I should probably buy running shoes. I'm using cross-trainers at the gym."

After Sam suggested a couple of brands, Sophie went to her room and sank onto her bed, heaving a sigh of relief. All she had thought about for over a week was making this request of Sam. *It would have been so embarrassing if he had refused to let me run with him.* Running at the gym had brought her more satisfaction than she could have imagined, and she wanted to see where she could take it. And being out there with Sam, all sweaty and exhausted, would do nothing to elevate her attraction to him. At least she didn't think so.

Things had been tense for a few days after the cookie meltdown, but since then he'd been very kind to her, making a point of inviting her to eat with him, or letting her know she was welcome to food in the fridge. Piper continued to invite her to join them for movie night. Sometimes Sophie felt like they were trying to make a point about how selfish she'd been with the cookies, and other times she thought they were being friendly.

I can't believe he doesn't have a girlfriend. Is it because of Norah?

Sophie made herself scarce on the Sundays that Norah came over, but she'd returned a few times when Norah was still there. The three of them were usually playing a board game, laughing and teasing one another, and Sophie thought about how happy they seemed. But sometimes after Norah had left, Sophie had also caught Sam drinking a beer and staring at the fire, deep in thought.

He's too handsome and too nice to not be involved with someone. I don't get it.

Sam

Sophie's request had caught Sam off guard. It would be nice to run with someone after not having that consistently since college. The night after she approached him, he spent time on the computer mapping out some five-mile routes in their area.

Sam also thought about Cookiegate, as he had dubbed it. Her distress had surprised him, because she had seemed mellow during the first couple of months she'd been living there and seeing her so distraught had been a shock. He and Piper had walked on eggshells for a few days after the blowup, and he sensed Sophie was doing the same. A few weeks had gone by, and the atmosphere in the house had returned to its relaxed cadence.

On the day Sophie showed Piper her room, when Sam was putting Piper to bed, Piper had confided, "Daddy, there's a picture in Sophie's room of her with a man. Do you think it's her boyfriend?"

Sam had told her he didn't know and reminded her that if Sophie wanted them to know about her private life, she would tell them. But the truth was, Sam was as curious as Piper. Sophie had told him she didn't have a boyfriend, but she was gone for a certain amount of time nearly every night. He wondered if she was really at the gym every day.

Well, in any event, her social life is a lot more active than mine. Sam had taken his discussions with Quinn to heart, and between those and his therapy sessions, he was learning how to be alone.

Sam met Sophie outside the house. "Are you ready?" He grinned at her.

Sophie rolled her eyes and took a shaky breath.

"Let's go." Sam led her to the same path he and Quinn had run on in the fall. But instead of being surrounded by bare branches and withered leaves underfoot, there were soft shoots of grass appearing and buds on the trees. They started off slowly, and when Sophie easily kept pace with him, Sam increased his speed.

They ran for an hour, and back at the house, Sam held up his hand to high-five Sophie. "That was a good run. I love getting outside this time of year." He stripped off his shirt and sensed Sophie watching him out of the corner of her eye as she stretched. Before he went inside, he smiled at her. "Same time, day after tomorrow."

Each time they ran, Sam set the pace a little faster, and Sophie stayed with him. He tracked all their runs, and two weeks in, when Sophie came home the night after their most recent run, she found him studying his laptop and drinking a beer.

"Is that allowed in the training regimen?" she asked with a raised eyebrow.

"It's Friday night—one beer's allowed. What do you think about our training? How's it compare to the gym?"

"Oh my God, I may never run on a treadmill again. I love running outside." A wide smile warmed her pretty face. "How am I doing?"

"What pace did you run on the treadmill?"

"Eight-minute miles for the last month or so."

"I have a confession. When you asked me about running with you, my first thought was what your pace would be, and I figured you'd be slower than my usual pace." At her look, he grimaced. "I know, stupid and sexist. You've amazed me these two weeks. Every time I pick up the pace, you're right there with me."

Sophie snickered. "That first day, I wondered why we were going so slowly." When Sam shared the tracking data with her, she studied it for a few minutes. "So, we stayed at five miles but increased the pace. Are we going to go longer distances?"

"Yeah, and we'll pick up the speed. Plus, probably add some hills. Do you know how many people they expect to race?"

"Over one hundred fifty have signed up already."

"That's a lot for a first-time event."

"The school has a ton of support. A lot of parents have registered and some alums. Plus, some of the older kids."

"Would you mind if I signed up? I haven't raced in a few years, and even before you approached me, I had decided I was going to enter a few this year."

"I wouldn't mind at all. It'll be nice to have a friendly face there."

They looked at their calendars and laid out a schedule for the next two weeks.

Later, Sam was in bed and almost asleep when his phone pinged.

> Caden: Hey.

This wasn't the first time Caden had texted at ten thirty. He told Sam he reached out to him to avoid texting Quinn.

Sam: What's up, man?

Caden: I've been pacing for half an hour. Ten thirty still hits me hard.

Sam: The nights I didn't have my daughter were the ones that killed me. I drank way too much for a couple of months after Norah moved out.

Caden: I'm so mad at myself for not being able to get on top of this.

Sam: I was furious at Norah for leaving, but eventually I figured out I was mad at myself too. For so many things.

Caden: Yeah, I'm mad at myself for being oblivious to what was going on.

Sam: Right there with you, brother. I've forgiven myself and made some changes in my life. I'm not sure I've forgiven Norah, but I've come to terms with her leaving.

Caden: Not sure I'll ever forgive Mary.

> Sam: Understandable.

> Caden: I've got myself together now. Thanks for answering.

Sam put his phone down, reflecting on the convo. *Caden thinks I'm doing him a favor by taking his texts, but the truth is the more times I say I've come to terms with Norah leaving, the closer I get to it being my reality.* The realization was comforting.

Chapter Seven

Resolution with Norah

Sam

SAM WAS LEANING BACK on the couch with his head resting on the cushions and his eyes closed when he heard Sophie enter the house.

The freezer opened, then Sophie said, "Want to celebrate Friday night?" When Sam opened his eyes, Sophie stood in front of him, holding two pints of ice cream. "I've got New York Super Fudge Chunk or Chunky Monkey."

"Whatever you're having is fine."

She scooped ice cream into two bowls and sat in the recliner after handing him one. "You okay?"

"Yeah." He paused. "No, not really. As I was leaving Norah's tonight, she told me her lease is up in May, and she needs to decide if she's going to buy the house."

"What's her alternative?"

"Honestly, I think she wants to move back in here. She hasn't said it in so many words, but she's dropped plenty of hints."

"What do you want?"

"Not that." He laughed ruefully. "I finally have clarity about what I want, and it's not a future with her." He took a spoonful of the ice cream and let it melt on his tongue. "I'm trying to figure out the best time to have the conversation, because it shouldn't happen when Piper is around. I'm thinking about next Friday, so there will be a few days for Norah to digest it. I'll need to find a babysitter."

"Piper might like the talent show the older kids are putting on." Sophie dug her spoon into the bowl. "I was going to invite both of you to come with me, but if you want to talk to Norah that night, I could take her to the show."

"You're sure?"

She nodded.

"That would work, but I need to run it by Norah. We agreed that if Piper was going somewhere with another adult, we each need to be informed about it."

He grabbed his phone to text Norah.

> Sam: *You said you want to talk. I can come over next Friday. Sophie would like to take Piper to a talent show at school. Is that okay with you? It would give us some uninterrupted time.*

> Norah: *I'm fine with Sophie taking her. I'm sure Pip will love it. Do you want to come for dinner?*

He didn't, but it seemed like agreeing to dinner would be the easiest thing.

> Sam: *Sure. I'll be there around six.*

> Norah: *I'm looking forward to it. This will be the first time we've talked without Piper around.*

Sam shook his head and realized Sophie was watching him. "She's looking forward to it. That's not how I'd describe what I'm feeling."

Sam felt like he had learned to control his emotions since the gut-wrenching drive to Boston in November, but driving to Norah's house on Friday, he was as nervous as he'd ever been.

Dinner was already on the table when he arrived, with an open beer at his place.

As they ate, Norah said, "Piper was excited about going to the talent show with Sophie. She likes her, and I think the stutter is getting better."

"Yeah, I've noticed that too."

"How are your classes going?"

"Quite well. I've submitted my major project for the latest course, and now I'm taking the spring and summer off." Sam saw the look of surprise from Norah. "I have two classes left, and they're both offered in the fall."

When they finished eating, Norah said, "Let's go in the living room to talk." She went to the kitchen and poured herself another glass of wine. "I've been meaning to tell you. I'm impressed with how tidy you're keeping the house. The messiness was one thing that bugged me when we were together, but every time I'm there for dinner, it looks great." She tittered nervously. "Maybe I was the problem." She took another bottle of beer out of the fridge and held it out to Sam.

He shook his head. "I'm fine." Then he took a breath. "We both know the problems were on both sides. I started taking ADHD meds in January, and it's made a big difference in my focus. I'm finding it easier to keep up with everything. The project I mentioned. I was a week early submitting it."

"Wow, that's great. Did the therapist you're seeing suggest the meds?"

"Actually, the first person to mention it was Quinn when I talked to her in Boston. But yes, the therapist gave me the prescription."

Norah's eyes narrowed when he mentioned Quinn, but her reaction didn't go any further. Still, Sam was going to be completely candid tonight, no matter what happened.

"I feel like we're getting along well now," Norah said. "And it's not because of sex, since there has been none of that. I know that was a concern for you." From where she sat on the sofa, Norah reached for his hand. "I miss you. I miss us. We should be together as a family."

Sam looked at Norah's happy, expectant expression, thinking about how warm her tone was compared to the way she had talked to him that Monday morning in November. *I'm about to shatter her world. There was a time I would have looked at this as payback for the way she hurt me. But not now. I hate what's coming.*

Sam squeezed her hand and let it go. "I've worked hard with my therapist. He's had me read some books on relationships, co-parenting, and codependence. I've learned a lot about myself, and I've gotten clarity on what I want my life to look like going forward." Sam rubbed his jaw before continuing. "One thing I want is another child, or perhaps even two."

"You do?" Norah's eyebrows shot up in surprise. "We agreed on one child for so many reasons, like providing a quality upbringing while we're still able to pursue the things we enjoy and not contributing to overpopulation."

"Those were your thoughts, Norah, and I went along with them. I always pictured myself married with two or three children."

Norah sat back on the couch, closing her eyes. After a few minutes, she opened them. "Are those your terms for getting back together? That we get married and have more children?"

"No, I'm telling you what I want in my life."

She looked away, then back at him. "I'm willing to think about those things."

Sam shook his head. "Norah, that's not what I'm asking. I shouldn't have abandoned my dreams and desires for yours, and I don't want you to do that either. I know you feel strongly about not getting married and only having one child. Don't abandon those beliefs for me."

Norah stared at her glass of wine. "Are you saying... I feel like we're getting along so well and now... Are you saying you've given up on us? That you don't want me back?" She leaned forward, gazing at Sam.

He sighed. "I want to be so crazy in love with a woman that I can't contain it, and I want her to feel the same about me."

"And you don't feel that way about me."

"I love the mother that you are to Piper, but no, I don't love you the way I want to love my partner. Think about it,

Norah—you want to get back together because we are getting along. You haven't used the word 'love' once tonight."

Norah took a deep breath and a swallow of wine. "What about Piper? Don't you think she's better off if we're together?"

"I think she's adjusted well, and in the long run, the best thing for her will be two parents who are as happy with their lives as possible. I've read a couple of books on co-parenting, and we're doing okay so far."

Norah's mouth tightened. "What about the house?"

"I'm going to keep the house. I've started the refinancing process, and I'll be able to give you your share in May."

Norah leaned back and spit out a small laugh. "You have everything all figured out, huh?"

"I've worked hard since you left. I needed to learn who I am and what I want."

"This isn't how I expected this conversation to go." Norah looked away. "It's going to take me some time to process."

"That's why I wanted to talk tonight. I figured it gives you some time without Piper being here."

Norah nodded.

Is it going to be this easy? Should I leave? Is there anything else to talk about?

After a moment, Norah closed her eyes. When she opened them, she looked at Sam. "Does Quinn have anything to do with this?"

"Norah..." Sam groaned.

She shrugged. "I have to wonder, now that you've seen her again."

"No." Sam shook his head. "We've established a friendship, I won't deny that, but her heart belongs to the doctor Piper mentioned after our first ski trip." He reached his hand across the distance between them and placed it on top of Norah's. "You and I stopped working a long time ago, but we kept at it because of Piper. And now, because of Piper, we need to let it go."

A tear slid down Norah's cheek, and Sam brushed it away.

She sighed. "I'm going to be pissed if six months from now, I find out you two are together."

Sam raised his hand in a pledge. "Not gonna happen."

Sam walked into his house as Sophie was leaving Piper's room.

She smiled at him. "We've been home for about half an hour. She read me a story and is still awake, waiting for you."

Sam gestured toward the bag on the table. "Ben & Jerry's. Join me when I'm done with her?" After Sophie nodded, he walked toward Piper's room.

"Daddy!" Piper jumped out of bed and threw herself at Sam. "I had so much fun!"

Sam caught her and brought her back to the bed. "What was your favorite part?"

"The d-dancers! They wore tutus, and they had lipstick on! C-Can I take dance lessons?"

He grinned. "Instead of gymnastics?"

"No, I want to do both." Piper looked at him with an impish smile that he recognized. "Pleeeease."

Sam sighed and shook his head even as his grin widened. She'd learned early how to tease him for things. "Your mom and I will have to discuss it." He sat beside her and stroked her hair. "You need to go to sleep." He stayed with her while she continued to chatter. When she quieted down, he kissed her forehead and stood to leave.

Before he reached the door, Piper said, her voice tinged with sleep, "You'll have to learn to put my hair in a bun. They all had their hair in b-buns."

"I can do that." Sam chuckled as he left the room.

As he scooped ice cream for him and Sophie, he said, "Wow, Pip loved the show! I can't remember when I've seen her so excited." He handed Sophie a bowl of ice cream and sat down on the couch. "I didn't think she'd quiet down this quickly."

"I know. She chattered all the way home. Did she ask you about dance lessons?"

"Oh yeah. Norah and I talked about dance, but we chose gymnastics instead. We'll have to revisit it."

"Speaking of Norah..."

He sighed. "It went about as I expected it would. I've done a lot of work in therapy, figuring out what I want my life to be like, and it's not the same as Norah's vision."

"What do you want?" She let out a humorless chuckle. "I'm still working on that."

"I want to be overwhelmingly in love with someone," he said after a moment. "So much so that we want to shout it from the rooftops and have no hesitation about making it official. And I want to make babies with that person."

"That's very definitive." She glanced down at her bowl. "Is there someone in your life? I haven't even seen you go on a date."

"Oh, hell no. Other than Quinn—and, well, you—there are no women in my life. But that's what I want, and I will not put things back together with Norah and live half a life."

"How'd she react to that?"

"Actually, not too bad." He dug his spoon into the ice cream. "She asked if Quinn influenced my decision. She thinks I'm waiting for her to be available."

"Are you?" Sophie grinned at him.

"No!" Sam registered her grin. "We talked about it, back in the fall." Sophie continued to grin at him, and he knew she was questioning his assertion. "Okay, maybe we did more than talk. But that's in the past. Friends it is, and friends is all it will ever be."

Sam nervously texted Norah on Sunday morning about coming for dinner, as she'd been doing since before Christmas. He half expected her to decline and was surprised by her reply that she would be there at five.

When Norah arrived, Piper eagerly launched into telling her about the talent show. As they sat down for dinner, Norah said, "What do you think, Dad, dance lessons in the fall?"

"I think so. It's all I've heard about all weekend. Women in my office are enthusiastic about two different studios."

"We should try to visit before they close for the summer." They played a game of Go Fish after dinner and put Piper to bed together.

Norah collected her stuff to leave and paused at the door. "I've thought a lot about what you said Friday night. I'm trying to get past my obsession with Quinn. The rest of it... You're right. I wanted our life to work, but we needed to be on the same page, and when I looked back, I realized we weren't. We can work together to give Piper the best possible life, and I hope we both find the love you described." A tear slid down her cheek.

Sam reached over to brush it away with a pang. Maybe they could be friends after all.

Norah shook her head. "Damn it, I didn't want to cry." He gathered her into a hug, and her head rested on his shoulder. "Thank you for having the courage to see what needs to happen. We'll be good as friends and co-parents." She kissed his cheek before walking out the door.

Chapter Eight

Return to Boston

Sophie

Sophie saw Sam check his watch as they neared the end of what she suspected had to be their longest run yet. They had been running for almost two hours, and she was nearly out of gas, she but didn't plan to let Sam know that.

"Race you to the house!" Sam grunted.

Oh, it's on. She looked at him, smiled, and kicked into high gear, but he matched her pace and passed her as they reached the house. They both collapsed on the lawn.

After catching her breath, she asked, "How the hell far did we go?"

Sam gasped for air. "Ten miles."

"Holy crap! The race is six miles. I only need you to get me ready for six!"

"I knew you had more than that." He rolled to his side. "The race is three weeks away. Now we'll work on picking up the pace and the kick for the end. Although I don't think that's going to be a problem—you nearly beat me just now."

Sophie gazed up at the blue sky filled with fluffy white clouds. It was a perfect spring day, and she was happy with her accomplishment. "Are we running this weekend?"

"Maybe late on Sunday." His voice and breathing were getting back to normal. "Joe called me last night and invited me to come down on Saturday to go to a Red Sox game, stay overnight, and go to brunch on Sunday. Since it's my weekend with Piper, Norah and I swapped things around a bit. Pip will be here tomorrow night, then Norah's going to keep her Saturday and Sunday, and I'll have her next Saturday and Sunday."

Sophie nodded.

"I'll head home right after brunch, so I won't be late," he said. "We won't run ten miles again." He grinned at her.

"Thank God for that. I'll hit the gym on Saturday."

Corey stood at the door, his overstuffed pack slung over his shoulder. "What do you want me to do, Sophie?" He was leaving for another mission, and the distress in his voice was obvious.

"I won't keep living like this. You leave me for months in this dump!" Sophie struggled to speak through the sobs wracking her. "I won't be here when you get back!"

"Sophie! Sophie, it's me." Sam's voice came from the other side of her door.

It roused Sophie from her deep sleep and the dream that had consumed her.

She sat up, and her hand went to her face, which was damp with tears.

After composing herself as best she could, she opened the door to see Sam there, in pajama pants but without a shirt. Belatedly, she realized she was wearing only a tank top and shorts. *Too late.* "What? Is something wrong?" She ran a hand through her disheveled hair.

He frowned at her, looking concerned. "You were crying."

Her face flushed with heat. "I—I was? It must have been a bad dream."

"It's not the first time I've heard you."

"I'm sorry," she mumbled. "I don't mean to disturb you."

"You didn't," he said. "Pip woke me up, wanting a drink of water. But I was concerned."

"Did I wake her?"

Sam shook his head.

"I'm okay. Thanks for checking on me." She closed the door in a rush of shame, embarrassment, and sadness. "Shit, shit, shit." She sat on the bed for a few minutes before crawling back under the covers.

When Sophie came out in the morning, Sam was sitting on the couch with a cup of coffee.

"Where's Pip?" Sophie asked. "She's usually watching her favorite Saturday morning show at this hour."

"Norah already picked her up. They're going shopping."

"I thought you were heading to Boston."

"I'm psyching myself up. The traffic intimidates the hell out of me. I got mired in a huge traffic jam when I drove down in November. Plus, I think Joe is fixing me up with someone." Sam rolled his eyes.

"About last night," she began. "It's a recurring dream. Remember when I told you about food insecurity?"

He nodded ruefully. "How could I forget?"

Sophie rolled her eyes. "I wish you could. The dream's related to that. I'm sorry if I woke you." *It's only a tiny white lie.*

"I'm only aware if Piper gets me up." He paused. "Have you ever talked to anyone about it?"

"Yes." She hoped he understood she would not say any more and was relieved when he changed the subject.

"Well," he said, "I can't put off the inevitable any longer. I'm going to shower and hit the road. I'll see you tomorrow."

Sophie watched as he walked to his bedroom. He had on a long-sleeved tee with the pajama pants from the night before, and the memory of his bare chest sent heat through her, despite her inner turmoil.

Sam

The drive was much better than it had been in November, and Sam reached Joe's apartment with no problem. "Hey, bro—nice place," he said as Joe welcomed him inside. "Tell me why I'm here again. You were kind of sketchy on the details when you called."

Joe laughed. "About a month ago, Amy invited me to a charity event where she and her husband had purchased a table."

Sam whistled. "Whoa, those kinds of things usually cost a grand or more. She has that kind of money? And you've stayed in touch since we saw her?" Sam and his brothers had gone to the Whistle Stop at Thanksgiving and run into Amy, a girl Joe had dated briefly in high school.

"A grand is Northeast Kingdom money," Joe scoffed, referring to the area of Vermont where they'd grown up. "It's probably ten times that down here—and yeah, Amy's husband has some kind of hotshot job. She and I became friends on social media." He shook his head. "Anyway, there was an empty place at the table, and she invited me to fill it. I think her idea was to fix me up with her friend Emma. We were the only singles at the table." He paused and grinned. "And Emma and I hit it off."

Joe tossed a Red Sox jersey to Sam. "I'm told we have to wear these." He pulled one over his T-shirt. "We've seen each other a few times since then. The four tickets to this game were one of the auction items, and Emma had the winning bid. She invited me to go along with another couple. They had a conflict at the last minute and backed out, so Emma asked a co-worker to join us. And she asked me if I wanted to invite you."

"Are you trying to fix me up?"

"I don't think so. I've never met the co-worker. How are things going for you?"

"I closed on the refinancing of the house this week and gave Norah her share. She's going to buy the house she's been renting." He sighed. "It's a relief to have that out of the way."

There was a knock on the door, and Joe answered it. He drew the pretty brunette at the door into a hug. She was nearly as tall as Joe and wore a Red Sox jersey of her own. The woman behind her was smaller, with short blond hair, and she wore a jersey as well. She waited patiently while Joe and Emma hugged, rolling her eyes at Sam.

Joe pulled himself away and gestured toward Sam. "This is my brother, Sam. This is Emma and..." Joe looked inquisitively at them.

"This is my co-worker, Lindsey," Emma said. "It's nice to meet you, Sam. Joe talks about you a lot."

"Believe nothing he says. It's nice to meet both of you."

"Our ride will be here soon." Emma grinned. "I'm excited about the game. I've never had seats this good—especially for the Yankees."

They arrived at Fenway Park in time for batting practice, and their seats were two rows behind the home dugout. Joe and Emma had eyes only for each other, leaving Sam and Lindsey scrambling for something to talk about.

"Have you been to Fenway before?" she asked him.

"No, it's my first time. I'd never even been to Boston until last fall."

"Where do you live in Vermont?"

"In Thetford. It's a small town close to the New Hampshire border."

"Ah," she said, brightening. "I attended college in Lyndon."

Sam chuckled. "Another small town close to the border. That's where I went to high school. What did you major in?"

"Communications and journalism. I'm on the production team at WBZ."

"Emma works there too? Joe hasn't told me much about her."

"Emma's a field reporter, an exceptional one. She's a natural and will probably be an anchor at some point." Still smiling, she shrugged. "I tried reporting, but I'm better off behind the scenes—I love it. What about you?"

"I'm a project manager for an economic-development council. My degree is in architecture, and I'm working on my master's in project management."

"Are you unencumbered?"

What the hell does that mean? Sam looked at her, confused.

She tilted her head. "Do you have a wife or girlfriend?"

He chuckled. "No. I have a six-year-old daughter. She encumbers me, I guess. Her mother and I split last November. You?"

"Well, I have a cat who's pretty needy, but no one else. My ex and I divorced a little over two years ago."

"Breakups are so much fun." Sam hoped she would get his sarcasm, and when she nodded and smiled, he knew she had.

Both teams hit the ball hard, and at the end of five innings, Boston was up by two runs. Sam excused himself to go to the restroom. As he was returning to his seat, he did a double take. Walking along the concourse in a worn Red Sox cap was Caden. By his side was a woman who Sam thought looked pregnant.

Did he leave Quinn because he knocked up some other woman? Did he lie to her? I'll kill him.

"Hey, Doc!" he called.

Caden and the woman stopped. "Sam? We keep running into each other in unexpected places."

Sam made sure that Caden knew he had noticed the woman's belly. "This is my friend Brooke. I'm here with her and her husband, Danny. Brooke, this is Sam Carpenter."

Brooke shook Sam's hand. "I'd love to chat, but my pregnant bladder won't wait. I'll meet you back at our seats, Cade."

Caden looked at Sam. "Did you think…"

"Yeah, I wondered why you're walking around with a pregnant woman. Sorry, I shouldn't have jumped to that conclusion."

"I haven't even looked at another woman since I met Quinn. Is she…"

"With me? No, I'm here with my brother and his girlfriend."

Caden shook his head as if to clear his thoughts. "Are you going to tell her you saw me?"

"Not unless you tell me to." Sam frowned at him. "I haven't even told her we text."

"That's probably for the best."

Sam motioned back toward his seat. "I need to get back before they send a search party."

"Okay," Caden said, beginning to pivot away, but he turned back. "Hey, I'm leaving the first of June for two months in Honduras. Going to a medical missionary program. So I won't be bugging you with texts at ten thirty."

"That's a big switch from Boston."

Caden laughed wryly. "Yeah, I've never been away from the city for that long, and it'll be a lot different from the ED at Mass General. I need a change of pace."

"Good luck." Sam nodded. "Hope it works out."

When Sam slid into his seat, Joe asked, "Did you get lost?"

"Nope, ran into someone I know."

The Red Sox won the game, and they stopped at a pub on their way back to Joe's apartment, where they ordered food. While they waited for it to be delivered, Joe opened his laptop. "I'm getting ready to list the cabin for rent. Let me show you the pictures I'm using." He flipped through the pictures, which included interior shots, winter pictures of the surrounding area, and colorful fall foliage pictures.

"I'm trying to convince Mom and Dad to add a hot tub or sauna," Joe added. "It would increase the value. The hot tub would be a pain because it would add to the cleaning, but it would work on the deck. A sauna would have to be inside, and I'm not sure where. There's probably space in the upstairs bedroom."

"The listing looks outstanding. I'd rent it." Sam told the women how Joe had convinced their parents to repurpose the run-down hunting camp as a vacation rental. "He designed an awesome addition and did most of the work along with our dad." He turned back to Joe. "Do you have any pictures of what it looked like before?"

Joe's face had gone red, but he looked pleased as well. "What are you, my PR agent?" He showed them pictures of the original building. "Hey, it's time for the news. Sam, turn on the TV."

Emma reached out to stop Sam. "No, we don't need to watch the news."

"Aww, come on. I turn it on every night, hoping to catch one of your segments," Joe teased her, and she blushed.

After they ate, Joe suggested they watch a movie. As they were trying to agree on one, Sam noticed Emma was running her hand along Joe's thigh.

Lindsey rolled her eyes at Sam and said, "It's a beautiful evening. Let's go for a walk."

Once they were outside, Sam asked, "Did you and Emma have that planned?"

Lindsey laughed and shook her head. "No, but it looked like they might want some time alone. Emma told me Joe's newly divorced—do you know what he's looking for as far as a relationship?"

Her directness surprised him. "I don't know. It's not something we've talked about. I think she's the first woman he's dated since his marriage imploded."

"I've known her since I started at the station and never seen her date. She's laser-focused on her career and ready to move into an anchor spot. If one doesn't open here, she'll go elsewhere." She eyed Sam. "Joe seems like a nice guy. I'd hate to see him get too invested. But Emma's probably told him. She's upfront about her ambition."

Lindsey led Sam past the sign for Boston Common. As they entered, memories from November flooded over him—seeing the duckling statues on his first run, the pounding miles he had done after finding out Norah had taken most of the furniture, and the early morning run that ended with him and Quinn at the same spot. It all seemed so long ago.

Lindsey stopped. "Are you okay?"

Sam realized his pace had slowed as they walked through the park. "Yeah, I ran here last fall. Norah—that's my ex—had just left me. I was a wreck."

"Do you want to go somewhere different?"

"No, no, this is fine. I want to bring my daughter here to see the duckling statues. Hopefully, this summer."

"There's lots to do in the city with kids. I take it the split wasn't your idea?"

"The split was mutual. The timing was a surprise. How about you? Why'd you divorce?" Since Lindsey wasn't holding anything back, Sam figured he could ask.

"I married my high school sweetheart right after I graduated from college. We spent a few years in Portland, near where we grew up, and then I took the job here. He didn't like the city, and I loved it. I worked a lot of evenings, and he found ways to amuse himself."

"He cheated?"

"Yeah, and I discovered I didn't care." She shrugged. "My job was more important to me, and that's no way to sustain a marriage. So we split."

"Is work still your prime focus?"

Lindsey smiled. "I have friends with benefits, but yes, work is the most important thing to me right now. No one I've met has knocked my socks off yet. Have you been dating?"

"No. In the beginning, I was trying to figure out what I wanted. I've realized Norah and I are on different pages and work better as friends, so the split is permanent. Piper and my job keep me busy, but I'm ready to move forward. The dating pool in my area is pretty shallow."

Lindsey bumped her hip against him. "Maybe you need to look in a different pool."

The tilt of her head and the gleam in her eyes were obvious invitations. Looking around, he realized they were in a secluded corner, with twilight gathering. He pulled her to him and lowered his lips gently to hers.

Lindsey met him boldly, opening her mouth and exploring him.

And he felt... nothing. *Shit, what is wrong with me? A kiss like this has always given me a hard-on.* Lindsey's body pressed tightly against him. *And she can tell that there's nothing there.*

She pulled back slightly, looking into his eyes. "Did I read you wrong? I thought..."

"No. I mean, you're pretty and witty..."

"And bright?"

Sam made a face at her.

"It's from *The Sound of Music*. I like musical theater."

He chuckled ruefully. "I was going to say 'direct,' but 'bright' works. You're what I'd be looking for…"

She nodded. "If you were looking, which apparently you're not."

"I'm sorry."

"Don't worry about it." She rolled her eyes. "I wasn't planning on having sex on the Common. We should head back."

Chapter Nine

The Race... And A Kiss

Sam

"PIP, DON'T GET OUT of sight!" Sam called as she and Janey raced ahead of him and Jesse.

The four of them were hiking in the White Mountains, and the girls had started up the mountain like rockets.

Sam was happy to have time to talk to Jesse, but he didn't want to lose sight of Piper.

"Don't worry," Jesse said. "The two of them will slow down as the path gets steeper."

Sam watched Jesse pick his way cautiously over the loose gravel on the trail. "How's the leg?"

"Better, but not where I want it. I saw an orthopedist this week. There's a procedure that might help, but he wants to do some tests first."

"And how's Caitlin?"

"Round and getting rounder." Jesse beamed. "She's doing well. Three months left. What's new with you?"

Sam slowed, keeping his eyes on Piper and Janey ahead of them. "I think... Damn, this is awkward." He paused and took a deep breath. "I think the meds I'm taking are making me impotent."

"Seriously?"

Sam could hear the smile in Jesse's response, and he turned toward his friend. "Yes! And it's not funny! I went to Joe's over the weekend, and this attractive, extremely appealing woman practically threw herself at me. But when we kissed, I had no reaction. Nada, zip, zero. It was embarrassing as hell."

Jesse was still trying to suppress a smile. "What are you taking?" When Sam told him, Jesse's forehead creased. "My pharmacology classes were a long time ago, but I think you'd be more likely to experience the opposite."

"Jesus, that's definitely not happening."

"You still get morning wood?"

Sam rolled his eyes. "Oh my God. Yes."

"So you're probably not impotent."

"Well, then what the hell is going on? This is so awkward."

"Where were you when this happened? Were you at Joe's? Was there a lack of privacy that concerned you?"

"We'd gone for a walk to give Joe and his date some time alone. We were in a secluded corner of Boston Common. The lack of privacy didn't bother either of us."

"Think about the last time you went for a walk in Boston."

"I was with Quinn. We walked back to the hotel after dinner." Jesse knew this walk ended with them going to bed. "Shit. You're saying my subconscious was messing with me?"

"It's a possibility. Give it some time."

He nodded. "Now that Norah and I have settled things, I'm thinking about dating, and I don't want to have a replay of the weekend."

"Do you have someone in mind?"

"No, but one of my co-workers has been after me to meet a friend of hers. I may take her up on it this summer. Right now, I'm focused on the race I'm going to run with Sophie in a couple of weeks. I don't have any performance anxiety about running."

Sam chuckled, then remembered something else. "Speaking of Sophie, I've gotten up several times with Piper and heard her crying. Last week, I knocked on her door to check on her. She said she had a recurring bad dream. I don't know if she's even aware that she's crying."

"Do you know what the dream is about?"

"She had times growing up that she was food insecure, and she said it relates to that."

Jesse nodded. "That can play games with your psyche."

"Tell me about it. Piper ate some of her cookies a couple of months ago, and she lost her mind. Should I do anything if I hear her again?"

Jesse eyed Sam. "What's your relationship with her?"

"Relationship?" His tone was indignant "She's my tenant. There's no relationship."

"Is a checking on a tenant in the middle of the night typical landlord behavior?" Jesse's voice held a tinge of humor.

"Okay. We're friends. I'd say we've become friends."

"Then be a friend. Don't push the matter. You've opened a door—it's her choice to walk through."

Sophie

The Thursday before the race, Sophie and Sam did a brief run.

While they were recovering on the lawn, Sophie looked over at Sam. "You said you see a therapist." She'd been wanting to ask him about it since he mentioned it in February.

"Yes."

"And you don't mind talking about it? Not the therapy itself, because I know that's private, but like, how long you've done it and why?"

"I don't mind. I started in January. Norah and I did couples and family counseling in the past, which obviously was unsuccessful." He sighed. "It wrecked me when Norah moved out. I was angry all the time and on the road to becoming a problem drinker."

"I've never seen you have more than one beer."

"The first two months after she left, nights that I didn't have Piper, I had many more than that." His gaze was serious. "I cut back to one around the time you moved in."

"So therapy's been successful this time?"

"I'm a work in progress, but I'm in a better frame of mind. A good enough frame of mind that I had my last session with Archie a few weeks ago. I have an extensive project going on this summer and won't be able to get away to see him." He paused. "I can go back if my life falls apart again. Hoping that doesn't happen."

She was silent for several minutes. "I've done therapy. Obviously, it was unsuccessful." She echoed his words, hoping they held more humor than despair.

Sam scrambled to his feet and grabbed her hand to help her up. "I'm no expert, but I think you have to be in the right headspace for it to help. Just because therapy didn't work in the past doesn't mean it won't in the future."

The next night, Sophie was at the sink when Sam came home.

"Catch!" He threw something at her.

She grabbed it as it sailed past. *A pair of socks?* She looked at them, bemused, then looked at Sam.

"I stopped to buy a new pair and bought you a pair as well," he said. "For tomorrow."

The next morning, Sophie nervously pulled on her sports bra, T-shirt, and running shorts. She sat on the bed and picked up the socks Sam had bought for her. *He bought me something. He was walking around a store, and I entered his head.* It had been a long time since a man gave her a present.

Oh, get a grip. This isn't a present. It's a pair of socks.

Sophie came out of her room and kicked her leg up when she saw Sam. "Great socks. Thanks so much!" *There, that wasn't so awkward.*

Sam was lacing his running shoes. "If you do as well as I think you are going to, you'll have to wear them for every race."

"Every race?" She laughed. "You think I'm going to do another one? I'm so nervous that I can't think straight. It's unlikely I'll put myself through this again."

"You're going to do fine, and you're going to like it so much you'll be registering for your next one as soon as you get home."

She wriggled her feet. "What if I suck?"

"Then we'll have a bonfire tonight and burn them." He straightened up. "But you will not suck."

Sophie rolled her eyes. "Aren't you nervous? Or is it just me?"

"I'm always jumpy on race day." Sam held out his hand, and Sophie saw the slight tremble. "It's even worse this morning because I want it to go well for you." He took a deep breath, then said, "Let's hit the road."

Sophie opted to drive them—she hoped concentrating on the road would keep her nerves at bay. When they reached the school, people were everywhere, setting up the carnival, and she ended up having to greet many coworkers with Sam in tow. Unsure of what to say, she introduced him to some as her trainer and to others as her landlord.

Sam led her to a map of the course. After they had studied it, he said, "Let's walk the beginning of the route, since we have plenty of time."

As they walked, he reviewed concepts they had talked about earlier. "Remember, don't start too fast," he said. "Don't let the people who set an early pace intimidate you because they'll fade before the end. We've talked about the marks you want to hit. And kick it in when you get close to the finish."

She gazed at him with a smile. "You're more nervous than I am."

"You've worked hard, and you're a great runner. I want it to be a wonderful experience for you."

They joined the queue at the starting line to listen to the last-minute instructions. The runners were all eager to start, shaking their arms and bobbing their heads, attempting to get and stay loose.

"On your marks, get set, *go!*"

With a deep breath, Sophie shot off the starting line.

Sophie lost track of Sam in the crowd, but it didn't concern her, since they had agreed that they would each run their own race. She set a comfortable pace and passed several runners. Eventually, with half a mile left, several people were still ahead of her. She picked up her pace, passing three women and two men. Sam's voice played in her head. *You've got a great kick. Don't forget that and don't let up.* His words propelled her, and she crossed the finish line in eighth place overall, but first among the women.

Sophie was just slightly behind Sam, whom she saw cheering loudly for her and waiting to congratulate her after she cleared the chute. She ran over and threw her arms around him, and he hugged her tightly. "You're amazing! I'm so proud of you!"

Her lips came to Sam's in a triumphant kiss, which lasted several seconds, and a nearby reporter snapped a photo of them.

Sophie let go of him, laughing shakily. "My God, I can't believe I did that. Thank you so much!" She gave him another brief hug.

The reporter approached them. "I need your names. I snapped a wonderful picture of you!" He showed it to them.

Sophie looked at Sam and shook her head.

"Hey, man, we're not a couple," Sam said. "We trained together. It's her first race, and I'm thrilled for her. That kiss was purely the heat of the moment."

"But that's the thing people love to see," the reporter insisted.

"I'd appreciate it if you don't use it. I have an ex and a young daughter, and I don't want them to get the wrong idea. And she's a teacher here." Sam hesitated. "Please?"

The reporter reluctantly agreed not to use it. "I need to get some shots of the winners," he said.

Sophie agreed to gather with the other first-place finishers in each age group. The reporter walked away, shaking his head.

After the pictures had been taken and the medals awarded, Sophie made her way back to Sam, and they walked around, looking at all the booths. They purchased burgers and sat at a picnic table to enjoy them.

Several kids approached, and they were full of questions. "Ms. Palmer, I didn't know you could run like that. Is this your boyfriend?" one girl asked.

"No, we're friends and he trained me for the race."

"But you kissed him!" a boy said.

"I was excited by how I did." She laughed. This scene repeated itself over and over as more kids came over to congratulate her and ask about Sam.

Sam seemed to enjoy watching her interact with the kids, judging by his easy smile and relaxed posture. At one point, after another nosy seventh grader came by, he asked, "Is this awkward for you?"

"No, I'll be yesterday's news by Monday." She laughed. "They're middle schoolers, and they like to look for some hot gossip. I'm ready to head home if you are."

"I'm ready." He stood and stretched. "A shower is calling my name."

She nodded. "And maybe a nap as well."

On the ride home, they went over every aspect of the race. "Things went exactly as we planned," Sophie said, marveling at it all. "I've never done anything like that. Thank you so much."

When they got home, Sam surprised her by suggesting that they go out to eat. "To celebrate. My treat."

She suddenly felt shy. "That sounds like fun, but I feel like it should be my treat to thank you."

A short time later, when she was getting dressed after her shower, there was a knock on Sophie's door.

"I made a reservation in Norwich at six thirty," Sam called out. "I'll drive."

Chapter Ten

An Even Better Kiss

Sam

As HE PARKED, Sam looked over at Sophie again, unable to forget the impact she'd made on him when she came out of her room earlier, ready for dinner.

She'd dressed in a cornflower-blue sundress, and her auburn hair was loose, curling down over her shoulders.

He'd whistled, glad he'd put on a white button-down shirt and navy shorts. "Look at you! It's amazing what a shower can do." Then he'd perused her more slowly, watching her cheeks go pink. "I've never seen you look like this."

His thoughts slid further back to the kiss she had planted on him after the race. For the first time in months, his stomach clenched in pleasure as he experienced a true stirring of desire. *Whoa. Focus.* He shifted into park and rushed around to open Sophie's door.

"Thank you." She graced him with the stunning smile that she so seldom shared.

When the host seated them, Sam pulled out her chair, and Sophie slid into it. She smiled again as she sat. "I really feel like celebrating." A white tablecloth covered the table, topped with candles and a vase of orange gerbera daisies. "I can't believe I came in first out of all the women runners!"

"I'm not surprised at all. You have a lot of natural talent." Sam smiled, pleased that he had selected an upscale restaurant. Their table was on the deck, and the server brought them the bottle of wine that Sam ordered when he made the reservation. Sam lifted his glass to hers, offering a toast. "To the first of many victories."

Her cheeks flushed as she touched her glass to his.

Conversation flowed easily after they ordered their food. The school had offered Sophie a position for the coming school year, so she would stay in Thetford. They had gotten comfortable with each other over the months, so when the question arose, it was natural for them to decide to continue sharing their space.

"School's almost done," Sam said. "What are your plans for the summer?"

"The kids will finish on Tuesday, and I have in-service to finish the week. I'll have a couple of weeks off, summer school during July and early August, then a few free weeks until the school year starts again." She blew out an amused breath. "The biggest thing I plan to do in the open weeks is relax. I want to spend time at the beach with a good book. What will Piper do this summer?"

"She'll go to daycare at least part of the time. Norah and I each have two weeks off, so she'll get a break. We've talked about her spending a week in Connecticut with Norah's family and maybe a week with mine."

"Does she swim?"

"Oh, yeah—like a fish. She loves the water."

"Summer school is three days a week. I wondered if you'd let her go to the beach with me once a week. It would be a change of pace for her."

He smiled. "She'd love that. I'll talk to Norah about it. Are you going to go anywhere, visit family?"

Sophie looked away from Sam. "No."

"Do you have a siblings? Parents who are still alive?"

She continued to avoid his eyes.

He frowned. "I'm sorry. Am I prying?"

"No, it's okay." After a pause, she said, "I have six-teen-year-old twin half-sisters."

"So they're significantly younger than you. If they ever want to visit, I'm sure we can find room in the house."

"I have little to do with them. I guess you'd say we're estranged." Sophie looked down at her wineglass.

"I'm sorry." Sam didn't want her to be uncomfortable, but he also wasn't ready to give up. "I'm realizing how little I know about you after all this time. I know more about the woman Joe fixed me up with a few weeks ago."

Sophie shook her head, her expression blank. "I know you're close with your family, so it's probably hard to understand, but I'm not."

"That closeness is new," he offered. "When I took Piper there for Christmas, I had to introduce her to my parents because she didn't remember them."

Sophie raised her eyebrows, looking surprised.

Sam took a sip of his drink, shifting his gaze down to the table. He unbuttoned his cuffs and rolled his shirtsleeves up, uncharacteristically nervous. Did he want to get this personal with her? "My dad suffered from undiagnosed depression when I was growing up. His medication was alcohol, and he was a mean drunk. Not physically abusive, but very demanding and demeaning. I left for good over a decade ago and had only been back a handful of times. My brothers and I were close as kids, but we went our separate ways after high school, so we had drifted apart as well."

"I'm sorry." She gazed at him, eyes wide. "How did you get to where you are now?"

"I went up at Thanksgiving because I was alone. I spent the weekend working on the cabin with Joe and Matt, and they told me he had changed." Sam shrugged. "I was skeptical, but little by little, the doors started opening between us. The difference is remarkable. You should see him with Pip. They've taken to each other. It's sweet—there's no other word for it."

Sophie's eyes had gone glossy with tears. "I'm happy for you. But it doesn't work out that way for everyone."

"You're right. And it's none of my business." He wanted to reach out for her hand, but kept his distance. "Let's change the subject. What's your next race going to be?"

"I don't know. What do you think?"

"There's an eight-mile race in Stowe in July, usually the hottest day of the summer, and a ten-mile one there in November, usually on the crappiest day of the fall." He laughed when she made a face.

"You think I can do ten miles?" she asked.

"I know you can. We've already run ten. But what I really think you need to do is a half."

"A half marathon? Thirteen miles? Where would we do that? Because you'd have to do it too."

"I'd like to do that. Several are happening in the fall. We can go online when we get home and find one we like. Are you up for the other two I mentioned?"

"I guess. I feel like I set an awfully high bar, finishing first today."

"You may not come in first every time, but you'll be competitive. You ran a good race today. I'd like to take you up north to some great biking trails that are fun to run on as well. It's a unique experience. We could make it a day trip, or we could stay in the cabin. It has three bedrooms. We could do it when I have Pip. She loves going up there."

Their server came back, asking about dessert.

Sam looked at Sophie. "Want to split a brownie sundae?"

She smiled. "Sure."

The ice cream was delicious and more than enough for both of them. *Splitting the dessert is very intimate. Why did I ask her to do it, and why did she agree? Is she feeling the same current between us as I am?*

When they arrived at home, Sam said, "Let's register for those races now and see what's out there for half marathons."

Sam opened his laptop and sat down at the dining room table after pulling out a chair for Sophie. They registered and then looked at other races. They picked out two half marathons, and Sam said, "Let me do a little research. You want a well-run race for your first one." He stood and offered his hand to help her up.

She smoothed her dress as she stood and turned to him. "Today, tonight... It was all fun. Thank you."

Sam put his hands on her waist, drawing her to him. He lowered his lips to hers, giving her time to pull away if she wasn't comfortable. When she leaned in, he kissed her gently. Slowly, her lips moved under his, and she relaxed against him.

He held her for a few minutes, then drew back with a breath of wonder. "That was not the heat of the moment." His hand moved to her hair, gently teasing one of her curls. Her eyes locked on his, and he felt like she was looking into his soul.

His heart pounding, he lowered his lips to hers again. His arms encircled her, and he rubbed circles on her back as the kiss deepened. Sophie reached one hand up to his head and ran her fingers through his hair, making Sam moan a little. It had been a long time since holding a woman in his arms had felt this right.

Then abruptly, Sophie pulled back. "I'm sorry. I can't do this." She turned and went to her room.

Damn, did I completely misread that? No, something's been there since that kiss at the end of the race. She reacted positively until she didn't. And Sophie could tell I was into it.

He flopped onto his bed, and as he tried to fall asleep, his mind replayed the sweet taste of her lips and the press of her body against his.

In the morning, Sam's first thoughts were about Sophie, hoping the kiss would not make things weird between them. He enjoyed having her at the house and running with her. Piper liked her, too, and he didn't want to mess up any of that. Why had she said she "couldn't do it"? She had been as into their embrace as he was. That wording seemed off.

But on the positive side, if there was one, his parts had all been working last night. He'd had his first response to a woman since being with Quinn, which was a relief.

By midmorning, Sophie had not come out of her room, which was unusual.

Sam gave a quick knock on her door. "Hey, Sophie, I'm heading to the cabin. Joe's up there this weekend, working on the landscaping."

"Okay," she said, her voice muffled through the door. "I'll see you tonight or tomorrow."

"How are your legs?"

"Better than I expected. I may go out for a walk."

"Good idea."

The drive north gave Sam plenty of time to overthink the kiss, but he knew he wanted more from Sophie. With her. He hoped they could work through whatever had made her pull away.

Joe was alone at the cabin and had three birch trees to plant. One hole was almost ready, and he showed Sam where to dig another one.

"Lindsey wasn't your type, huh?" Joe asked as they worked.

Sam's mind spun. He hadn't really wanted Joe to find out what had happened—or more accurately, didn't happen. "Why? What did she say?"

"Nothing much, just that you didn't seem to be into her." When Sam's face reddened, Joe pounced on the moment. "Okay, what gives? Why are you all defensive?"

"I'm not defensive. You're right—she isn't my type."

"Uh-huh. I thought anything with legs and boobs was your type."

"That's enlightened." Sam scoffed. "Not to mention sexist."

Joe put his shovel down. "Okay, what is up with you? What the hell happened?"

Sam gave up. He had always been defenseless against Joe. The guy was relentless. "Nothing, absolutely nothing. That was the issue. We kissed. I had no reaction, and Lindsey knew it."

Joe's eyes went wide. "Do you have a problem? I mean, she's pretty and sexy. You guys seemed to get along. Why wouldn't you respond?"

"I've wondered the same thing." He sighed. "I hadn't responded to any woman since Norah left. Well, except for Quinn. But I think it's resolved." He paused, wondering if he should continue. *Might as well tell someone.* "Because I kissed Sophie last night, and *everything* jumped to attention."

"You kissed your tenant?" Joe gaped at him. "Was that wise?"

"Not sure. That's why I'm up here digging holes with you." Sam barked out a laugh. "She kissed me after the race, which opened a door. Then we went out to dinner, and she was all dressed up, and I wasn't thinking of her as my tenant." He paused. "She seemed into the kiss for a few minutes then pulled

95

away, told me she couldn't do it, and retreated to her room. She hasn't come out since, and I'm hoping I haven't screwed things up—but you know, I also must admit, I enjoyed the kiss. I'd like to see where it could go."

When Joe didn't respond immediately, Sam changed the subject. "What's going on with you and Emma?"

"I like Emma a lot. I mean, you saw her. She's beautiful, interesting, and driven. We have fun together." Joe picked up his shovel again. "She's looking to become an anchor and may need to go to another market for that. So we're enjoying each other and playing it by ear."

"Listen to you — 'another market.' You already know the lingo."

They laughed together.

By the time they finished with the trees, their mother arrived in a car full of flowers, and the three of them spent the rest of the afternoon planting.

When they finished, Sam looked around. "I'm thinking about coming up here for a weekend with Sophie and Piper. I'd like to take Sophie running on the trails, then take her and Piper to Willoughby Lake."

Joe and their mother both raised their eyebrows at that idea.

"There's three bedrooms," Sam said, feeling awkward. "We'd each have our own room, the same as we do at my house. Sophie and Piper are close, and we've become good friends. She's an excellent runner, and I think she'll like the trails."

Laura left first, and Joe jabbed at Sam as he was getting ready to leave. "Honestly? Just running on the trails? After what you told me earlier?"

"Yes," Sam said, glaring. "Piper provides a built-in chaperone; in case you've forgotten."

Joe cocked his head. "She can always spend the night at Mom and Dad's."

Sam shook his head, got in his car, and raised his middle finger at Joe before driving off.

Sophie

What the hell was I thinking?

That had been Sophie's prevailing thought since their embrace the night before. Since their kiss at the race, really. She knew she'd planted the seed when she'd kissed Sam at the finish line. Pure euphoria was coursing through her at the end of the race, and having Sam there to hug, to kiss, had been perfect. The feel of his strong, sweaty body against hers was etched in her mind.

As was their kiss last night, when they were looking their best and slightly tipsy from the bottle of wine they had shared. *It's been over two years since I've been held like that, kissed like that. He was so gentle and kind. And I ran away like a scared dog.*

On Sunday, Sophie stayed in her room until Sam left. She went for a long walk, trying to erase her attraction to him. The attraction that, she fully acknowledged, began when she saw him looking like a whipped puppy in the school parking lot before Thanksgiving.

By Tuesday, Sophie knew she couldn't avoid him and Piper any longer. She stopped at the market on her way home and walked in with all the fixings for hot fudge sundaes to celebrate the last day of school.

As Sophie savored the sweet fudge sauce, she thought about sharing dessert with Sam on Saturday night. His eyes caught hers, and she knew that night was on his mind as well. She held his gaze for a few seconds before she asked, "Are we running tomorrow night?"

Sam nodded as he took Piper to her bedroom.

Chapter Eleven

The Truth About Sophie

Sophie

THEY RAN FOR EIGHT miles, keeping a steady pace. When they hit the last half mile, Sam winked at her. "Race?"

She put on a burst of speed in answer. He reached the yard a few strides ahead of her, and they both fell onto the grass, panting. It felt comfortingly familiar, lying there, catching their breath together.

Sophie lay flat on her back, looking up at the dark-blue sky of the early evening. How many nights had she lain in the grass like this before sheltering for the night? An understanding of the importance of the security she felt living in Sam's house overwhelmed her, and she knew she needed to share her story with him. It was time.

"When I was little, I used to lie on the grass like this before going to sleep, hoping to catch sight of the first star so I could make a wish."

"What did you wish for?"

"This," she whispered over the lump in her throat. "I grew up poor, and not just free-lunch poor. We were living in our car and scavenging restaurant dumpsters."

Sam rolled up on his side, and Sophie felt him watching her, but her eyes didn't leave the horizon.

"My mother was sixteen when she had me," she said. "Her parents kicked her out when they found out about her pregnancy. She moved in with my father, but he died when I was five. My mother had no high school diploma, no skills, nothing. When we were evicted from my dad's apartment, we lived in our car."

Sam reached out to her, but Sophie scooted away, not wanting to succumb to his touch.

"Sometimes we lived in homeless shelters, but what I remember the most is the car," she said. "My mom started serving in restaurants, and she was good at it, but there was never enough money. When I was eleven, maybe twelve, she finally got us our own apartment. We'd been there a few months when a very successful restaurateur walked into the place where my mother worked and sat at one of her tables. Charlie came back several times until he finally asked her out." She paused. "When I was thirteen, we moved in with him, and he proposed shortly after that. My mother didn't want him to know how we had struggled to survive, so we never talked about it. A year later, they got married. My mother stepped right into her role as the wife of a successful restaurateur and expected me to accept our new life just as easily." She looked up into the darkening sky again. "But I had missed something in my development—not mentally but emotionally. I started high school with all new kids, and I could have been anyone I wanted to be, but I didn't know how to be anything but a poor little girl with raggedy clothes and not enough food. I felt like a fraud throughout high school and much of college."

She took a deep breath and finally looked at Sam. He reached for her hand, but she shook her head, and he let his hand fall back to the grass.

"When I was eighteen, I spent the summer working at an ice cream shop. One afternoon, I recognized the young man ordering a mint chocolate chip in a waffle cone. He had lived in the same shelter that my mother and I did when I was ten. His name was Corey, and he recognized me too." She smiled sadly. "He came back when my shift finished. We sat on a bench at the harbor and talked all night long. For the first time in years, I could be myself. I saw Corey every night for two weeks, then he left. He'd enlisted and didn't know when he'd be back."

She rolled up to her side, turning to look at Sam. "Two years passed before I saw him again. He came home on leave, and we spent a week together. That pattern continued for years. We'd spend a few days together, and then I wouldn't see or hear from him for eighteen months or longer. He was part of a super-clandestine security force." She blinked back the sudden tears at the memory. "Three and a half years ago, he convinced me to elope with him. We flew to Vegas and got married. Two years ago, he left for a mission, and five days after that, I opened our door to a military chaplain. Corey had been killed in a training accident." Her voice stayed devoid of emotion, although her eyes were still wet. "The one person who knew me, really knew me, was gone."

She finally looked at him again. "I'm broken, Sam. I have nothing to give you."

Sam swallowed hard and was quiet for several minutes. "I had no idea. I'm so sorry."

"No one has any idea. You're the first person I've told."

"I don't see you as broken." His voice sounded so sure. "I see a strong woman who has overcome hardships that most of us

102

couldn't even imagine. The story of my dad's bad moods sounds damn pitiful."

She stared at him. "I lost my shit over cookies!"

He didn't break eye contact. "And that makes perfect sense now."

Sophie lay back on the grass. "I shouldn't have kissed you. I let my emotions take over."

"The heat of the moment. It's okay." Sam stood and reached for her hand to pull her up, as he had done every time they had lain on the lawn to recover.

Sophie hesitated and then grasped his hand and scrambled to her feet.

Sam let go of her hand as soon as she was standing and gazed at her warmly. "Thank you for trusting me with that."

"I let you think... You deserved to know."

"You're not leaving, are you?" he asked, looking concerned. "Nothing needs to change. If you want to talk, we can talk. If you don't want to, we won't. We'll go back to how things were, you making your smoothie in the morning, me trying to keep Piper out of your cupboard." He grinned.

Sophie managed a weak smile back at him. "I don't know if the genie can go back in the bottle, but no, I'm not leaving." She took a deep breath. "I'm comfortable here—the most comfortable I've been in quite some time."

"Let me know what you need, what I can do."

Sam

After Sophie went to her room, Sam stepped into the shower, his mind whirling with what she'd shared with him and his reaction to her. When he grasped her hand to pull her up, a spark had traveled directly to his cock. *My God, what am I doing? She. Is. My. Tenant. And she just shared a heartbreaking story with me. Sex should be the last thing on my mind! And yet here I am.*

A wave of sadness came over him. *I was not expecting what she told me. I thought maybe she'd been abused or raped, but it turns out she's a widow.* "Man, a widow, at thirty." He shook his head. "That's so awful."

When had he become so attracted to her? Had it started with the kiss after the race or before that? Sophie was pretty. He noticed that way back in November, when they met at the Thanksgiving feast. But redheads weren't usually his type, and when they met, he was still sorting things out with Norah and recovering from losing Quinn a second time.

When they'd started running together, he started seeing her in a different light, loving how totally she threw herself into the training. Her ability and determination had impressed him, especially since she had no concept of her talent. His favorite thing in the world right now, aside from Piper, was the sprints at the end of his runs with Sophie. They both went all out trying to beat each other, and he loved lying on the grass, recovering with her.

Sophie telling him about her childhood there didn't surprise him. They had shared other serious conversations lying there.

No, maybe Sam hadn't felt the telltale flickers of desire for her until that kiss, but he'd been attracted to her for far longer. He had laid the foundation, and all the pieces felt like they were coming together. *And I am going to do absolutely nothing about it because it's not what she wants.*

On Thursday night, Sam asked her about going north to run on the trails over the weekend.

"I don't feel like I'm in the right headspace," she said, sounding regretful. "I want to do it. You made the area sound very special. Perhaps in a few weeks."

Sophie had stayed in her room since Wednesday, except for her time in the kitchen.

But on Saturday night, Piper insisted on knocking on her door. "Come on, Sophie! It's movie night."

Sam was relieved to see her come out to sit with them. Movie night couldn't be skipped.

"What are we watching tonight?" Sophie asked. The June night was unusually sultry, and she had on shorts and a tank top.

"*Coco*! Have you seen it?" Piper answered with enthusiasm.

"Can't say that I have. Are you going to share that popcorn with me?"

"Oh gosh, yes! I forgot!" Piper ran to the kitchen to get a bowl for Sophie.

"She's so excited." Sophie smiled at Sam.

He smiled back. "Yeah, she loves movie night. Have you noticed that the stutter is almost gone?"

"I have. She's worked hard, and you and Norah have done your part too. I love success like this."

Sam nodded. Butterflies invaded his stomach when Sophie entered the room, and talking to her sent them into overdrive. *I feel like I'm back in high school with a pretty girl paying attention to me for the first time. But damn, she's so appealing.*

Piper came back with a bowl that she filled with popcorn for Sophie before climbing onto the couch next to Sam. When the movie finished, Sam carried her to bed, as he always did.

Sophie

Sam returned to find a beer and a glass of wine on the coffee table. Sophie had moved to the couch, and he gazed at her before sitting on the opposite end and taking a swallow of the beer.

Sophie didn't look at him, keeping her eyes on the wineglass, which she eventually picked up and spun between her fingers. They sat in silence until she finally met his gaze.

"I didn't tell you the entire story," she began.

He shook his head. "You don't have to."

"I've done some bad things. I've hurt people, truly hurt them."

"Are you warning me away?"

"Maybe. I don't know."

"I've hurt people too. There isn't a person alive who hasn't."

Sophie took another swallow of her wine. "I was in a comfortable situation when I left with Corey. We'd talked about how different our lives were going to be from the way we grew up. Then after Vegas, we went to Maryland, where he was stationed." Sophie massaged her forehead. "You're going to think I'm a terrible person. And you'll be right."

Sam edged closer to her, as if inviting her to share.

"Corey was living in a crappy trailer in a terrible part of the city." She rubbed her forehead again and tried to hold back the tears. "My mother and I had lived in better places. I discovered he was terrified of spending money. The thought of being poor..." She paused. "'Poor's' not the right word. Destitute, broke, penniless—take your pick. It paralyzed him." Her gaze had been across the room, but now she looked directly at Sam. "It's not uncommon for people who grew up like we did."

Sam nodded. "I can understand that."

"We fought constantly. I wanted more—we could afford more. Before he left on the last mission, we had our worst fight ever. I told him I wouldn't live that way any longer, and I'd be

107

gone when he returned." She ran her hand over her face, wiping away the tears. "I feel responsible for his death. If we hadn't argued... Was he careless because I upset him?"

Sophie placed her glass on the coffee table and leaned back, spent. *Now he knows it all. Well, almost all.* "You don't want to be involved with me. I wreck people."

"Our situation is very different." Sam looked serious, but not judgmental. "Again, we've all hurt people."

"Not like I have."

"I could tell you what I did to Quinn when she was nineteen, but I don't want to argue about which one of us acted worse when we were younger." He shook his head. "Where do we go from here?"

"You're my landlord, and I should not be feeling the way I do."

Sam chortled. "You're my tenant, and I've been arguing with myself about my feelings since last Saturday. And by the way, I feel like an old man when you refer to me as your landlord."

She couldn't smile back at him. "I'm afraid."

"Afraid of what?"

"Hurting you, ruining our friendship. This... Your friendship means a lot to me."

"It means a lot to me too. We can take it slow, figure out where we are." He gazed at her. "I don't expect to jump into bed tonight, or tomorrow, or even next week. We'll see how we feel."

Sophie blinked back more tears, trying to find the words to respond.

When she didn't, Sam asked, "What's wrong? I…"

"I… I like the idea of slow."

"We both agree that our friendship is important. Rushing into something is what will put that in danger. It could be we'll decide we don't want to go any further—I don't know. This is all unfamiliar territory for me. I've never tried to figure out a romantic relationship with my tenant."

Sophie knew he hoped to make her smile. "Yeah, the idea of romance with my landlord is new to me too. That sounds like the title of a cheesy novel."

Sam smiled. "Honesty is important to me. It's something I've worked on since Thanksgiving. Recognizing what I'm feeling and being open about it rather than telling people, particularly women, what I think they want to hear. That's been a huge thing for me to learn." He tapped his fingers on his chin. "So can we agree that's a key component in whatever this is going to be?"

"Yes, I'll be honest." She smiled. "I've struggled with that in the past. I've been in therapy off and on since Corey died, and honesty is a big part of that."

"One more thing." He looked into her eyes, and her heart skipped a beat. "I want to know you. I want to understand what life was like for you. Not all at once, but I hope you'll be able to trust me enough to share it with me."

"I've already shared more with you than I have with anyone," she admitted softly. "So yes, I want to do that."

"Come here." When Sophie moved over to sit next to him, Sam put his arm over her shoulder. "I feel like we negotiated a peace treaty." He sighed. "I'm not cut out to be a diplomat."

"You'd do fine." She relaxed against him.

Sam lowered his mouth to hers gently. She responded, and their lips parted and clung together longer than during either of their other two kisses. For the first time, they both seemed to get lost in the feelings.

Sam pulled away and stroked her cheek. "You okay?" When she nodded, he rubbed his hand along her arm. "Where does your coloring come from? I've known a few gingers, and they were all pale and freckled. You are so tan, and it's only June."

"My father was Italian. My skin tone came from him, and my hair and eye color came from my mother."

"Do you remember him?"

"A little. He worked at a car wash, and in my mind, he was handsome. I don't know if he was or if that's the story I created. I remember him carrying me to bed. Seeing you carry Piper to her bedroom sparked that memory."

"I'm sor—"

"No, no, don't be sorry. It's a good thing." She leaned up to kiss him again.

He swiveled his hips as if to hide his growing erection, but she didn't let him get away. She smiled, and he grinned back at her.

"I could do this all night," he said, "but Piper is up at six, regardless of the day."

They stood, and he pulled her close for a last kiss before they went to their rooms.

Chapter Twelve

Stand Up Paddleboarding

Sam

SAM WAS MAKING BREAKFAST the next morning when Piper walked into the kitchen, carrying Sophie's wineglass and his beer bottle. "Daddy, did you and Sophie stay up after I went to bed?"

"Why yes, we did." He laughed. "Is that okay with you?"

"Did you watch another movie?" She was serious. Movies were a big deal to her.

"No, we just talked."

Before Piper walked in, he'd been thinking about his unexpected conversation with Sophie. *This is going to be more complicated than my other relationships. She's so strong, but there's fragility too.*

He'd never rushed into sex, so he was comfortable taking it slow. *Yeah, why did I never rush into sex? Because I was still involved with Quinn when I met Ginger and still involved with Ginger when I started hanging out with Norah. And Quinn was so young...* He blew out a harsh breath, reminding himself that he'd made amends for that. He would do better.

This is the first time that I'm walking into a relationship without being tied to someone else. I want to get it right.

His heart jumped when Sophie walked in, and he wondered if hers did the same. "It's still hot today. Pip and I are going to the lake. Norah's coming for dinner, so we'll have to head home by mid-afternoon." He paused. "Do you want to join us, Sophie?"

She nodded slowly. "Yes, but I'll drive myself in case I want to stay longer than you do."

Sam and Piper arrived at the lake first and staked out a spot with towels, sand chairs, buckets and shovels. He chased Piper into the water, and they were there when Sophie arrived.

Sam watched as she found their spot and took off her T-shirt and shorts to reveal a black bikini. He felt a stirring in his cock, even in the water. *Oh, I'm in big trouble here. The water is springtime cold. Maybe that will keep things under control. But damn, she's gorgeous, with that tawny skin and those green eyes that just hypnotize me.*

Sophie splashed her way out to them and asked Piper to swim with her. Sam expected her to make eye contact, to acknowledge the night before somehow, but nothing showed in Sophie's demeanor. The three of them stayed in the water until their teeth were chattering and their skin wrinkled.

Piper started building a castle, and Sophie stretched out face down on a towel. Sam sat in one of the sand chairs, sneaking glances at Sophie, admiring her from behind and thinking about how Joe had gotten it wrong when he said anything with legs and boobs was Sam's type. What he liked most was a nice ass. And Sophie's qualified.

Later, Sam bought them sandwiches and drinks from a food truck. When Piper nudged Sophie to wake her up, she scrambled into the empty chair to eat.

After she finished her sandwich, Sophie surprised Sam by saying, "I'm going to rent a stand-up paddleboard for an hour. Have you ever done that? It's fun."

"I have not."

"I'll paddle for a little while, then you can try it. Piper isn't big enough to go on her own, but I can give her a ride. Or you can, if you feel confident enough."

Sophie took the board into the water and jumped up to a standing position without effort—she made it look easy. She paddled a long distance down the lake and then returned, motioning to him and Piper. "Come on out."

They walked out to meet her, and she showed him how to get up and start paddling. He fell several times, and Piper collapsed in giggles with every splash.

Despite the merriment in her eyes, Sophie suppressed her laughter and encouraged him. "You're doing great. You'll get it this time."

He finally stood and paddled around in a circle.

"Daddy, you did it!" Piper cheered. "Now take me!"

Sam wobbled a little on the board. "I'm not steady enough to have her on it. Can you take her out?" he asked Sophie.

Sophie nodded with a smile, and he hopped off, giving the board and paddle back to her.

Sam stood knee-deep in the water, enjoying Piper's delight in the ride.

When her hour with the board was up, Sophie came back to shore with Piper.

"Can we get one, please, Daddy?" Piper begged. "That was so much fun!"

"I'll think about it. Let me take the board back." He returned and told Piper they needed to pack up and leave. "We've already stayed longer than I planned." He gazed at Sophie. "I hate to leave. We'll see you back at the house."

Sam was cleaning the kitchen while Norah played chess with Piper when Sophie arrived carrying several bags of groceries, which she started putting away. She took a pint of Ben & Jerry's out of her bag, looked at Sam, and mouthed, "Later."

There was a big smile on Sophie's face as she walked to the living room. "Hi, Norah. Don't you love that chess table?" Sam had placed the recent addition in a spot where it didn't have to be put away since Piper challenged everyone to a match.

"I do like it. We're all learning chess together. She'll probably be playing circles around Sam and me in no time. Congratulations on your race. I heard you did well."

"Thanks. It was beginner's luck. I'm sure the next one will be more challenging. I'm covered with sand and need a shower." She nodded at Norah. "It was nice seeing you."

After Sam and Norah put Piper to bed, Norah collected her things, getting ready to leave. "Is Sophie going to be here all summer?" she asked.

"Yes, she's teaching summer school in July and August. What do you think of Pip going with her to the lake one day a week? Is that okay with you?"

Norah thought for a few minutes. "I guess so. I'm always a little nervous when Pip's near the water, which is stupid, because she swims like a fish. Do you think Sophie will keep a close eye on her?"

"I do, but I'll mention your concern. I worry too."

Norah paused before walking out the door and gave him a good-natured grimace. "I have a date tomorrow night. I'm nervous."

"That's great." He smiled encouragingly. "How'd that come about?"

"It's the brother of a co-worker. He's in town for a job interview."

"Well, have fun."

Sam sat on the couch, thinking about Norah dating. He was happy for her. *Should I have told her about Sophie? Maybe, but it's so new. I'm not telling anyone but Joe until it's more serious.*

Sophie came out of her room. "Ice cream?"

He nodded.

She scooped out two bowls and handed one to him before settling in the middle of the couch. "Was today a little weird for you? I wasn't sure how to act. I assume you don't want Pip to know that things have changed between us?"

"No, I don't." He eyed her. "Can I tell you that you killed me in that bikini?"

Sophie grinned.

"You looked so amazing, so sexy," he said. "And I looked like such a klutz on that paddleboard."

After they both finished their ice cream and put their bowls on the coffee table, Sam reached for her, and she leaned toward him. His lips met hers with more passion than ever, more need. Her lips parted, and his tongue entered to explore. When her tongue brushed against his, shock waves coursed through him.

Sophie sighed and squirmed closer to him. He pulled her onto his lap and savored the feel of her settling against him. His hands ran up and down her back, his desire for her overwhelming, but he would not allow himself to get carried away. He nibbled on her bottom lip and then trailed kisses down toward her neck.

Sophie sighed with pleasure. "You may not stand-up paddleboard so well, but you have other skills." She curled tighter against him.

He smiled against her skin. "Where did you learn to do that?"

"Paddleboarding?" She paused. "I was on vacation and had access to one every day, so I practiced until I had it down. I lived near a lake, and the man I was living with gave me one for my birthday. This is me being honest. I don't like admitting to you that I lived with someone."

"I was with Norah for eight years. It's okay." *Is she talking about Corey? Do I want to ask? Not right now.* Sam kissed her again and felt the same shock waves. He adjusted his hips, and Sophie rocked against him, making him groan with pleasure. "You know I kind of had a date when I went to Joe's a few weeks ago?"

She nodded.

"We kissed, and she made it abundantly clear that she was available. And I had no reaction, nothing. Before we officially ended things, Norah had tried to get something going, and I had no reaction to her either." He stroked Sophie's cheek. "I thought there was something wrong with me. And then you kissed me after the race. Now, every time I look at you, I get hard. Too much information?"

She grinned, her cheeks pinking. "No, I sat in my room all week, getting turned on every time I thought about you. I had to do something—that's why I started the conversation last night. Your interest was obvious, but you needed to know what you were getting into."

"I'm glad you did." He gave her another lingering kiss, then said, "I should go to bed. Unlike you, I must work tomorrow." He stood and pulled her into a tight hug.

"What's the week look like for running? I need to let my fellow gym rats know when I'll be there." Sophie smiled at him.

"Quinn invited me for dinner on Wednesday night, said she has something to tell me, so let's aim for Thursday."

On Wednesday, Quinn greeted him with a hug. They hadn't seen each other in over a month. "I'm grilling some chicken, and I made a salad. Can I get you a beer?"

Sam nodded, and she went to the kitchen. Looking around her living room, he noticed that the picture of her and Caden was still on the wall with her other hiking photos.

Quinn returned with his beer. "First you have to see this." She dangled a piece of paper in front of him—the degree from her master's program.

"All right! I'm so happy for you. I know getting through this semester wasn't easy." He hugged her tightly.

"Be careful—don't spill the beer!" Quinn took back her degree and handed him the bottle. "Since I finished, I've realized the classes were an excellent distraction. I've been at loose ends for the last month." They walked out to the deck where Quinn had set the table and lit a couple of citronella candles to ward off mosquitoes. After they sat down, she said, "I'm going to Honduras to work as a medical missionary for a month."

"You're what?" Sam's fork clattered to his plate. *Is she aware Caden is doing the same thing? Should I mention it?* He cleared his throat. "I'm sorry—you surprised me. How'd that come about?"

"The hospital encourages humanitarian work, and I need a change, so I found a clinic in Honduras that I like. I leave in a couple of weeks."

"That's a big step. It'll be quite a change from Dartmouth."

"Yeah, it will." Quinn paused. "I still miss Caden so much. Right after he broke it off, I'd text him every few days, but I never received a response. I don't do it as often now, but I still send at least one a week at ten thirty. That was when he texted me every night before we'd even had our first date. I thought maybe that would get to him. But it hasn't." She shook her head. "I must stop thinking about him all the time. At least I won't text him from there."

120

She looked so sad. Sam wanted to tell her how much Caden was struggling to stay away from her, but it wasn't his place. If nothing had changed for either of them after their time in Honduras, Sam decided he would tell her about his conversations with Caden.

"I don't even know if he's still going to therapy," Quinn continued. "It's killing me."

"I wish there was something I could do or say to make you feel better."

"I know. It helps to have you to talk to. I don't want to sound like a broken record to my friends. I'm sure they think I should be over him." She stopped there and smiled at him. "What's going on with you? Now that things are officially over with Norah, are you going to date? I know some nurses I could introduce you to."

"Actually..." Did he want to tell her about Sophie? "There's kind of something going on between me and the woman renting my spare room." He could see the surprise in Quinn's eyes. "I know. It sounds a little strange. We became close when we were training for that race I told you about, and there's an attraction between us. It's new, though, and we're taking it slow. She has some baggage."

"Baggage like Caden?"

"Not the same issues at all, but definitely stuff in her past that has played with her head in similar ways. She tried to discourage me from pursuing her. We talk pretty intensely, kind of like conversations I've had with you."

Quinn studied him. "You look happy."

"I am, but I'm nervous too. She's a little fragile."

Before he left that night, he gathered Quinn into a tight hug. "I hope Honduras gives you what you need. Let me know when you get back."

"I will. Take care of yourself."

He was glad he told her about Sophie—it felt good to talk about it, and Quinn was a good sounding board. Aside from Jesse, she had become one of his closest friends.

Sam spent the drive back home pondering what to do when he got there. Being involved with someone living in his house was a little weird. If Sophie lived somewhere else, on a night like this, when he had other plans, he wouldn't see her. He would probably call or text her after the dinner with Quinn. *But she's right there in my house.* It would feel supremely odd to call or text her.

She still didn't hang out in the living room very often, so he didn't expect to find her there. *What if she's in her room? Should I go to her? Do I want to see her?* Oh, hell yes, he wanted to spend time with her. The sun was nearing the horizon when he walked in the door, and Sophie was sitting on the deck with a glass of wine.

His stomach filled with butterflies, and he shook his head as he chuckled to himself. *I've got it bad.* He filled a glass with water and joined her. "I wondered where you'd be."

"I wasn't sure what to do. The idea of sitting in the living room, waiting for you, felt weird. It's a beautiful night, and a glass of wine on the deck seemed like a good idea. This is kind of awkward."

"It's nice out here. The deck doesn't get enough use."

They watched the sunset in peaceful silence.

"How was Quinn?" she asked.

"Oh God, you won't believe this." Sam ran his hand through his hair. "She's going to Honduras to work in a clinic for a month."

"Does that bother you?"

"When I was in Boston, I ran into the doctor she was involved with, and he's doing the same thing. He's there now."

"Wow. Does Quinn know? Is that why she's going?"

"Nope, she's going to get over him. Several clinics operate down there, so it's possible they won't be at the same one." But maybe they would be—perhaps that was what was meant to happen.

"You didn't tell her he's there?"

"No. He and I have been texting, and I haven't even told her about that." Sam looked at her sheepishly. "I suppose this goes against my talk about being honest."

Sophie laughed. "Well, kind of."

"I know. I decided on the way home, if she's still messed up over him when she gets back, I'll tell her about our conversations." He grinned and waggled his eyebrows. "She asked me if I wanted to be fixed up with a nurse from the hospital, and I told her that wasn't necessary."

Sophie nodded. "What else did you tell her?"

"Not a lot. Mostly that we were seeing where things could go."

Her mouth twisted. "Did you tell her I'm a head case?"

"I mentioned you tried to discourage me." He paused, trying to gauge if she was upset. "I hope that's okay. I'll never share any of the details. That's your story to tell."

Silence gathered around them before Sophie spoke again. "It's hard to get used to the idea that someone else knows about how I grew up. I've kept it so deeply buried for such a long time. Or about Corey."

Sam stood and reached for her hands. "I want you to you trust me. I know there's a lot we need to figure out."

She relaxed against him. "I'm working on it."

Chapter Thirteen

Meeting The Family

Sam

SOPHIE WAS ON THE deck again when Sam returned home after pizza night with Norah and Piper. The heat from earlier in the week had disappeared, and Sophie had a blanket from her bedroom draped over her shoulders.

She stood when Sam came out, and he grabbed the blanket and wrapped it around both of them as he held her.

"You don't have to be out here," he said. "You can sit in the living room."

"I know. I like it out here. It's peaceful."

They walked inside and relaxed on the couch. Sam rubbed her hands to warm them up.

Sophie sighed. "Your tenderness is warming me as much as the friction of your hands on mine." When he stopped, she inched her fingers under his sweatshirt.

Sam jumped when her still-cool hands touched his warm skin, and they both laughed. His hand slid under her shirt and rubbed her back. She sighed with pleasure, and Sam let one hand drift to her front. He stroked her breast through her bra, making her sigh again and lean against him.

When he pulled his hand back, she murmured, "No, please don't stop. I like you touching me."

Returning to her breast, Sam pushed the bra out of the way and gently pinched her nipple until it hardened under his fingers. Sam loved her slightly olive-toned skin and wondered what her nipples looked like. He wanted to have her breast in his mouth, to suck on it, to feel her reaction. He was harder than he'd been in ages, aching with it.

She could tell, because she snaked her hand between them and started stroking him through his jeans.

Sam shifted his hips against her, wishing that they were naked but still wanting to wait before they took the step of making love.

Where did that come from? Making love? Is that what I want to do? It's been a long time since I thought of sex in those terms.

They moved together, and his desire burned hotter.

Yes, that is what I want. But not yet.

He slid his hand back out from under Sophie's shirt and pulled her onto his lap. "I didn't even ask you about your day. I don't want you to think that making out with you is all I'm interested in." He ran his hands through her hair.

"I went to the gym this morning, then had lunch with a teacher I'll be doing summer school with, and we worked on school stuff this afternoon." She sighed. "Where did the warm weather go? I hate that the temperature changed so drastically."

"Me too. But it'll be good for running. We should do a long run tomorrow."

"The trails you mentioned—would tomorrow be a good time to go up there?"

"It would. I like that idea. I want to show you where I grew up. We should leave early, dressed for running, then after, we can go to the cabin to shower and change. I'll take you up to the mountain and to Willoughby Lake. It won't be warm enough to swim, but it's a pleasant drive."

"That sounds like a full day."

"It is. Do you mind?"

"No, I've never been that far north. It'll be fun to be somewhere different. I haven't been anywhere since I started at the school before Christmas." She brought her lips to his, and he opened his mouth to let her play as he pulled her tightly to him.

After a few minutes, she stopped and smiled. "I enjoy finishing my night this way."

"Me too."

They continued to explore each other long into the night.

Sophie

Sophie was in the kitchen when Sam came out of his bedroom in the morning.

He put his arms around her, drawing her into a kiss. "I want to start every day like this. Good morning." He smiled at her.

"Good morning." Their lips met again. "It's a nice way to face the day. I packed a tote bag with clothes to change into—are jeans and a T-shirt okay?"

"Yeah, we'll find a place for lunch, but everything is casual. Bring a sweatshirt too."

As they were driving, she asked him to tell her more about his job.

"We focus on bringing new business to the area or helping existing ones expand. Often, that involves renovations or new construction. That's where I get involved." He glanced at her. "Sometimes I tweak the plans to make them fit the area better, but mostly I manage the projects, making sure they stay on schedule and don't go over budget. We're going to break ground this summer on a large building that will offer space for several businesses." He rubbed his jaw. "It's the largest project I've worked on, and I'll confess, I'm a little nervous."

"You like it, though?"

"I do," he said, nodding. "At Thanksgiving, Joe suggested we start a business, Carpenter Brothers Carpentry. He'd do the construction on buildings I designed. Not sure how serious he was, but I like what I do, and I'm not much of a risk-taker. Security is important to me."

"I saw the sign and wondered what it meant."

Sam chuckled. "Matt made me that for Christmas. He's a talented woodworker—and who knows? Maybe someday Joe and I, or even all three of us, might get something going."

"Do you want to visit Matt and Jilly today?" she asked. "You haven't seen the baby since right after he was born, have you?"

"I'd like to do that, but I wasn't sure how you'd feel about it."

She smiled, glad he was being careful with her. "You want to know me. I want to know you. I'm okay with meeting them."

"How about my parents?"

Sophie took a deep breath then let it out slowly. "In for a penny, in for a pound."

Sam reached for her hand. "It'll be fine."

They parked at the trailhead, and he explained that they would have to be aware of bike riders. "They'll let you know they're behind you. And watch out for tree roots."

Once they were ready, they ran through the woods, up and down hills, and over bridges spanning streams.

About an hour later, Sophie felt her feet go out from under her just before she went down in a heap on the side of the trail.

Sam stopped and kneeled to help her up. "Are you okay?"

"I'm fine." She stood, brushing pine needles and dirt off her shirt. "That was embarrassing."

"It happens to everyone at some point. At least the pine needles are soft."

They kept going, running for another thirty minutes as they circled back to the car. Winded, they stood with their hands on their knees until they caught their breath.

"We can shower in the cabin. It's about a twenty-minute drive," Sam said.

"Do you have a key?"

"There's a coded lock, and we all have the code." Sam pulled into the drive at the cabin and pointed. "This still takes my breath away every time I see it."

Sophie climbed out of the car and stood for a minute to take it all in. "This is lovely. What a breathtaking getaway." The trees she knew he'd helped plant looked like they were doing well, and the flowers were blooming. The stream at the back of the property gurgled loudly.

Sam led her to the door and punched in the code. The living room had a couch, a loveseat, and two recliners as well as a large flat-screen television. It was decorated in earth tones with an enormous fireplace flanked by bookshelves dominating one wall. The dining room was open to both the living room and the kitchen and held a table big enough to seat eight people.

The kitchen was modern, with dark cabinets complemented by open shelving and an island with more seating.

Sam showed her the first-floor bedrooms, one fitted with bunk beds and the other with a queen-size bed.

They went out to the deck, which overlooked the brook and had a hot tub. Sophie commented on it, and Sam looked surprised.

"Joe wanted Mom and Dad to add a hot tub or a sauna. Must be the hot tub won. Want to try it out?" He raised his eyebrows.

Um, yes. Sophie grinned and kissed him.

Sam led her up the stairs to the primary bedroom. "Hot damn—they did a sauna too." He pointed out the cathedral ceiling and told her how they had installed all the sheetrock over Thanksgiving weekend. The east wall had a large window with a view of the mountains. "What do you think?"

She could hardly believe it was real. "My God, the whole thing is beautiful, amazing. I'd love to stay here."

"Joe put up the listing a few weeks ago, and they already have it booked for a couple of weeks in the fall and three weeks in the winter."

She laughed. "I think Carpenter Brothers Carpentry could do okay."

"I had very little to do with it, remember? My head was still stuffed up my ass when it started." He grinned. "Let's shower. We'll use the one downstairs. You can go first."

Once she was done and dressed, Sophie walked around the cabin, exploring it, while Sam showered. When Sam came out, she was sitting on the deck.

"Do you like it here?" he asked.

"I love it. This deck's even better than yours."

"I love it here, too, and sharing it with you makes it even more special." Sam reached for her hand. "I'd like to go in the hot tub or sauna, but I know you didn't bring a bathing suit, and I know where getting in naked would lead."

"Yes, it would probably put an end to the idea of taking it slow." Sophie chuckled. "Can we come back? After we've... you know." She couldn't help giving him a suggestive look.

"Definitely." Sam stood and held his hand out to Sophie. "We're going to have lunch at the mountain, then drive to Lake Willoughby before we go to Matt's."

They ate lunch at a restaurant with a view toward Willoughby Gap. When they were driving to the lake, Sam kept glancing at Sophie.

Finally, she laughed at him. "What?"

He grinned. "I just can't wait to see your reaction when we get closer."

Sophie gasped as the glacial lake carved between two mountains came into view. Sam pulled over to the side of the road, and Sophie's head swiveled as she tried to take it all in. On the right, massive stone cliffs towered overhead; the mountain on the left, while shorter, was covered with deep-green fir trees that reached the water's edge.

The scene took Sophie's breath away, and she turned toward Sam. "Is this what we were looking at from the restaurant?" When Sam nodded, she said, "It's amazing."

"I love it here year-round," Sam said. "We'll come back in the fall when the leaves change color. In the winter, ice climbers play on those cliffs, and you'll see shanties sheltering the people ice fishing on the lake. They take some record-breaking lake trout out of there."

Sophie continued to gaze at the mountains in awe, and when Sam drove by a campground, she squealed, "Paddleboards for rent! Are we going to come back here too?"

"On a warmer day. The water is frigid, even on the hottest day of the summer." Sam smiled and told her some myths about the lake.

As Sam drove to Matt's house, Sophie's nerves kept her quiet.

"Are you okay?" Sam asked after a while.

"I'm a little nervous," she admitted. "Meeting the family, you know."

"I know."

Matt opened the door before Sam knocked and went straight to Sophie. "I'm Matt, the best of the Carpenter brothers. And you are?"

As she laughed, Sam introduced her. "This is Sophie Palmer."

"You are far too pretty to be spending time with my brother."

Sophie shot Sam a bemused look. Sam had told Sophie before they arrived that Matt liked to bait him at any chance he got, and she now had proof.

"He thinks he's funny. Don't be a pain in the ass, Matt."

Matt led them inside and introduced Jilly, who was holding the baby.

"Can I hold him?" Sam asked, arms outstretched. As Jilly handed him over, Sam said, "He's grown since Joe and I were here, but still so tiny."

"What's his name?" Sophie asked.

"This is William Matthew Carpenter," Sam declared before either of the parents could answer. "The first of the second generation of Carpenter brothers. Or the second of the first generation of Carpenter cousins."

"If there's going to be more, you and Joe better get to work," Matt snarked.

Jilly rolled her eyes. "The two of them act like they're still six and nine years old—pay no attention. Have you and Sam been dating long?"

Sophie looked at Sam, and they both smiled.

Sam answered. "It's pretty new." His face reddened, and Sophie found his awkwardness endearing. "She's renting my spare room. We've been running together, and I wanted to take her on the trails. She suggested we stop here so I could see this little guy again."

"We're glad you stopped." Jilly smiled warmly at Sophie. "Sam mentioned the race you were training for, and it's good to meet you."

He cooed at the baby while Matt got them drinks. Sam and Matt continued to razz each other while Jilly and Sophie talked throughout the visit.

Once they left, the mood changed during the drive to Sam's parents' house. Sophie could tell Sam was nervous. She reached over, placing a comforting hand on his leg. "Are you okay?"

"My choice in women has always been an issue between my father and me. He's liked none of my long-term relationships." Sam placed his hand over Sophie's. "Things are better between us, but I'm still nervous every time I see him." He squeezed her fingers gently. "Until I see that he's sober."

When his mother answered the door, she gave him a quick hug and invited them in.

"Mom, this is Sophie Palmer. Sophie, this is my mother, Laura."

The two women shook hands, and Laura led them into the great room, where Trent was watching television. Sam introduced Sophie to his father.

Trent stood and shook Sophie's hand. "It's nice to meet you. What brought you up here?"

"We've been running together, and I wanted her to have the chance to run on the trails."

Sophie could hear the nerves in Sam's voice, and he placed his palm against his thigh. Was his leg trembling?

"We were sweaty and dirty when we finished, so we went to the cabin to shower," Sam said. He took a deep breath before ending with, "We left it clean, brought our own towels."

Trent laughed. "I'm sure it's fine. We don't have anyone renting it this summer, so it's available for all of us to use."

"It's a beautiful spot, Mr. Carpenter," Sophie said, hoping to give Sam a breather. "Sam said that you and Joe did most of the work."

"Thank you—and please, I'm Trent. We all worked on it, and it looks pretty good. Did Sam show you pictures of what it looked like before?"

He hadn't, so Trent found a photo album and flipped to the pictures of the original cabin. The pictures included shots of Sam and his brothers when they were kids.

She smiled over the pictures. "Wow, the change is remarkable. And which one of these is you, Sam? You all look alike!"

Trent pointed out which brother was which, and while they were busy looking at the album, Sam followed his mother into the kitchen.

Sophie could hear their conversation.

"Is Sophie the woman you were talking about the day we planted the flowers?" Laura asked. Sam must have nodded because she then asked, "She's your tenant?"

"Yes, but it's becoming more. We're seeing where it might lead."

Trent made Sophie laugh as he described the antics of Sam and his brothers. She was sure he was sober and hoped Sam could relax.

When he joined them, Sophie took Sam's hand while they walked to the dining room. "You okay?" she whispered in his ear.

Sam nodded. "Better," he whispered back.

While they were eating, Sophie said, "I noticed the barn. Do you have animals?"

Trent chuckled. "No, this hasn't been a working farm since we've been here. We use the barn for storage."

Sam jumped in. "Hey now, are you forgetting about Brutus?" He looked at Sophie, smiling. "He was a steer we raised one summer."

"Oh yeah, I tried to be a gentleman farmer for a few summers." Trent shook his head. "We tried the steer, pigs, chickens, you name it. The boys always became attached, so there was a big hullabaloo when it was time to butcher them."

"We loved Brutus," Sam said sadly.

Sophie and Laura giggled at his long face. Then Sophie asked if they had ever considered converting the barn into a vacation rental.

"I've seen beautifully renovated barns, and that cabin is so special," she added. "I bet you could make the barn amazing."

Trent looked at Sam with a light in his eyes, and Sam nodded, grinning. They both began talking at the same time.

"There are a couple of different ways to do it. Several individual rooms and a common area with a kitchen and living room—"

"It's an enormous structure. We could put several units in it—"

"It would be pricey—each unit would need a bathroom—"

"We'd have to insulate..."

They stopped talking and looked at Laura.

She smiled, and Sophie could see how happy she was to see her husband and son getting along after so many years of estrangement.

Chapter Fourteen

Ready For The Next Step

Sam

SAM CHATTERED NONSTOP AS he drove home, aware Sophie hadn't seen him like this and was happy to share it with her. "That has never happened! My dad and I having the same idea at the same time and bouncing thoughts off each other like that. Never! Actually, it was your idea. That was amazing!" He reached for her hand.

"I love seeing you this excited."

"I've never had that with my dad. It's incredible. And I think he likes you. He's never liked any of the women I've dated. So many ideas are flying around my head. I'm going in a hundred different directions."

When they got out of the car at the house, they hugged tightly while still in the driveway. "Thank you for being willing to go," he murmured into her hair. "This was an outstanding day."

Once inside, they walked to the couch, and Sam pulled her down to his lap. As he kissed her deeply, his hand slid under her T-shirt and fondled her breast then pushed her shirt up to move her bra out of the way.

His tongue flicked over her nipple, and he felt it harden. Reluctantly, he moved his mouth away and looked at her. "Do you mind?"

"Not at all." Sophie sighed and moved her hand to the back of his head to bring it back to her.

Sam played with her nipple and leaned in to take more into his mouth. He sucked hard, and they both moaned with pleasure.

Sophie stroked him through his pants, and Sam brought his hand between her legs. She squirmed at his touch. "My God, you're making me so hot. Don't stop."

Sam continued to suckle first on one breast then the other. He finally paused and buried his head in her neck, nibbling his way back to her mouth. "I want you so much. But not tonight."

"Or tomorrow night, or next week?" She teased him with an echo of his words when they talked last Saturday.

"Well... I'm not sure I can wait that long."

"Me either." She kissed him and clung more tightly to him.

"We should talk about birth control." He cleared his throat. "I, um, I have a box of condoms."

"I have an IUD. STIs aren't an issue for me, either, because I was tested, and I'm clean."

"So we don't need the condoms, but I should be tested too. There haven't been a lot of women, and I'm fairly certain I don't have anything, but that's not proof. I'll get the tests done next week." He ran his hand over his jaw. "I mean, we could use condoms, but I'd like to wait."

"I'm okay with that." She laughed softly. "You aren't afraid of awkward conversations, are you?"

Before he went to sleep that night, Sam texted Joe.

> *Sam: Ever think about turning Mom and Dad's barn into a vacation rental?*

> *Joe: Can't say that I have, but I like it. That would be an enormous project.*

Sam: Sophie and I went north today to run. I showed her the cabin, and we went to Matt's then to Mom and Dad's. We were talking after dinner, and she threw out the idea. Dad and I both grabbed onto it and started tossing ideas around. It was amazing.

Joe: Dad liked it?

Sam: Yeah, and my mind is going in a hundred different directions. Do you know the dimensions? I'm going to sketch out some ideas.

Joe: I'll find out. Emma and I have a few days off, and we're going to the cabin tomorrow afternoon and staying until Wednesday. We can stop at your place and see what you've done.

Sam: That sounds good. Stay for dinner with us.

Joe: Any more kisses with your tenant?

Sam: Where's the middle-finger emoji?

The next morning, Sam was sitting at the table with a large sketch pad and his laptop when Sophie came out of her room.

"You look busy." She put her arms around his neck and leaned down to kiss him.

"I have all these ideas. We could go several directions with the barn—all one-bedroom units or a mix of one- and two-bedroom units or self-contained apartments. Would we want to use the height to make two stories or leave soaring ceilings? I'm getting some of these ideas down." He told her about Joe and Emma's planned visit, then pushed back from the table and gathered her into a hug, nibbling on her neck.

She moved against him. "I've never seen you this excited about something."

"I know. Maybe nothing will come of it—this would be a massive undertaking and very costly. But it's fun to be using my design skills." He smiled. "This is more exciting than any project I did while I was in school. I'm going to get some breakfast and coffee. Do you want something? Do you want to do something today? Joe isn't leaving the city until midafternoon, so the whole day is open."

She shrugged. "I'll drink my smoothie, and can I watch you work?"

"Please do. Then I can bounce ideas off you."

After they ate, they sat at the table together for several hours. Sam explained to Sophie what he was doing, and she offered some tips. By noon, he had drawings of all the ideas they'd talked about.

When they were ready for a break, Sam stretched and looked at her. "We ran hard yesterday, so how about going for a walk? I'd like some fresh air."

As they walked, they held hands.

"That was fun," Sam said. "I enjoyed having you there with me. That's the most focused I've ever been working. Have I told you I've been taking ADHD meds since January?"

"No, you didn't. How did you find out you needed those?"

"My distractibility and messiness were a big issue for Norah. I mentioned it to Quinn when I saw her in Boston, and she suggested it. When I discussed it with Archie, that's my therapist, he prescribed them. It's made a big difference, but today was the first time I could see it so clearly." He thought for a few seconds. "I'm also seeing it in our running. I used to find any excuse not to work out, and I haven't been doing that." He grinned at her. "Of course, it might be because I enjoy running with you."

"You're so open about therapy," she said, her voice hushed. "I feel like it's something to keep hidden."

"Like I told you before, I've been at it for a while. Two years of couples counseling with Norah, then family counseling when Piper started stuttering, and now on my own. In the last six months, it's finally been working for me. I was quite a mess at the end of last year. You wouldn't have liked me." He hadn't liked himself much either. "Are you still doing therapy?"

"Yes, we talk on the phone every week. She's great and makes herself available by text if I have a crisis." She grimaced. "Like the cookies. When I walked out that night, I drove to town and sent her a text, and she called me to talk about it." Sophie sighed. "I feel so stupid about that."

Sam stopped and hugged her. "Don't. Once you explained things, it made sense. Even your brief explanation of food insecurity helped me understand. You educated both me and Piper." He put his arm over her shoulder and kept her close as they walked back to the house.

Later that afternoon, Joe knocked then let himself and Emma in. After introducing Sophie and Emma, Sam had Joe and Emma sit in front of the laptop while he and Sophie stood behind. Sam kept his arm around Sophie's waist as he talked Joe through the sketches.

Joe whistled. "There's a lot of ideas here, and I like them all. You're jazzed about this, aren't you? I'll try to feel Dad and Mom out while we're there."

"I've enjoyed working on the design, but my project management skills will help on the scale of it too," Sam said. "There are some paper drawings that you can take with you. Come out to the deck while I grill."

Joe followed Sam outside. "Looks like that kissing worked out okay."

"Yeah, we're taking it slow. Mom figured it out pretty quickly. True confession? I like her." Sam smiled. "I like her a lot."

The dinner conversation was lively among the four of them. Joe remarked on the chess table, and Sam said it was to provide more mental stimulation.

"Thank God for that. I love my niece, but I about died playing Candy Land at Christmas."

Sam nodded. "We visited Matt and Jilly yesterday too. Matt was his usual pain-in-the-ass self. I must admit, though—it was a trip seeing him hold his son."

Joe smiled. "We'll see them while we're up there. Can't wait to see how much the baby has grown."

Sophie found the pictures she'd taken of Sam holding William and handed her phone to Joe. When he handed it back, she said, "Oh, you should see this one too." It was one of Sam with Piper at the lake. "Ask Sam about stand-up paddle boarding." She grinned.

"I sense a story." Joe looked expectantly toward Sam.

"A very short story. I suck."

Joe laughed and nudged Emma. "Tell them your news."

Emma took a deep breath, and her cheeks flushed. "I'm moving from the field to a late afternoon anchor spot. I'll start when we get back."

Joe was beaming, and Sam could tell that he was happy Emma was staying in Boston.

Joe gathered the drawings that Sam had done. "I'll let you know what the thoughts are. Thanks for dinner."

"Anytime. Enjoy the cabin. It surprised me to see both a hot tub and a sauna."

Joe waggled his eyebrows suggestively as he and Emma walked out the door, making Sam laugh.

Once they were gone, Sophie took Sam's hand. "I'll take care of the kitchen in the morning."

Sam protested, but she led him to the couch.

"I like your brothers. You have good relationships with them." She kissed him deeply. "And I'm jealous of Joe and Emma spending time at the cabin. I'd love to go there with you for an overnight."

He was already growing hard at her nearness, but the thought of them together in the hot tub aroused him even more. "We'll go up in a few weeks. But I don't want to be in separate bedrooms." Sam slid his hands under her shirt and sought her breast.

"I'd like to share a bed with you." Her hand snaked inside his jeans.

"Oh, Sophie..." He pushed her shirt out of the way, unhooked her bra, and took her nipple between his teeth. His hand moved between her legs to stroke her heat.

She squirmed under him. "You're killing me." She moaned and stroked his erection.

Sam withdrew his mouth and pulled her shirt down. He put his hand over hers, increasing the pressure on his cock before he slid his arm around her back. "Do you remember me saying maybe we'd decide we don't want to go any further, that maybe we'd decide friends is what we want?"

"Oh yes, I remember."

"I want to go further. Just friends won't be enough."

"For me, either. But..."

Sam cocked his head at her when she paused.

Finally, she said, "Your friendship still means everything to me. I don't want to lose it."

"I know. And I feel like that's getting stronger as well. I loved having you there while I was working this morning. And oh God, I love this." Sam kissed her deeply before he got up to go to bed.

Chapter Fifteen

Does Sam Believe In Forever

Sam

AFTER GETTING TESTED FOR STIs, Sam was told he would have the results by Friday. He thought about what that meant. They were both ready to take it all the way.

Sophie said she hadn't been with anyone since Corey had died, and Sam wanted their lovemaking to be good for her. If the amount of heat they'd generated on the couch was any sign, he was certain it would be.

He figured it could happen Friday or Saturday night. For the first time since Norah had moved out, Sam wished Piper wouldn't be with him. But he realized he was going to have to juggle Piper and private time with Sophie. Piper would always be his first concern, and Sam didn't want her to know about him and Sophie right away, which Sophie understood. *Should we wait until Pip is at Norah's?* That would mean waiting until Wednesday. He couldn't suppress the groan that thought caused. *It isn't like Norah, and I never had sex with Piper in the house. We learned to be quiet. But what if Sophie's a screamer? Dammit, another awkward conversation we need to have.*

Joe told him that his mom and dad had talked about the barn project, loved his sketches, and wanted to move forward. Sophie was almost as excited as Sam when he gave her that news. They spent time playing with his sketches on Wednesday and Thursday night. The next step would be to put some costs on the project so that the family could make an informed decision.

His results were in on Friday, and as Sam suspected, he was free from any STIs. When he picked up Piper that afternoon, it was obvious she didn't feel well. She had a slight fever, her nose was stuffy, and she was sneezing. A summer cold—the last thing either of them needed. Sam gave her Tylenol and some chicken noodle soup, remembering Norah swore by that when any of them were sick. The only thing Piper wanted to do was cuddle with him on the couch. She went to bed at eight, and Sam knew she would sleep fitfully.

Sophie had stayed in the living room to watch movies with them, and after Piper was in bed, she moved to his arms.

"If the past is any indicator, Pip won't sleep well tonight," Sam said. "She may end up in my bed or want me in hers." He kissed Sophie. "This isn't how I was hoping for tonight to go. My test results are in, and I'm clean."

Sophie rested her head on his chest. "I understand. It's okay. How long do you think she'll be down?"

"I think she'll be much better by tomorrow afternoon. The first twenty-four hours are usually the worst. When I let Norah know Pip was sick, she said she showed some signs Thursday night."

"You're so good with her." Sophie kissed him. "You should go to bed. It sounds like you might not get much sleep tonight."

Sam stood to go to his room and then sat down again, reaching for Sophie's hands. "If we..." His cheeks reddened. He searched for the words while Sophie held his gaze. "If we have sex while Piper is here, we'll have to keep the noise down." The words came out in a rush, and Sophie's mouth quirked slightly. "I mean, her door will be closed, and we'll close mine, but..."

Soft laughter bubbled from Sophie, and she placed a finger over Sam's lips. "I can be quiet." Watching him relax, she said, "You're very cute when you're embarrassed."

As predicted, Piper cried in the night and wanted him to stay in her room. She slept much later than usual, but seemed a little better when she finally woke up. By early evening, she was nearly back to normal, with no fever and only a few sneezes.

Piper felt well enough to go to Sophie's room to get her for movie night. As she led Sophie to the living room, Sam heard Piper say, "We're watching *Beauty and the Beast*. Have you seen it?"

"Nope, haven't seen that one." Sophie settled in the recliner and smiled at Sam.

Piper looked at her with a serious expression. "You haven't seen any of them. Didn't you watch movies when you were little? Daddy has seen the movies."

Sophie shrugged. "I think you just pick ones I haven't seen. That's why I enjoy watching with you. I get to see things that are new to me."

Piper was asleep when the movie ended, and Sam carried her to her room.

She woke up as he placed her in bed. "Daddy, I love Sophie. I want her to live with us forever."

Sam smiled. "I hope she'll be with us for a long time."

"Not forever?"

"Forever is hard to predict. It's difficult to know all the changes that could take place. We should concentrate on being happy with what we have right now."

"Do you not believe in forever because Mommy left?"

My God, where do all these questions come from? Does she ask Norah these kinds of things?

Sam sat down on Piper's bed and gathered her into his lap. "Mommy moving out was hard, and it made me sad. You're right." He sighed. "Before she left, I thought we would live together forever in this house. But I think we are all better off now. We have fun when it's you and me, you have fun when you're with Mommy, and we have fun when we're all together. We'll be a family forever, but have two different homes for you to live in."

Piper nodded. "Can new people come into a family?"

"Of course—sometimes a family starts out as two people or three like us and then they have another baby, so then they are four."

"Will you and Mommy have another baby?"

"I don't see that happening." He rubbed his jaw. *This is killing me. Why is she coming up with all of this tonight?*

"How about Sophie? Could she be part of our family?"

"It's more complicated for adults to become part of a family. There would be lots of things to work out." He kissed her forehead. "That's enough questions for tonight. You need to go to sleep."

"You should work those things out with Sophie. I love her, and I want her here forever..." Piper trailed off, almost asleep already.

Sam slid her under the covers and quietly slipped out of her room. He closed her door and leaned against it to pull himself together, taking a couple of deep breaths and running his hand through his hair.

As Sam entered the living room, Sophie asked, "Everything okay? You were with her for a long time."

A beer waited for him, and she held a wineglass, as had become their usual Saturday night ritual.

Sam sat down, pulled her close, and said nothing for a few minutes. "She had some questions—existential questions that six-year-olds shouldn't be asking." He shook his head. "I need to ask Norah if Pip asks her these kinds of things." He heaved a sigh. "Okay, I'm all right now." He nuzzled her neck.

After a moment, Sophie pulled back a bit. "I've seen none of the movies."

Sam raised his head to look at her.

"When Pip asked about the movies earlier... why you'd seen them, and I hadn't? Watching movies doesn't happen much when you're living in a car or even in a homeless shelter. If we had a movie night, it would usually be an adventure or superhero movie." She shrugged. "You said you want to know what my life was like. That was part of it."

Pulling her tighter, Sam put his head back, and a tear rolled down his cheek.

"Hey, I didn't tell you that to make you cry." Sophie wiped the tear away. "I'm sorry."

"It's okay. It hit me hard on top of her questions. I want to know. Please don't ever hold back." He kissed her deeply and continued holding her. "She should sleep okay tonight." Sam gazed into her eyes. "I want to make love to you."

Sophie's face flushed. "I want that too."

Sam stood and took her hand. "Let's go to my bedroom." He had folded the duvet back earlier, and a lamp glowed with a soft light in the corner. "I don't want to be in the dark. I want to see you. Is that okay?"

"Yes, I want to see you too."

Sam reached for the hem of her T-shirt and pulled it off. Her bra was white lace. His hand smoothed over her breast, and she shuddered in response. He gathered her close, relishing the feel of her chest against him. After unhooking her bra, he let it drop to the floor and moved her slightly away from him so he could look at her.

"I've imagined what your nipples must look like. Those glimpses in the living room were not enough. You knock me out." He lowered his head to take one in his mouth. Her nipples hardened, and he flicked his tongue over the nub before sucking on it. They both moaned, and her hips shifted against him.

Sophie reached for his belt, and Sam stood silently while she undid the buckle and lowered his zipper before grasping the sides of his jeans and lowering them to the floor. He stepped out of them, and she pulled his shirt off. He smiled, standing before her in his boxers.

His erection strained against the cloth, and as Sophie's hand closed over it, he groaned.

"I'm ahead of you," he said, keeping his voice low. "Those pants have to go." Sam shoved her sweatpants to the floor and took a deep breath at the sight of her in a lacy white thong. "Damn, that is hot. I want to take it slow but not next-week slow."

She laughed softly, which was what he'd hoped for.

"I want to savor this, but it's hard." He grinned. "Double entendre intended."

"And now I'm more naked than you are," she complained. "Off with the boxers." She slid them down and took a deep breath at the sight of his erection. Her arms went around him, and Sam hugged her tightly. "This feels so good. I'm not sure about that slow pace either."

Sam worked his hands down to the thong and eased it off. "I want to do so many things with you." He cupped her ass in his hands as she gripped his erect cock.

They ended up on the bed with her in his lap. His hands ran up her back, and he ducked his head to reach her breast. He teased the nipple with his tongue and made her wriggle. She stroked his cock from balls to head, and Sam suppressed a groan as he thrust against her hand.

He took her breast in his mouth, sucking gently at first then more aggressively. Sophie moaned and swiveled toward him. Her leg swung around to straddle him so her center could rub against his cock as he fondled her breasts.

Sophie kept grinding against him, whispering, "Oh God. I want you so much."

Sam was murmuring as he lifted her and moved to the middle of the bed. His tongue explored her mouth again as he moved his hand toward her slit. He found her opening and slid a finger inside.

"Yes, don't stop," she begged, writhing against him. Her hand found his cock again and started stroking him.

He gasped. "I won't last long with you doing that."

"I want to feel you inside me."

Sam rolled her onto her back and slid another finger into her. "You're so wet."

"I know—please, Sam."

He pulled his hand away and climbed on top of her, rubbing his cock on the nub between her legs before sliding inside. She was tight, and not wanting to hurt her, he moved slowly—but she raised her hips to meet him. When he was all the way in, he stopped moving and looked at her.

Sophie bucked her hips up. "I feel like I've been waiting forever for you."

"You're so beautiful, so tight, so hot. This is so right." Sam moved, and Sophie matched his rhythm. It would not take long for him to orgasm, but he wanted to be sure she came, so he slid his hand between them.

When his fingers found her clit, she drew a sharp breath. She moved faster, wildly, before shuddering silently beneath him.

"Oh my God." She continued to move against him until he exploded, barely able to swallow his shout of pleasure.

He collapsed and rolled them onto their sides. He found her mouth and kissed her ravenously while he waited for his heartbeat to return to normal. Sam moved back so he could see her face. "Are you..." Then he saw the tears. "Sophie, sweetheart, did I hurt you? What's wrong?"

"No." She wiped the tears away. "It's just—it's been a long time, and the emotion had gone out of it. But this... This is all feels." More tears coursed down her cheeks, and she buried her face in his shoulder. "I'm being silly."

"Shh, shh. Don't say that. You're fine." Sam held her until the tears stopped.

"I'm sor—"

Sam's finger touched her lips. "Stop. You don't need to say it. I'm not saying 'Love means never having to say you're sorry'"—he grinned, hoping she understood his reference — "but not for this. Do you want your wine?"

"That would be nice."

Sam pulled his boxers on before going to the living room. When he came back, he handed her the wineglass and his beer and took the boxers off before climbing back into bed.

Sophie handed him the beer, and he took a long swallow.

"I've dreamed of being naked next to you." He put his arm over her shoulder to pull her closer.

Sophie sighed. "I should go to my room. Piper shouldn't find out about this. Not while it's this new." Her voice was soft, and the tears had left her eyes, replaced by a hint of laughter. "Was I quiet enough?"

"You were perfect. I don't want you to leave. We can set an alarm for early morning, and you can go back to your room then." He smiled at her. "If you don't mind having your sleep interrupted, I'd like to sleep with you next to me."

"Interrupted sleep will be worth it to spend the night here with you."

Chapter Sixteen
Piper Loves Sophie

Sophie

Sᴏᴘʜɪᴇ ᴡᴀѕ ᴅʀɪɴᴋɪɴɢ ᴄᴏꜰꜰᴇᴇ on the deck the next morning when Piper came outside. "Hi. Pip. How are you feeling?"

"I'm better. Can I sit in your lap?"

She had never asked to do that before, and Sophie's heart fluttered as she opened her arms to the little girl.

"I love you, and I want you to live with us forever. Did Daddy tell you?" Piper's gaze was intense.

Sophie shook her head. "He didn't, but Pip, you've touched my heart."

"I think he doesn't believe in forever because Mommy moved to a different house, but I want him to work on making you part of our family." Piper hugged her, hopped down, and went inside.

Piper's words stunned Sophie, and she was gazing into the distance with a smile on her face when Sam came out onto the deck.

"Pip has a birthday party to go to later, so we can go for our run while she's gone," Sam said. When she didn't answer, he studied her more closely. "Are you okay?"

She continued smiling. "Honestly, never better."

They ran eight miles, raced at the end, and collapsed on the lawn as usual.

Sophie rolled up on her side. "Piper told me you're going to be working out the details so I can be part of your family. I understand why you were emotional after that conversation."

"See? I told you." Sam shook his head. "I don't know if these questions happen when she's with Norah, but they kill me. What's going to happen when she's a teenager?" He grinned at Sophie. "Did she tell you she loves you?"

"She did. My heart is so full. I don't know if I've ever had that said to me with such sincerity."

"She's really something." Sam stood and reached for her hand. "Come shower with me." He laughed. "I've wanted to say that for so long."

Sam pulled her into a kiss as soon as they walked inside, then he led her to his shower. He tugged her shirt off and pulled down her shorts. Sophie did the same to him, and they embraced before stepping into the shower. He soaped her body and gently ran a washcloth over her, then lowered his mouth to her breast. Sam sucked hard on the nipple and moved his hand between her legs. Sophie moaned and grasped him while thrusting against him.

"Put your arms around my neck," Sam murmured.

He lifted her up, she wrapped her legs around his waist, and he lowered her onto his erection. Sophie welcomed the feeling of him filling her up as much as she had the night before. They moved together and came quickly.

"My God, what you do to me," he said, letting her down.

She laughed. "Is this part of the details you're working on?"

Sam chuckled, turned off the water, and wrapped her in a towel. He dried her gently before he ducked his head to go after her breast. His cock was hard again, and Sophie was sighing with pleasure. They walked to his bedroom, and Sophie pushed him onto the bed. After climbing on top of him, she grasped his erection and guided him slowly inside. Cupping her breasts, she invited him to play.

Sam took one in his mouth and pinched the nipple on the other. She languidly moved up and down on his cock, teasing him by nearly letting him slide out and then taking him deeply again and again. She stopped moving altogether, letting Sam's cock fill her completely. They both moaned, and his mouth found hers. Their tongues twined, and he moved his hips against her, sliding his hand between them and finding her clit.

Sophie groaned. "You don't want this to last long, huh?" She began moving again, and his hips frantically thrust up against her. She felt her orgasm build as he filled her even more completely. He came with a moan, and she followed right behind.

Sam put his arms around her back, hugged her tightly, then asked, "No tears today?"

"My God, no. That was incredible." Sophie smiled. "There are no other words."

Sophie worked to hide her attraction to Sam over the next two days while Piper was there. They didn't want to lead her on when neither of them was sure where things were going to go, but when Piper left for Norah's on Wednesday, they went at each other with abandon, and Sophie contentedly slept the entire night in Sam's arms.

Sam arrived home first on Thursday, and when Sophie came in from spending the afternoon at the lake, she nearly melted at the sight of him. He'd had meetings that day and was wearing a white button-down shirt and tie.

Sophie grabbed the tie and led him to the bedroom. She sank onto the bed, then reached out to unzip his pants and slide them down to his knees. Her legs spread and invited him in. She loosened the tie, unbuttoned his shirt, and raked his nipples with her teeth. Her legs wrapped around his waist as he entered her, and her hips rose to meet his thrusts. "Oh, Sam, yes, yes," she cried as the first of multiple orgasms began rolling over her.

When Sam finally came, he collapsed on top of her, tangled in his pants, shirt, and tie. He panted, trying to catch his breath. "Oh, babe."

Sophie sighed. "You look so hot. Will I get to see this again?"

He laughed. "If it's going to get this kind of reaction every time, you'll definitely see it again."

Sophie slid the tie over his head, and she buried her head against his chest and listened to the thump of his heart. When it slowed to normal, she raised her head and gently kissed his lips.

Sam

Two weeks later, Sam stood at the door to the deck, watching Sophie gaze across the landscape. He'd come from dinner with Norah and Piper, a rare Thursday night occurrence because Norah and Piper were heading to Maine the next day. They were going to spend a week at the beach, and while Sam would miss being with Piper, he was looking forward to an entire week

alone with Sophie. It was a warm July evening, and Sophie wore shorts and a halter top. She had taken Piper to the lake that afternoon, and Sam could see how the sun had kissed her skin. He couldn't wait to run his fingers over her warmth. The weeks since they had begun making love were some of the best he could remember.

Sam went back to the kitchen and scooped out two bowls of ice cream. As he opened the door to the deck, Sophie turned to him, and she beamed with a smile.

"Hey." She reached for one of the bowls. "You read my mind. I was thinking about ice cream."

Sam caressed her forearm with his fingers. "I knew you'd feel warm. I love how you look after a day at the lake. Pip said you rented a kid-size paddleboard for her today."

"I did." Sophie smiled. "She did great. And I cleared it with Norah first."

"That was appreciated." Sam held Sophie's hand as he told her that Piper had told Norah about wanting Sophie to be part of their family. "Pip wants you to come to pizza night."

"Oh God. How did Norah react to that?" Sophie asked.

Sam felt his face redden.

Sophie's eyes narrowed. "You told her about us, didn't you?"

"Yeah, she read it in my expression," he said, smiling to reassure her. "She seems okay with it. She likes you."

Sophie took a deep breath. "Well, that's handy, I guess." The only sound for a few minutes was their spoons scraping the bowls.

Finally, Sam said, "You're good with Piper. We've never talked about kids. Do you see them in your future?"

Sophie brought a spoonful of ice cream to her lips, and her tongue snaked out to lick it. He watched appreciatively, but a long pause stretched out before she answered—enough that Sam thought she was going to answer negatively.

"Yes, I do," she said. "This may not be a good reason, but I want to see if I can provide a better childhood than I had."

"My thoughts are similar. I want my kids to be happier than I was and not live in fear of me."

Sophie nodded. "I also think, God, this is probably even worse. I want a chance to... It's like I want to relive my childhood." Sam took her hand. "I want to do the things I didn't get to do. I want to watch all the movies."

"That makes sense, but remember, sometimes you need to be the parent."

"I'm going to leave that hard stuff to you." She laughed and leaned in to kiss him.

Her lips were cool, in contrast to the heat that ran through his body, and Sam realized she was saying she wanted to have children with him. He looked at her questioningly, and Sophie nodded.

Sam took Sophie's bowl, placed it on the table, and turned back to her. After pulling her up, he wrapped his arms around her and moved back so he could see her face when he told her his news. He ran his fingers through her hair. "I have a surprise for you. We're going to the cabin tomorrow night."

"Did you tell your parents we're going to be there?"

Sam nodded.

Sophie's mouth quirked. "They'll figure out that we've moved beyond dating."

"Probably. Is that okay with you?"

"Yeah, but I thought you wanted to keep it private. Now Norah knows and your family..."

"Babe, anyone who looks at me can tell something is going on in my life." He rubbed circles on her back with one hand. "I'm sure I'm walking around with a lovestruck grin on my face." His eyes met hers. "I hope you feel the same."

"I do." She paused, then continued, "It's been a long time since I was in the position of telling people I had a boyfriend. Is that what we even call it?"

"I enjoy thinking of you as my girlfriend, and the longer this goes on, the more I want to let people know."

Chapter Seventeen

Passion At The Cabin

Sophie

Darkness had fallen as they reached the cabin. When they got out of the car, Sam drew Sophie into a hug and buried his face in her hair. She loved it when he did that. "It's a beautiful night. Let's go in the hot tub."

Sam took their bags to the upstairs bedroom and returned with towels, then led her to the deck. "We can undress right here. It's the nice thing about being in such a private spot." They left their clothes in a pile and climbed into the vigorously bubbling water. The warm water was welcome in the cool night air. They sat across from each other, enjoying the jets and relaxing for a few minutes.

After a while, Sam slid around until he was beside her. He put his arm over her shoulders and drew her close to him. Sophie leaned her head back, put her hand in his lap, and found his cock, which hardened at her touch under the water. Her strokes were gentle. "I love watching you squirm and feeling you get harder as I touch you."

Sam finally reached over to fondle her breast, at first doing it in the same tender manner, then pinching the nipple to make her jump. Sophie turned slightly, and he lowered his head to take her breast in his mouth. She sighed with pleasure. They stayed outside long into the night, lazily playing with each other, discovering new ways to turn each other on.

Afterward, Sophie helped Sam move the lid to the hot tub into place before they made their way to the bedroom. Frenzy had fueled their pairings all week, but tonight they were both relaxed and savoring their time together.

Sam lay on the bed and pulled her toward him, but Sophie shook her head, kneeled beside him, and took his erection in her mouth. This was unfamiliar territory for them, and she could tell Sam was trying unsuccessfully to control himself. His hips swiveled toward her, and he put a hand on her head to move her closer.

She pulled back for a second to whisper, "Relax," and his groan in response increased her eagerness. She took him deeply and grasped his balls, knowing it would add to his excitement.

"Sophie." His voice was thick with need.

She took her mouth away and scrambled to lie beside him. Sophie stroked him slowly at first and then faster as he swelled in her hand.

"I'm close," he moaned.

"Let go," she urged. "I want to watch you." Sophie moved her hand faster, keeping her eyes on his face when he erupted. She ducked her head to his lips and kissed him gently before she went to the bathroom and returned with a warm washcloth, which she gently ran over his torso and now-spent cock.

When she finished cleaning him up, Sam clasped her hand, pulled her to him, and kissed her deeply. "That was..." He smiled, his eyes heavy-lidded. "Really something. But what about you?"

"I loved it. Watching you, knowing I turn you on this much—it's exciting. We have all weekend," she said, smiling. "Don't worry about me."

In the morning, Sophie stretched and moved closer to Sam. She slowly opened her eyes and found him staring at her. The east wall of the bedroom was entirely glass, giving a beautiful view of the mountains. As the sky lightened, she said, "Wow, that's stunning. Did you see the sunrise?"

"No, I've only been awake a little while. Joe nailed it, making that entire wall a window." He stretched and smiled at her. "I woke up to a text from him inviting us to come to Boston in a few weeks. There's a Tall Ships festival going on. He'll stay with Emma so we can have his apartment."

Sophie frowned. "Do you want to do it?"

"Yeah. I think it sounds like fun. I decided back in the fall that I was going to take Piper to Boston in the summer."

Sophie drank in Sam's excitement and thought about how much Pip would love it. But Boston—she hadn't been back there since she ran away with Corey. She immediately wondered what would happen if they ran into someone who recognized her. Sam deserved an explanation for her uncertainty, but she couldn't get any words out.

Obviously sensing her discomfort, Sam said, "We can talk about it later. I don't need to answer him right now." He wrapped his arms around her. "Let's plan our day. I'm thinking of a hike up Mt. Pisgah this morning and then swimming. Tomorrow, we'll run on the trails again."

"What about paddleboarding?"

Sam rolled his eyes. "We can do that after the trails tomorrow. You want to watch me make a fool of myself again?"

"I do." Sophie chuckled. "I know you'll succeed. The first time's the hardest."

"Speaking of hard..." Sam moved her hand to his erection.

"I thought you wanted to get out early to beat the crowds."

171

Sam groaned. "Why do you have to be so practical?" He disentangled himself from her and climbed off the bed.

Sophie dug into the bag she'd packed. "Will there be a place for me to change into my bathing suit, or should I wear it under my hiking clothes?"

He cocked his head. "Actually, there's a nude beach."

"What? You're kidding, aren't you?"

"Nope, there's a secluded cove at the south end of the lake, and it's clothing optional." He laughed. "You didn't realize the Northeast Kingdom could be so exciting, huh?"

"Is that where we're going?"

"No, I'm a Neanderthal. I don't want anyone else looking at you." He grinned at her. "And you can never tell what characters might be there. We'll go to the north end. You can change in the porta potty or in the woods."

"No, thanks." Sophie grimaced. "I'll wear my suit under my hiking clothes."

Sam chose the north trail for them, which she found moderately difficult with some steep, challenging sections. They stopped at one of the scenic overlooks to take pictures.

Sophie's breath caught as they looked down at the lake. "It's gorgeous. You're so lucky to have grown up here."

After reaching the summit, they slipped and slid back to the base and headed to the north end of the lake.

At the beach, Sophie took off her shorts and shirt, and she could see the lust in Sam's eyes. As they lay on the sand together, he caressed her back. "Do you want to learn to ski? I don't enjoy thinking about winter, but you should come with Piper and me next year."

"I'd like to try it." She gazed at him. "Are we making long-term plans?"

"I think we are. Do you mind?"

"No, but I'll confess. It scares me."

"Me too." He edged closer to her. "You're hot."

"Double entendre intended? Let's cool off." Sophie scrambled to her feet and held out her hand to pull him up before running into the water with Sam close behind. "Oh my God, it's so cold!" She stopped when the water reached her thighs and splashed Sam as he caught up to her, then plunged beyond and went deeper into the lake. She dove under the water, quickly swimming out to him.

"You're a natural," Sam said.

"I grew up near the ocean. Beaches were free. I spent a lot of time swimming."

Later, they stopped at a food truck for dinner and ate on the deck at the cabin. They enjoyed the hot tub as they had the night before, and as they went upstairs, Sam said, "Tonight's your turn."

Heat spread through her. "How about it's our turn?" She turned and put her arms around him. "This was a nice day."

· He kissed her passionately. "It's not over yet," he said and pulled her down to the bed.

On Sunday, they ran the trails again, then drove to the south end of the lake, where they rented two paddleboards from the nearby campground. Sophie gave him tips and encouragement, and Sam was more successful than he had been the first time. When their time was up, they headed back to the cabin.

The door had barely closed behind them when Sam put his arms around Sophie and undid her bikini top. "Damn, you make me so hot when you wear this. I couldn't wait to get you out of it." He lowered his mouth to her breast and flicked his tongue over her nipple. As it hardened, he took it in his mouth and sucked hard as she moaned with pleasure. She tried to push his swim trunks to the floor, but he grabbed her arms and pinned her against the door. "My turn today. Let me play."

Sam continued to suck on her breast while he pinched her other nipple. Sophie lurched against him, and his free hand shoved her bikini bottom to the floor. Then Sam kissed his way down her front, kneeled in front of her, and buried his face between her legs, making her gasp. He stood and swept her off her feet and carried her upstairs to the bed, where he lay her down, spread her legs, and tongued her clit as she groaned. One finger slid inside, then a second.

Sam's fingers moved only a little, and Sophie sensed he was teasing her by purposely slowing things down. She squirmed, but failed to speed up his touch.

His fingers were buried in her, agonizingly still, when Sam raised his head to look at her. "Touch yourself."

"What?"

"Touch your breasts. Pinch your nipples."

Sophie shot him a reluctant look, and he nodded encouragingly. Her hand crept to her breast and fondled the smooth flesh. Her fingers tweaked the nubs, the sensation arousing her more than she expected.

Sam groaned. "Oh God, that is so hot." He lowered his mouth back to her clit and sucked and nibbled as his fingers moved in and out. As her breath came faster and she played with her nipples, Sam moved his fingers more quickly.

"Oh, Sam," Sophie moaned as her orgasm overtook her.

Sam crawled up beside her. He kissed her, and when their tongues tangled, Sophie realized she was tasting herself on him. Her hand searched for his erection and began stroking it. "I want you."

"That wasn't enough?"

"No, I want more. I want you inside me. I want to feel you come."

Sam lowered his mouth to her breast again and sucked it hard, eliciting more moans.

Sophie spread her legs to welcome him as Sam positioned himself above her. "Yes... Fuck me... Fuck me now, Sam..."

He slammed into her, and she raised her hips to meet him. "Not slow, Sam, not now. Show me how much you want me. Make me come again." Sophie felt the effect of her words as his cock grew harder, and he moved deeper inside. She rose to match every stroke as he plunged into her until he came with a shout. She hadn't come again, and Sam slid his hand down to touch her clit as he continued to pump into her. That was all she needed, and she cried his name as her orgasm hit.

Afterward, Sam rolled them onto their sides.

Sophie whispered, "Oh my God."

"I know."

They were both trembling, and it took several minutes for them to catch their breath.

Sam pulled back to see her face. "That was incredible."

Sophie nodded.

"We can shower before we head home," he said.

"I don't know if I can even stand up." Sophie's legs felt like rubber.

Sam pulled her to her feet, and before leading her into the bathroom, he said, "Lean on me. You can always lean on me."

Chapter Eighteen

More Of Sophie's Truth Comes Out

Sam

THE DRIVE HOME BEGAN in companionable silence, and Sam pondered his growing attachment to Sophie. She was witty and sarcastic, and they shared a similar sense of humor. She still had a vulnerability about her, even though she tried to hide it. He wanted to take care of her, wanted to help her battle her demons. Was this love? He wasn't sure. He wasn't sure of anything anymore.

They'd been on the road for a few minutes when Sophie said, "I'm going to buy a paddleboard."

"What happened to the one you had—the birthday present?"

Her answer didn't come for several miles. "I left that living situation abruptly."

Sam found her response cryptic and realized he never had asked her if it was Corey who had given her the paddleboard. "Is that when you became a minimalist?" he asked, hoping she would smile.

She didn't respond, not even after many more miles had passed.

When Sophie remained quiet, he glanced over to see her staring straight ahead. *Damn it, I'm falling in love with her, and she still doesn't trust me.* He thought back to the night they had agreed to see where things could go. Remembered telling her he wanted to know her. *This is what I was talking about. I've been open with her, but she can't do the same.*

Sam drummed his fingers on the steering wheel. He continued to glance over at Sophie, feeling anger building as her lips remained sealed. This wasn't anger like he had felt toward Norah back in the fall. It was anger tinged with deep sadness. *This is the deal-breaker. I need to cut my losses. We had an incredible weekend—if there was any time for her to open up to me, it should be now.*

178

The rest of the drive passed in strained silence, and when they arrived at the house, Sam took his bag out of the car and strode inside, with Sophie trailing behind him. "I'm going to have a beer," he said. "Do you want some wine?" He needed to end this now before his feelings became any stronger.

"Yes."

When Sophie came back after taking her bag to her room, Sam had left a glass of wine by the recliner while his bottle of beer was at the far end of the couch. They sat in silence until finally, Sophie took a long drink of the wine and blew out a heavy breath. "I was engaged. He found me in bed with Corey and kicked me out of the house. All I took were my clothes and my books." Sophie's voice broke. "I told you I've done terrible things." Tears streamed down her face.

Sam suppressed a shudder. Her tears, combined with the news that she'd been engaged to someone other than Corey, were like a knife in his gut. He went to Sophie, gathered her in his arms, and led her to the couch. He settled her in his lap, holding her as she silently cried and as he tried to digest what she had told him.

"I'll start looking for a new place." Sophie's voice was shaky.

"What?"

"You can't want me to stay, knowing what I've done."

Sam remained silent, trying to figure out how to react. Finally, he said, "I don't want you to go."

"You were mad in the car."

179

"There was a bit of anger but more disappointment." Sam moved so he could see Sophie's face. "I felt like you were never going to trust me." Should he tell her all of it, tell her he was falling in love with her? He shook his head, trying to clear his thoughts. "There must be more to the story."

"I know you must have questions. Ask me whatever you want." She looked at him. "It may take me some time to find the words. But I'll answer you, and I'll be honest."

"I don't have any idea what to ask." His stomach growled. They had started cooking together, and the kitchen was a comfortable place for them. "Let's make some dinner."

As they worked, he could sense her relaxing. Sam, on the other hand, was spun up like a top. He opened the fridge, and his hand lingered over a bottle of beer, which he defiantly pulled out and opened before pouring Sophie another glass of wine. They sat at the table, waiting for the food to cook, and Sam took a long swallow from the bottle. "How did you end up engaged to someone other than Corey?"

Sophie folded her hands together and brought them to her mouth, bowing her head briefly. "Corey moved in and out of my life. Here for two weeks and then gone for months or even years at a time." After a moment, she raised her eyes to meet Sam's. "I dated. Several years back, I was in a serious relationship. We were living together, and he proposed." She took a swallow of the wine.

"Did you love him?"

"I... Yeah, I did." She sounded resigned. "It wasn't what I felt for Corey, but I thought I'd have a good life with him. So I said yes. Our wedding was a few months away when Corey came home and found out. He came to me and poured out his feelings, then he asked me to elope with him."

Sophie shook her head. "The bond between Corey and me was so strong—the history we shared..." She took a swallow of wine and pressed her hands on the table. "Corey and I were packing my clothes—I intended to be gone before my fiancé came home. Which I'm aware would have been a coward's way out. Instead, I made it worse. We ended up in bed, and Richard walked in on us." Her gaze moved away from Sam and then back. "It was awful."

Sam tried to picture the scene, and his stomach turned over.

Sophie swallowed. "My mother was furious that I married Corey. She left me voicemails telling me I was going to end up living in my car." Her voice broke. "I had an advanced degree and could find a good job. I could take care of myself, but her comments shattered me."

"That's when you stopped speaking to her?"

"Yeah. We had a big blowup, and I've had no contact with her since." She sighed. "I can't imagine what she could do to make me want to see her again."

"This was in Boston, wasn't it? That's why you hesitated when I mentioned the weekend."

Sophie nodded. "Richard and I lived outside of the city, and his office was in the financial district. But... there will be thousands of people. We won't run into anyone who knows me. We should go. Piper will love it."

After they ate, Sam started cleaning up the kitchen, and Sophie said she was going to take a bath.

When he finished in the kitchen, Sam stood in the doorway to the bathroom, watching Sophie submerged in the bubbles. Her head rested on the rim of the tub with her eyes closed. Normally, Sam would wash her back, and when the water cooled, he would take her hand to help her out and wrap her in a towel.

Tonight, his desire to do that was muted by the torment Sophie's confession had caused. Hearing that she'd been found in bed with another man made him remember his reaction all those years ago to finding out what Quinn had done when they took a break. *At least I didn't lose my shit like I did that night. What Sophie did back then shouldn't matter now.* It shouldn't, but it did.

Sophie opened her eyes, saw Sam watching her, and climbed out of the tub. She grabbed a fluffy white towel off the rack, and Sam crossed the short distance from the door to the tub and took the towel from her. He wrapped it around her and gently wiped the water away. "Let's go to bed. It's been a long weekend."

The prospect of sleeping together while Piper was with Norah had been enticing to both of them. Sophie slid her arms into her robe and turned to face Sam. "Do you still want me to sleep in your bed?"

"I... Yeah."

Sam stretched his arm under Sophie's shoulders, and they lay stiffly side by side, with none of their usual warm snuggling.

Finally, Sophie rolled on her side and locked her eyes on his. "I wish you'd tell me what you're thinking."

"I can't." Sam sighed. "I'm not even sure I know. Maybe tomorrow." He rolled onto his other side, away from her gaze.

Sophie

Sophie listened to the ragged sound of Sam's breathing, sure that he wasn't asleep. *I'm going to be haunted by the sins of my past forever.*

She awoke the next morning to an empty bed after a night of fitful sleep, waking often and aware of Sam tossing and turning.

Sophie listened for the sounds of Sam getting ready for the day, but the house was silent. Wrapping her robe around her, Sophie walked to the kitchen and found a note telling her he'd gone to work early. The note said nothing about seeing her that night or wanting to talk. She drank her smoothie before making a cup of coffee and going out to the deck. The sun was warm, and she hoped it would burn away the knot of tension that had engulfed her since Sam asked her about the paddleboard on the drive home. She couldn't read his emotions—didn't know if he was angry, disappointed, or hurt. He had never said so little to her about his feelings. The day loomed long before her. She added to his note, telling him she was going to the lake, then to the gym and wouldn't be home until after dinner. She couldn't sit around all day, waiting for him—maybe her absence at dinner would give him time to process.

Sam's car was in the drive when Sophie returned home after the gym and dinner with one of her workout partners. She sat in her car, replaying her conversation with Ali, who had been the first to befriend Sophie. While they were eating, Ali had asked what was bothering her. Ali knew about Sam, and Sophie confessed that they'd had a bit of a disagreement. *What else could I call it?*

"If you need a place to stay, you know the guesthouse is available. For as long as you want." Ali had told Sophie several times that if she'd known Sophie needed a place to live, before she rented the room from Sam, she would have offered the guesthouse on her property.

Twilight was gathering as Sophie walked into the house and saw Sam on the deck with a glass in hand. She poured a glass of wine and went to join him. "Hey." Leaning down, she kissed him on the cheek before sitting beside him. "What are you drinking? I've never seen you with anything but beer. Except for those times you've had wine with me."

"Bourbon. Cheers." Sam raised his glass toward Sophie's, and she sensed it wasn't his first. "Jesse turned me onto it. Sometimes, something stronger than beer is called for."

His tone gave her pause. "And this is one of those times?"

"I think so." He nodded. "Yeah." Sam had been looking at the horizon before, and he turned to face Sophie. "I'm not drunk."

"Okay." Sophie wasn't sure how to proceed. This was a side of Sam she hadn't seen before.

"Can I ask you something?"

"You can ask me anything."

"How long were you with Richard before he found you cheating?"

Sophie drew in a sharp breath. "I was with him for three years. We'd been living together for about a year." *I'm not holding anything back.*

"Was it the first time you'd seen Corey? I mean, since you got involved with Richard."

"No. I saw him about six months after Richard and I started dating and then again right after I moved into Richard's house."

Sam drained his glass and put it on the table, his hand unsteady. The sound of glass hitting glass echoed over the valley. "I might be a little drunk." He leaned back in his chair. "I need to understand, Sophie. How you dated someone, moved in with him, and got engaged, all while seeing someone else."

"It wasn't all while seeing someone else." Her temper flared. "In three years, I saw Corey a total of nineteen days, once for five days and once for two weeks. I *told* you—he was in and out of my life."

"How did you *do* that? If that had been me you'd been dating, I would have wanted to know where you were."

"My mother lived in Rhode Island. I told Richard I was visiting her."

Sam snorted. "So you lied."

Sophie took a swallow of her wine, wishing it was the bourbon. "Yes, Sam, I lied. Are we going to catalog all my missteps tonight?"

"Missteps!" Sam choked out a humorless laugh. "That's a good word."

"I lied, and I did terrible things. I told you that before we went forward." She stood. "I'm going to bed before we say something we can't unsay. I'll be in my room."

Chapter Nineteen

Sophie Says Goodbye

Sam

NURSING A HEADACHE FROM the bourbon, Sam walked into the kitchen the next morning while Sophie was making her smoothie. "I'm sorry for going at you last night," he said.

Sophie reached into the cupboard, ignoring his gaze. As she measured protein powder into the blender, she said, "Bourbon must be a truth serum for you. You asked what you wanted to know without sugarcoating it."

Sam put his hand on her arm, and Sophie didn't pull away. "You're right. I asked what I'd wondered about all day, but I could have been kinder about it."

"Probably." Sophie looked into his eyes. "Where do we go from here?"

"I have more questions."

Sophie huffed out a breath. "Great." She rolled her eyes and started the blender.

"I need to understand. Can we talk tonight? I promise I'll be sober."

"Tonight is supposed to be a five-mile run." She poured the smoothie into a travel mug. "Can we do that first?"

"Yeah." Sam knew what she was doing. Their best conversations happened after a run. He hoped that would hold true for them again.

Sophie beat Sam to the lawn by three steps.

When he caught his breath, he said, "I'm never drinking bourbon again."

"Maybe I'm getting faster than you." Sophie chuckled.

"Could be," Sam admitted. He rolled on his side. "During the weekend, on the ride home, I thought about how I'm falling in love with you." He stopped and watched her face. When he saw no reaction, he continued. "I knew Corey had been in your life, but I didn't think about other men."

"I didn't think there was a future with Corey." She met Sam's gaze. "When I spent the two weeks with him, if he'd given me any sign that he wanted to build a life with me, I would have left Richard. Hell, I *wrestled* with the idea of leaving. But I cared for Richard, and I was comfortable with him."

"Is that what you are with me? Comfortable?"

Sophie shook her head and reached out to take Sam's hand. "I'm so much more than comfortable with you. I've bared my soul to you, told you things about myself that no one else knows. You said you're falling in love with me. I feel the same way."

His breath caught. "What happens when you run into the next Corey?"

"I'm not sure what you're asking."

Sam held her hand in both of his. "If we go all in, commit to building a life together and you run into someone else from your childhood, what's going to happen? I'll never understand all that you went through. We'll never have that shared experience. If someone comes along who has that with you, will you want to be with them?"

Sophie frowned and opened her mouth to respond, but Sam put a finger over her lips. "Let me finish. I don't think you'd cheat on me. But I fear you might leave me for someone that you have a greater connection to."

"I made that mistake once. I won't make it again."

Sam stood and pulled Sophie to her feet. "Let's shower and get some dinner."

They took dinner out to the deck, and when they finished eating, Sam said, "I'm worried about Piper's reaction if we continue getting closer. If we let her know and then we break up. You've already become important to her."

"She's important to me. *You're* important to me." Sophie's eyes pleaded with him. "What are you saying, Sam?"

"I think we need to pull back." He rubbed his jaw. "Ever since you kissed me after the race, I've been overwhelmed by desire for you. I haven't thought about the long-term effects, and now I have."

"Okay." Sophie rose from the table and started picking up the dishes.

"You don't have to leave. We talked about our friendship. I'd like that to continue."

"Sure." Sophie loaded the dishwasher and walked into her bedroom without saying another word.

Sam stayed on the deck, watching the sunset. He hadn't been completely honest with her. Her admission of the tangled relationship with Corey and Richard had rocked him to his core. When he considered that, along with her reluctance to open up to him, he knew he couldn't continue. He couldn't risk his heart, and he couldn't risk Piper's.

Sophie pushed open the door to his bedroom just as Sam had removed his shirt. "The *least* you could have done was be honest with me." She crossed the distance between them.

He swallowed. "I—"

She put her hand across his mouth. "No. Now you're going to let me finish." She took a deep breath. "You didn't *just* start thinking about the effect on Piper if we break up. You're ending this because you think I'm a cheat and a liar."

Sam took a step back. *I can't be this close to her.* "Piper has always been my first concern. I've made that clear."

"Don't hide behind her." Sophie stepped up to him. "Look me in the eye and tell me the fact that I cheated on Richard doesn't matter to you. Or that I lied to him."

"I can't." Sam's face contorted in pain.

"It wasn't you I cheated on. It wasn't you I lied to. I'm not the same person who I was back then." Sophie looked away then choked out, "I've been completely honest with you."

Sam struggled to maintain a civil tone. "I've had to pry everything out of you with a pickax. What's the next thing that's going to drop?"

"There's nothing else. I've told you all my secrets." Sophie moved toward him, reaching out her arms. "I love you, Sam. More than I've ever loved anyone."

Sam met her embrace and wrapped his arms around her. He buried his face in her hair, drinking in her scent. Her hands rubbed circles on his back, and he wanted her.

Reluctantly, he stepped out of her arms and rested his hands on her shoulders. "Everything you said is accurate, Sophie. I want you, but that's not enough. We both need to be willing to go all in, and we're not there." He dropped his hands. "And honestly, I don't think we ever will be."

Sophie

The rain that had been falling all day spattered against the windows as Sophie placed two pillar candles in the center of the table. Sam would be home soon, and she hoped to squash the acrimony that had permeated the house since Sunday night. She held the lighter against the wick and watched the flame leap to life. Mesmerized by the flickering light, Sophie settled into a chair and let her brain replay the reels that had been on a continuous loop all day.

First, Richard walking into the bedroom where she lay tangled in the sheets with Corey. He had screamed, "What the fuck is going on?" Anger and disbelief, unlike anything she had ever heard, filled his voice.

Sophie had leaped off the bed, snatched her bra and panties from the floor, and struggled into them as Richard continued screaming, demanding to know who Corey was. Corey responded with shouts of his own while Sophie pulled on the rest of her clothes.

Finally, Richard had looked around the room and saw the open suitcase filled with Sophie's clothes. His voice grew hard, and his eyes were cold. "Get out," he'd said as he turned to leave. "I never want to see you again."

Corey had slammed the suitcase shut, and Sophie followed him out of the room. Over the years, she had tried and failed to erase the picture of Richard standing near the door as she and Corey walked away, his face stained with tears but his jaw set.

Then eighteen months later, Sophie had been the one standing near the door with her jaw set. They had been arguing for days when Corey had received a notification to report for duty in two hours. As he jammed his clothes into a duffle, Sophie had told him she was going to look for better housing while he was gone. He had fallen apart, telling her they couldn't afford it and that the trailer was good enough.

When his ride arrived, Sophie had yelled her final words to him as he walked away. "I won't live like this any longer! I won't be here when you get back!"

The turmoil of how those relationships ended tormented her. *I can't do that again.* She wouldn't be the shrew she had been to Corey, but she wouldn't wait for Sam to throw her out, either.

Sophie watched Sam enter the dining room and look at her with a question in those blue eyes she loved. He sat down wordlessly, but she could tell that the agitation he'd been in had calmed, just as it had for her. There was a glass of wine beside each of their plates, and when they finished eating, she refilled them.

She looked at Sam and took a deep breath. "I can't stay. I've loved being here. Getting to know you and Piper has been wonderful. But to be here and not share the closeness that we've had won't be good for me. And it won't be good for you."

"Where will you go?" Sam's voice was soft. The turbulence that she'd heard in his voice so often since Sunday was gone.

"Do you remember Ali, one of my workout partners?" When Sam nodded, Sophie continued. "She and her husband have a beautiful home, more like an estate actually, and there's a guesthouse. She told me I can stay there as long as I want to."

"That's not far from here, is it?"

"A few miles." Sophie took a swallow of her wine. "I don't want to lose touch with Piper. I wondered if I could continue taking her to the lake on Fridays." She paused, her chest tight. "You're right about the effect on her. I hope if I see her through the rest of summer, that might help, and then once school starts, I'll see her there."

Sam seemed deep in thought for a couple of minutes. "I guess that will work. It's kind of complicated, since she's at Norah's on Friday morning."

"It's not. I've been picking her up there all summer and taking her back at the end of the day or bringing her here," Sophie said. "Plus, Norah needs to know that there's been a change in our status and that I'm living somewhere else."

Sam nodded. "I dread telling Pip you're moving out."

"Let me do it. I want you there, but I'm making the move and feel like I should be the one to tell her why."

"What exactly will you say?"

"It'll be a lie." Sophie smiled ruefully at him. "At least partially. I want to do it on Friday. I'll have my car packed and leave after I talk to her."

"That soon?" Sam finished his wine. "I thought when I saw the table, with the candles and the wine... I wondered if you were trying to get me to change my mind."

Sophie wanted to ask him if it would have worked. She had her emotions held tightly in check. "No. I wanted to have a pleasant meal without disagreement."

"Do you want to continue running together?"

"I don't think that will be wise. But I'm going to do the races we signed up for, and I hope you'll be there." That night in June felt so long ago.

"I will be. I'm looking forward to them," he said. "Do you want help packing?"

Sam took Friday off, and after going for a long run, he and Sophie packed up her room. She directed him to the bookcase, and as he placed her books in a box, he picked up the framed picture nestled among them.

"Is this Corey?" he asked.

"Yes."

"You look happy."

"For a brief time, we were." Sophie glanced at the picture and then at Sam. "I've been happier here than at any other time in my life." She returned to folding her clothes, while Sam carried the boxes of books out to her car.

The room was almost empty when Sophie looked around at the walls where she had tacked up pictures Piper had drawn for her. She took them down carefully and finally reached for the last thing remaining, a bulletin board festooned with photos of her with Sam or with Piper. After they started sleeping together, Sam had contacted the photographer from the race and obtained a copy of the kiss picture. It had a place of honor on the board, and when Sophie took the board down, she ran her fingers over the photo, remembering how sweet that first kiss had been. She stacked Piper's pictures on top and carried the bulletin board out to the car herself.

Norah arrived from Maine by midafternoon, and the car had hardly stopped when Piper jumped out. She ran to Sam and flung her arms around him. "Daddy!"

Sam hoisted her up, feigning difficulty. "Oh my gosh, you grew while you were gone. That's got to stop!"

"Silly Daddy. Put me down. I need to hug Sophie." She wrapped her arms around Sophie. "I missed you both." Piper let go of her and ran back to the car.

Sam had called Norah on Thursday to tell her what was going on, and now she shook her head as she looked at Sam. "This is going to break her heart." Her gaze turned to Sophie. "I'm glad you're going to continue to see her for the rest of the summer. That will help."

Piper ran back with her eyes aglow. "Look what I found!" She held a sand dollar out to show them.

Sam drew in a sharp breath. "That's very cool. I found one of those a long time ago."

"Where is it? Can I see?"

"No." Sam shook his head. "I lost it."

"I'm *never* going to lose mine." Piper walked with Norah to the car to collect her things, and after Norah left, she looked at Sophie. "Why do you have all those boxes in your car?"

Sophie put her arm over Piper's shoulders. "You miss nothing, Pip. I have something exciting to tell you. Let's go inside."

After Sam settled with Piper on the couch, Sophie sat on the coffee table facing them and took one of Piper's hands. "I've found a house to move into," she said. "I'm excited because I've never had a house of my own."

Piper's face crumpled. "You're leaving us?" Tears welled up in her eyes.

"Yes, but I won't be far away, and I'm still going to take you to the lake every Friday. I know you're probably sad, but I hope you can be excited for me."

"I-I-I want you to be here forever so I can see you every d-day." She buried her face in Sam's shirt, sobbing quietly.

Sophie moved to the sofa, wrapping her arms around both Sam and Piper. "I love you, Pip, but I need to try this." Her voice cracked, and she sat holding them until Piper's sobs had subsided.

"If you don't like it, will you come back?" Piper looked from Sophie to Sam. "Daddy, don't you want her to stay?"

Piper's tear-stained face broke Sophie's already-fractured heart, and she watched as Sam swallowed hard before answering.

"I want Sophie to be happy, and having her own place instead of just a room in our house is a big deal for her," he said. "I'm sad that she's leaving, the same as you are." He kissed the top of Piper's head.

Sophie rose from the couch, and Piper climbed down from Sam's lap. Sophie kneeled to embrace her. "I'll pick you up next week at your mom's, just like I have all summer," she whispered in Piper's ear.

"That's forever away." Piper's voice was full of despair.

Sophie walked out the door with Sam and Piper watching and as she reached the car, Piper called out, "Wait." She went inside and then ran to Sophie. She handed her the sand dollar. "You k-keep it. So you d-don't forget me."

Sophie's eyes filled with tears as she gave Piper one last hug and drove away without looking back.

Chapter Twenty

Joe Visits

Sam

ON SATURDAY NIGHT, PIPER climbed onto the couch next to Sam. "I miss Sophie."

"Me too, baby girl." Sam sighed. "Me too." Sam had taken Piper to a lake in New Hampshire in an effort to ignore the emptiness of the house. But Sophie's absence was hard to miss when it came to movie night.

They made it through the next few days, and when Sam dropped Piper off at daycare on Wednesday morning, she said, "Only two more days until I see Sophie!" Her eyes were bright with excitement. Her distress at Sophie's departure lessened a little every day, but she still told Sam every night how much she missed her.

"Enjoy your time at the lake." Sam rumpled her hair before she ran inside. On his way home that night, he purchased a twelve-pack of beer. He was four beers in when his phone pinged with a text.

> Joe: Piper can stay with Emma and me when you come to visit, then you and Sophie can have my apartment for yourself. The city can be a romantic place.

Sam read the text and tossed his phone to the corner of the couch. *Romantic—yeah, right.* The beer dulled the ache he'd felt since Sophie drove away and quieted the swirling doubts he had about ending things with her.

When Piper was at Norah's, Saturday mornings with Sophie meant sleeping late and enjoying each other. They'd go for a long run before going out for brunch. When he finally crawled out of bed on this first Saturday without Sophie or Piper, Sam felt lost. As he looked around the kitchen, nothing appealed to him for breakfast. Instead, he popped the top on a beer.

When his phone pinged with a call from Joe, he'd lost count of how many he'd had. "Hey."

"You didn't answer my texts. Are you going to come down next weekend?" When Sam didn't answer, Joe went on. "Emma is working this weekend, so I'm heading north to work on the plans for the barn project. Why don't you and Sophie come with me? We can discuss the weekend on the drive." When Sam still didn't answer, Joe asked, "Sam, what the fuck? Are you there?"

"Yeah, that's... That doesn't work for me."

"What's going on?" Joe's tone had changed, and Sam knew his brother could hear the despair in his voice as well as the alcohol.

"Nothing."

"Uh-huh, tell it to someone who doesn't know you. What's going on?"

"Sophie's not here."

"Sam. Talk to me."

"Geesh, Joe, back off. It's too complicated to go into. She moved out. You go meet with Mom and Dad. I'm not in the mood." He ended the call.

Three hours later, his front door opened, and Joe walked in. "Jesus, Sam, it smells like a brewery in here."

"Did you drive all the way from Boston to tell me that?"

"I put the barn plans off for a couple of weeks. You sounded like you needed me more."

Sam scowled and motioned his brother away. "I don't need anything."

"When was the last time you ate something?"

"I had pizza last night at Norah's."

Joe nodded. "I brought some fried chicken." He went to the kitchen, which was a mess of dirty dishes and empty beer cans, found a plate, and brought it to Sam. "Eat. And then tell me why you're drinking like a fish."

Sam reluctantly picked up a piece of chicken. After he finished eating it, he leaned back and rested his head on the back of the couch. "Sophie and I called it quits. I told her she could stay here... you know, as my tenant. She didn't think that was a good idea. She left a week ago."

"What happened?"

Sam told Joe about Sophie's relationship with Richard and Corey. "So she was living with someone and snuck off to be with this guy who I guess she considered her soulmate. She accepted a proposal from Richard and then let him find her in bed with someone else." Sam shook his head. "I don't think I can get past that." He looked at Joe. "Could you?"

"I don't know." Joe rubbed the back of his neck. "I mean, it wasn't you she cheated on."

Sam shot him an anguished look. "Fuck, Joe, can I trust it won't happen again?"

"Is she remorseful?"

"I don't know. Before we went forward with a relationship, she warned me away because she'd done terrible things. And now I know what those things are."

At one point, Joe went into the kitchen, and Sam must have either passed out or fallen asleep, because when he opened his eyes next, it was morning, and the smell of bacon and coffee permeated the house.

He raised his head and groaned. He hadn't drunk that much since right after Norah left. Stretching his legs, he slowly sat up, his head pounding, and knew he'd gone too far.

Joe came out of the kitchen and put two plates on the table, where he'd already placed mugs of coffee.

Sam went into the bathroom and gazed at his reflection in the mirror as he reached for Tylenol. *You're a mess. You gave Sophie that line about how therapy has worked for you, and what's the first thing you do when you hit a bump? Go right back to the bottle. You're no better than your father was.* He swallowed the Tylenol. *Jesus, how much have I had to drink since Wednesday?*

Sam walked out to the table and saw Joe already eating. He sat down, looked at Joe, and asked, "Can you please chew a little more quietly?"

Joe looked at him and made a point of chewing more loudly and stirring his coffee vigorously.

Sam scowled. "You're an ass."

"Head hurt?"

"You can't imagine. I'm an idiot."

Joe smirked. "Tell me something I don't already know." They ate in silence.

Sam showered, which left him feeling slightly more human. He poured another cup of coffee and opened his laptop to show Joe his latest work on the barn project. They spent the day talking about it and revising Sam's drawings.

When they took a break, Joe gave Sam a long look. "I don't know if I should tell you this or not. The lease is up on my apartment in September, and I'm going to move in with Emma."

Sam's face lit up. "That's great! Why wouldn't you tell me?"

"I don't want to make you feel bad."

Sam waved his hand, dismissing what Joe said. "I like Emma, and I'm glad you're happy. Don't worry about me—I'll get through this. Thanks for coming, even if I acted like a jerk yesterday."

Joe nodded. "I'm going to propose."

"Already?"

"We love each other, we get along great, and we're making long-term plans. Why wait for some arbitrary timeline?" he asked, spreading his hands in a shrug. "We're talking about kids, and that'll happen sooner rather than later. Call me old-fashioned, but I want to be married first."

"Sophie and I talked about kids," Sam murmured. "We made long-term plans. I can't believe it's all gone."

Joe raised his eyebrows. "Maybe it'll still work out. Emma and I both like her. I need to head back. Want me to take that last six-pack?"

"You know I can go to the store and buy another one." Sam grimaced. "Yeah, take it with you. It kills me to think I'm acting like Dad."

"Have no fear. If you act like Dad did, Matt and I will both come over here to kick your ass."

Chapter Twenty-One

Making Amends

Sophie

SOPHIE RELAXED ON THE deck at the guesthouse after spending the day at the lake with Piper. It was the best day she'd had since she drove away from Sam's a week earlier. Piper had been excited to see her and noticed the paddleboard strapped to the roof of her car the minute she walked out of Norah's house. The day flew by far too fast. Sophie showed Pip how to do the breaststroke. They built a sandcastle that Piper christened "the world's biggest" and played on the paddleboard. *I would like to buy her a kid-sized one, but that would probably be overstepping.*

Before Piper climbed out of the car back at Norah's, she said, "Daddy misses you."

Sophie hugged her. "I miss him too."

"Can I tell him?" Piper looked seriously at Sophie.

"Of course."

He misses me. God, I ache for him.

The guesthouse was beautiful, and as Sophie had unpacked her belongings, she thought about how she'd once yearned for a place like this. But she realized, no matter how expensive the finishes, warmth didn't envelop her at the guesthouse the way it had at Sam's.

Sophie reviewed the week. On Monday, she had purchased the paddleboard and paddled the length of the lake. The water glistened like a mirror, and she tried to absorb the serenity it offered. Anything to silence the drumbeat in her mind that repeated her faults in an endless loop. The next three nights, she ran longer and faster than usual, trying to exhaust herself, but sleep eluded her even after the hard runs. The day with Piper was a welcome distraction.

After dinner, Sophie opened her email, and as she scrolled through it, deleting nearly everything, one popped up from her investment company. *Finally, something worth opening.* She perused the report, learning that her investments had grown by ten percent since the last report six months earlier.

"What's the next thing that's going to drop?" Sam's words from the week before washed over her. *When I talked with Sam*

about renting the room, I told him the hotel was too expensive. He's right—I've withheld so much.

Sophie leaned back in her chair, breathless, the way she always was when she thought about the money. She received a large insurance payout following Corey's death and inherited the money he had saved by living so frugally. She shook her head, trying to dislodge the memories. The money horrified her. She didn't feel she deserved it, and when she called it "blood money" in therapy, her therapist recommended Sophie find an investment firm to handle it so she could stop obsessing over it.

Once she did that, Sophie put the money out of her mind, except for the reports she received every six months. In two years, it had grown to more than half a million. *I could buy my own damn house, and I let Sam think I couldn't afford a hotel room. What else* am *I hiding?*

Two weeks later, Sophie drove into Boston, fought the traffic she hadn't experienced in several years, and found a parking spot. She got out of her car and walked to the law office of Richard Sizen, Esquire.

As Sophie had struggled to identify other secrets she'd kept from Sam, she remembered her therapist discussing the benefit of making amends. Sophie had made the appointment with Richard immediately, fully expecting it to be canceled when Richard saw her name on his calendar. When no email or telephone call came telling her to stay the hell away, she moved forward.

She took a deep breath as the elevator rose to the tenth floor. When she approached the receptionist, she could barely meet her eyes. "I'm Sophie Palmer. I have an appointment with Richard Sizen." Her voice trembled.

"Mr. Sizen, your ten o'clock is here," the young receptionist said into the phone. "Yes. Okay, I'll tell her." The girl smiled at Sophie. "He's going to be a few minutes. He said to please take a seat. May I get you something to drink—coffee, tea, or water?"

"No, I'm fine." She sat in one of the leather chairs, relieved that the receptionist was someone different than Sophie remembered—she wouldn't know her history with Richard. She gazed out the window at the Boston skyline. *I wonder if Sam brought Pip to that Tall Ships festival.*

Soon a tall, dark-haired man dressed in an expensive blue suit with a crisp white shirt and gray striped tie came walking down the hallway. Sophie stood.

"Mr. Sizen," the receptionist began, "this is—"

Richard interrupted. "It's okay. I know Ms. Palmer." He extended his hand, and Sophie shook it hesitantly. "It's nice to see you after all these years. My office is this way."

He can't possibly mean that. Sophie had played several scenarios for this meeting in her mind, but none of them looked like this.

Richard pushed open a door and waved Sophie inside. "After you. Please have a seat." He sat behind the desk.

Sophie had been in his office a few times, and she looked around at his diplomas on the wall and photos she'd seen before, mainly of him with friends on vacation. There were two she didn't recognize. One of Richard with a boy who appeared to be around ten years old and another of the same boy with Richard and an attractive woman.

When her gaze returned to him, Richard finally spoke. "Are you in need of legal advice?"

"I'm here to apologize," she blurted out. "I expected you to cancel the appointment."

Richard's lips quirked up. "I considered it, but curiosity got the best of me. Call me a glutton for punishment."

She nodded. "I am trying to make things right with people I hurt."

His mouth quirked again. "After all this time? Are you doing a twelve-step program or something?"

Sophie shook her head, trying to find the words she'd so carefully rehearsed.

Richard leaned forward. "It might be easier to understand if you told me you'd been in the throes of some kind of addiction when we were together."

Sophie shook her head. "I wasn't. The man you found me with was someone I'd known as a child." She took a deep breath. "I had an extremely tough childhood." *Is it ever going to become easier to say these next words?* "My mom and I lived in homeless shelters for a good share of it. Corey—that was his name—was

209

in a shelter with us when I was ten. When we ran into each other as adults, there was a connection. One I'd never experienced before."

"You ran into him, found this connection, and brought him back to our house, to our bed?" When Sophie didn't reply, Richard continued. "You couldn't have gone someplace else, like a hotel? I mean, it's bad enough you screwed someone else but finding you in our bed? That devastated me." The cordial tone he'd greeted her with was gone. This was what Sophie had expected.

"Corey convinced me to elope with him," she said. "I was packing to leave. I intended to be gone before you came home."

Richard sat back, stunned. "You eloped with someone you knew when you were ten and reconnected with after—what? Nineteen years? That doesn't make any sense. That's not something the Sophie I knew would do. Your actions were always measured and well-thought-out."

"I reconnected with Corey when I was eighteen. He was in and out of my life."

"Are you saying the whole time you were with me, you were involved with someone else?"

Sophie took a deep breath. "'Involved' isn't exactly the right word. I saw him twice after I met you. And then that day..." She placed her hands flat on Richard's desk. "My behavior was inexcusable. There were a lot of factors, but I have no excuses.

I'm in therapy, trying to figure out why I did things that hurt people I cared about."

"I'll be honest, Sophie. This doesn't make it any better for me. I feel like a fool."

"I portrayed a persona very well." Shame washed over her. "I'm learning to be more genuine."

Richard nodded. "I guess you did. Are you still married?"

"Corey died in an accident a year and a half after I left you."

"Damn." Richard's face registered his surprise. "I'm sorry." He drummed his fingers on the desk. "No matter what you did to me, that must have been tough to go through."

"It was."

He shook his head. "You never mentioned being homeless."

"Another thing I kept deeply buried."

"What about Charlie?" he asked. "Are you telling me he's not your father? Because that man clearly loves you."

"He married my mother when I was fourteen and adopted me." *Adopted me!* Sophie drew in a sharp breath. *Charlie* adopted *me. Something else I didn't admit to Sam.*

"Are you okay? You look like you've seen the proverbial ghost."

"I... Yeah, yeah, I'm fine." Richard's question about Charlie had knocked Sophie's carefully planned dialogue out of her mind. *I've said what I wanted to. I need to get out of here.* She pointed toward the pictures. "Are you married?"

"No, I met Giselle about a year after you left. Her son's ten, and he's a complication. Don't get me wrong—I love him, but he's resentful of me."

Sophie stood. "I hope you work it out. You deserve to be happy. I'm sorry that I treated you so badly." She turned to walk out the door.

"Sophie, wait." Richard came out from behind his desk. "Thank you. It's good to have an explanation." He hesitated but then hugged her. "I hope you find happiness too."

Sophie slumped against the elevator wall, taking deep breaths, waiting for the doors to open on the ground floor. It was a sultry August afternoon, but goose bumps covered her arms as she walked to her car.

During the drive back to Vermont, she replayed every conversation she'd had with Sam about what her life had been like after Charlie entered it. *I never told him that Charlie adopted me. I referred to the twins as my half sisters. How greatly I wronged adopted people with those words. I'm a horrible person.*

Two weeks remained of Sophie's summer vacation, and she spent part of every day at the lake, gliding across the water on her paddleboard, trying to figure out all the things that she hadn't "dropped" on Sam. She pondered all that Charlie had done for her. He'd paid for college, both undergrad and graduate school. While they were together, Sam had mentioned paying off his student loans. *Why didn't I tell him then?*

Charlie paid for her first car, as well as the deposit for her first post-college apartment. Charlie did all the things a father would for his child, and Sophie never acknowledged it.

I've focused on how hard the first twelve years of my life were without thinking about how privileged my life became after Charlie fell in love with my mother. I need to put that hungry child in raggedy clothes to bed. That's not who I am anymore. My mother. She kept the story of our life from Charlie, and isn't that exactly what I did with Richard and then again with Sam?

She remembered Sam's words. *"I have to pry everything out of you with a pickax."*

Why did Mom keep it all from Charlie? How poor we were, the shelters, the lack of food? Was she embarrassed? Or afraid Charlie would leave us if he knew the truth? Why have I done the same thing? Sam wouldn't have left me if he'd known the story from the beginning. He's been so open about going to therapy, how he drank too much, about Quinn and Norah. Why couldn't I do the same?

I've got to get answers.

Chapter Twenty-Two

Whispers

Sophie

THE WEEK BEFORE SCHOOL started, Sophie left the safety of the guesthouse and drove to Rhode Island. It had been over three years since she'd been there, but she still remembered the way to Charlie's flagship restaurant, Whispers. She wanted to talk to her mother, but she needed to see Charlie first and hoped he would be at the restaurant.

Dinner service didn't start until five, but the door wasn't locked, and Sophie walked inside, where she found comfort in the familiar surroundings. The walls were deep purple, and crisp white tablecloths topped with floral overlays adorned the tables. The dining room was large, but the signature draw of Whispers was the secluded nooks outfitted with tables for two and comfortable armchairs where couples could meet for an intimate dining experience. She and Richard had been in one of those nooks when he proposed.

From the back of the dining room, Sophie saw Charlie seated with his back to her, talking to the restaurant staff.

A woman noticed Sophie, rose from the table, and walked toward her. "Are you here about the open server slot? Did you fill out the online application?"

"No, I'm here for..."

At the sound of her voice, Charlie's head snapped around to look, and he pushed his chair back. A wide smile blossomed, and he reached her in microseconds.

"Sophie!" He wrapped her in his arms and enveloped her in his familiar scent.

Sophie's eyes immediately filled with tears. After a moment, Charlie let her go and took a step back, staring at her and shaking his head, the big grin still on his face.

"Monica," he called to his chief hostess, "my daughter is here, and we're going to chat at table five. You know everything that needs to be set up for tonight. Take care of it, please." He grasped Sophie's hand and led her to one of the nooks.

Sophie followed him, trying to blink the tears away. As she heard him talking to Monica, she knew the hostess would be compensated for the extra work. Charlie was the most generous man she knew.

A server approached the table. "May I get you something to drink?"

Sophie's mouth was dry. "I'd love a glass of water."

"Sparkling or still?"

"Sparkling, please." Sophie realized her blinks were not working when she heard Charlie say he would take a glass of sparkling water and asked the server to bring a box of tissues.

Sophie rested her hands on the table, unsure of what to say.

Charlie grasped them. "I could say 'long time, no see.' Or 'look what the cat dragged in,' or a million other clichés, but I won't. God, it's good to see you, Sophie."

The server arrived with two glasses of water and the tissues. Charlie pulled one out and handed it to her.

She wiped her eyes. "I wasn't sure if you'd be happy to see me."

"You're my daughter, and I've missed you. Of course, I'm happy to see you! Have you talked to your mother?"

"No, I came here first. My fight was with her, so I thought the chance of you talking to me was better."

Charlie shook his head. "She'll be as happy to see you as I am. And so will the twins. There's been a hole in our lives." He handed her another tissue as his words prompted more tears.

"I've made such a mess of my life, Charlie."

"Nothing you can't fix, I'm sure," he said with his characteristic optimism. "What's going on?"

"Do you know what life was like for Mom and me before she met you?" Sophie had debated what she wanted to say with Charlie, but she knew she had to stop keeping secrets. When he nodded, Sophie leaned toward him. "How? Mom was adamant that we couldn't tell you."

"The blowup with you devastated your mother. She told me everything, which included how she thought you were throwing your life away with a boy you'd met in a shelter."

"She told you about living in the car, not having food?"

"All of it." Charlie nodded. "But, Sophie, I already knew. Rhode Island is a small state, and the restaurant business is a tight community. It was love at first sight when I met your mother, and I made inquiries." He gazed at her steadily. "None of that mattered to me. I loved her, and I loved her prickly twelve-year-old daughter."

Sophie leaned back in her chair, stunned by Charlie's confession. She took a sip of water. *He knew all along, and it didn't matter.*

She spoke, slowly at first. "I'm in love with a man, but I hid all the important things about my life from him. He broke up with me because he said he can't continue prying everything out of me. I'm no better than my mother."

The smile left Charlie's face. "Your mother is a phenomenal woman. Think about what she went through. Disowned by her parents, giving birth to a baby at sixteen—the same age the twins are now. And I can tell you for sure they are not ready to be parents." He kept his gaze on her. "She cared for that baby, for *you,* with only an eighteen-year-old boy to help her. Then when he died, she did whatever it took to keep you with her, to keep you safe. Yes, it wasn't always pretty. I know those years were hard for both of you, but please don't ever think of your mother as anything less than amazing."

That's what love looks like. He concentrates on the positives. Sam couldn't do that.

Sophie looked back at Charlie. "I'm beginning to recognize all of that. It's why I'm here. I need to understand what drove my mother, and I need to thank you for all that you did for me."

He nodded. "You're not still with the young man you eloped with?"

"He was killed in an accident almost two years ago."

"Oh, Sophie." He reached for her hands again. "I'm so sorry."

"I want to tell you and Mom the whole thing, but I can wait until you come home tonight."

He shook his head. "I'll go with you now. Give me a minute to talk to Monica and my chef."

I walk in here after more than three years away, and he drops everything for me. Is my mother going to react as positively as Charlie did?

Charlie came back. "I called your mom, and she should be home by the time we get there. She was working on the new restaurant."

"Another new restaurant?" Sophie raised her eyebrows. This would be his fifth, spread over three towns.

"This one's going to be the best. It's going to be called My Four Redheads." Charlie opened the door to Sophie's car for her. "I'll follow you." He winked at her as he walked away.

He's naming his next restaurant after my mom, the twins... and me.

At their house, Sophie's mother welcomed her the same way that Charlie had. They exchanged apologies, punctuated with tears, and Sophie launched into what had happened with Corey, going all the way up to falling in love with Sam.

"I kept so much from him," she said. "I didn't even realize how much until I left his house and had time to think about it all."

Lydia took her hand. "I set a terrible example for you because I was so sure that Charlie would disappear if he found out how poor we were. I underestimated him. You've done the same thing with Sam."

"I have." Sophie nodded. "He'll never get over that. He'll never trust me." She squeezed Lydia's hand. "Charlie pointed out how hard you worked to keep me with you. I don't even have that. Yes, my first twelve years were hard, but since Charlie came into our lives..." She paused and smiled at him. "My life's been easy. All my struggles are of my own making." She shook her head. "I'm not a good person."

Her mother moved to the couch and wrapped her arms around Sophie. "Don't talk that way about my daughter."

Sophie managed a small smile and tried to remember the last time her mother had embraced her like this.

"You've made some mistakes, but you're not a bad person," Lydia said. "I know you can become the person you want to be. And look at the work you do. You're making a difference in kids' lives. All your father and I do is feed people."

Charlie took Lydia's hand and winked at her while his other hand grasped Sophie's. "You're a strong woman who can take care of herself."

Sophie sensed Charlie had more to say, but her twin sisters burst through the door at that moment, their familiar voices laughing as they entered the living room—until they stopped short at the sight of Sophie on the couch with their mother and father.

"You're back!" Grace sputtered.

Before Sophie said could say anything, Destiny added, "Where have you been? We've missed you."

Tears threatened to spill freely when she saw them. They'd been thirteen when Sophie bowed out of their lives—both of them awkward with braces on their teeth, children on the cusp of womanhood, and now they were beautiful young women.

What was I like at thirteen or at sixteen?

Stop that, Sophie admonished herself. *What matters is who I am now. Charlie and my mother were right. I can be the woman I want to be.*

Charlie wanted to show Sophie the new restaurant, but they couldn't all fit in one car, so Destiny and Grace rode in Sophie's car and interrogated her on the drive.

"Why did you disappear? What happened to Richard? Where did you go? Where are you living now?"

She answered their questions as fully as she could. Then Grace posed the biggest question. "You had an argument with Mom, but why didn't you stay in touch with us?"

Sophie sighed. "I made a big mistake leaving with Corey. My life was not at all what I expected it would be, and it was embarrassing to admit that to anyone. I've done a lot of work on myself, and I promise I'll never disappear like that again from my family. I hope you can forgive me." She had a feeling winning back her sisters would take longer than winning back her parents.

They met Charlie and Lydia at the restaurant, where the sign was already up. Sophie cried again as she looked at the sign. *They never gave up on me.* The interior was black and gray with glass-topped tables. Lydia handed her a menu, and Sophie saw that the cuisine would be modern fusion.

Charlie pointed at a spot behind the hostess's station. "I want a picture of my girls there. I'd like to have a professional portrait done. Sophie, will you make the trip back down here if we set something up?"

Sophie nodded, smiling through tears, and Lydia laid out framed pictures of the three girls taken when they were toddlers.

"These will go on the walls too," Charlie said. "Your mother still needs to decide on the placement."

Charlie and Lydia took Sophie out the back door, which led to an alley. He opened the door to a shed at the corner of the building. Inside was a large refrigerator, and shelves lined the walls. "We're going to put uneaten food out here every day. It will be available to people who are struggling to feed themselves. It'll be called Lydia's Pantry."

Sophie's eyes met her mother's.

"That was all Charlie's idea," Lydia said.

Sophie's heart swelled with love for him. *He gets it.*

They convinced Sophie to stay overnight, and she drove home the next day with her heart feeling lighter than it had in years.

I understand now why Sam is so happy to have his brothers and his parents back in his life.

Chapter Twenty-Three

Trent Intervenes

Sam

SAM'S LEGS WERE BURNING after a ten-mile run, and he was gasping for air as he finally collapsed on the lawn. He rolled onto his back and gazed up at the late summer sky. *Sophie's been gone nearly a month.* While he struggled to catch his breath, all the times he'd laid there with her washed over him. *Lying here on the grass to recover was a mistake.*

He stood, bending to put his hands on his knees, still waiting for his heartbeat to slow, but the change in position did nothing to quell the pictures of Sophie flooding his mind. "Fuck it."

Once inside, Sam opened the refrigerator and gazed at the six-pack he'd purchased to replace the one Joe had taken home with him. "Fuck it," he said again and grabbed one of the beers. After draining it while standing at the island in the kitchen, he showered then opened another one.

Sam was on his fourth when he heard a vehicle in his yard. Upon rising from the couch, he walked to the window and saw his father walking toward the house.

"Damn." Making no effort to hide what he was drinking, Sam opened the door. "Hey, Dad."

Trent gestured toward the bottle in his hand. "Got one of those for me?"

Sam's eyes narrowed. "You don't want a beer."

"Sure I do." Trent walked to the refrigerator, opened it, and took out one of the remaining bottles. "Hmm, don't think I've ever had this kind. All these craft breweries springing up everywhere. It's tough to keep track."

Sam's stomach clenched. *Jesus, am I going to be responsible for him falling off the wagon?*

"Can we sit in your living room?" Trent started walking that way, and Sam followed. Trent stretched out in the recliner, so Sam sat on the couch. "I miss having a recliner. Your mother

wouldn't let me get one when we bought new furniture."
Trent sighed. "This is the life."

"Dad, what are you doing here?"

"Thought I'd drop in, see what's new."

"You live over an hour away. You don't drop in on me."

Trent pushed the recliner upright. "I suppose you're
right. The drive is kind of long. Joe told me Sophie moved
out."

Sam took a deep breath. "She did." When Trent didn't
respond, Sam asked, "Did he tell you why?"

"More or less. He said you're not handling it well."

"I'm not." Sam finished his beer and put the bottle on the
floor. It wasn't lost on him that Trent had not opened the
bottle he had taken from the fridge. "I've told her everything, Dad. How I walked away from all of you, the rotten
things I did to Quinn, all the issues in my relationship with
Norah, how I was drinking too much, how I started therapy.
I haven't kept a single secret from Sophie." He drew in a
shuddering breath. "And all she did was spoon-feed me little
tidbits about herself. I don't think that's how relationships
are supposed to work. Finding out she'd been engaged while
she had something going with another man was too much."

"There must be a reason for her reluctance to share,"
Trent pointed out.

Sam grimaced.

"And what she did is in the past."

225

"I know that," Sam said, "but how do I know it won't happen to me?"

"You can't. The same way your mother can't be sure I won't drink again. There are no guarantees in life, son."

Sam leaned forward with his elbows on his knees and buried his head in his hands. After several minutes, he sat up and shook his head. "I miss her. I wonder every day if I made a mistake not trying to work it out."

Trent shrugged and raised his unopened bottle. "Is this a regular occurrence?"

"More than it should be." Sam picked up his empty bottle and rolled it between his palms. "Joe told you how drunk I was when he came up. Tonight's the first time I've had anything since then. I don't have a problem."

"I hope not. The idea of my DNA contributing to one of you boys becoming an alcoholic haunts me. Drinking alone isn't a great idea."

"I fucking *miss her*, Dad." Sam's voice broke. "This makes it easier." He set the bottle back down with a clink.

Trent frowned but nodded. "Easier in the moment." He stood and walked back to the kitchen where he placed the unopened bottle on the island. "I wasn't sure whether to come down here. But I dropped the ball so many times when you were growing up—I don't want to do that anymore. Don't let alcohol ruin your life." He embraced Sam. "I love you."

Sam stood at the island after Trent left, staring at the bottle. Finally, he took the last one out of the refrigerator, flipped the caps off both, and watched the amber liquid disappear as he emptied them into the sink.

Sam stretched out on a lounge chair on his deck, watching the sky explode with red from the setting sun. The night before, he'd gone to Quinn's for dinner and found Caden there. They told him about being at the same mission in Honduras, and Quinn acted like she was angry with him for not letting her know he'd been in touch with Caden. But Sam knew it was all an act, and seeing Quinn and Caden's happiness made him feel better than he had since Sophie left.

It also left him feeling more alone. Summer was almost over. The next day would be the final Friday that Sophie took Piper to the lake and then brought her back to him. *I'm never going to see her again after tomorrow. Pip has adjusted to her being gone, and they'll see each other at school...* He took a deep breath. *But it will be the end for me.*

The emptiness Sam felt had not abated. Earlier that day, he'd finally made a call to set up an appointment with Archie, only to find he was on vacation for two weeks and didn't have any openings until a week after that. *I'll be fine until then. I don't even really know what we're going to talk about. But I can't go on feeling this sad.*

The sunset was fading when Sam's phone pinged with a text. He smiled when he saw a picture of Jesse and Caitlin holding a tiny baby with a head full of dark hair.

> Jesse: Introducing Matteo, our second New England baby. Mom and baby are both doing great!

> Sam: Congratulations! I'm so happy for you guys!

> Jesse: Give us a week, then get your ass over here. We can't wait to introduce you to him. And Janey says to be sure you bring Pip!

"The rowers are out there, Daddy."

Sam and Piper were on their way to Jesse's after having shopped for a gift for Matteo. Piper was beyond excited to meet the new baby.

Janey popped out of the house as soon as Sam drove up. She hugged Piper. "I have a baby brother!" she announced before taking Piper's hand and tugging her toward the house.

Jesse met them at the door, and Sam high-fived him. "Caitlin just finished nursing, so Matty is ready for company." He ushered them into the living room, where Caitlin sat on the couch.

Sam approached, and Caitlin held the baby out to him. He settled Matteo against his chest and drank in the new-baby scent. After a couple of minutes, Sam shifted him around so he could see the boy's face. "Hi there, little one."

Wide brown eyes stared back at him.

"You're calling him Matty?" Sam asked.

Jesse nodded. "Yes. His full name is Matteo Samuel Ortega."

Sam tilted his head. "Say what?"

Jesse and Caitlin grinned at him. "You heard me."

"Wow," Sam said, his chest tight with love. "I'm honored."

Piper moved closer to Sam. "Can I hold him?" Her voice was barely above a whisper.

"Of course. Jesse, can you help her?" Caitlin looked at Sam. "I'm still moving a little slowly."

Piper settled on the couch, and Jesse put a pillow in her lap. Sam carefully placed Matty on the pillow then sat beside her.

Piper's eyes widened. "He's so small."

Sam took one of Matty's hands, showing Piper how tiny his fingers were.

"We need one of these, Daddy," Piper told him.

Jesse and Caitlin joined Sam in chuckling.

"Maybe someday, Pip, maybe someday." Sam cleared his throat. "We brought Chinese food. Anybody hungry here?"

Sam gave the baby back to Caitlin, who settled him into a carrier before she walked to the table.

"He's in someone's arms most of the time," she said.

After eating, the kids scattered, and Jesse suggested Caitlin take a nap. He took Matty, led Sam to the living room, and sat on the couch with the baby nestled on his shoulder.

"You look content," Sam said.

"I am. He wasn't planned, but as soon as we came home with him, we both felt like the family was complete. I'll be getting the big snip soon." He and Sam both grimaced and laughed. "Caitlin was such a warrior. I feel like it's my responsibility to make sure she doesn't have to go through that again."

"The kids seem thrilled with him."

"So far, so good. I'm sure there will be some rocky moments." Jesse shifted the baby to his other side. "So what happened to you and Sophie? I liked her. And as usual, your texts were rather cryptic."

Sam took a deep breath and launched into what had happened, ending with, "I feel like she's never going to be open with me. I couldn't go any further, not knowing what else was going to come out."

"What's it been? Over a month?" When Sam nodded, Jesse eyed him. "You doing okay?"

Sam rubbed his hand over his face. "Honestly? No." He paused. "I miss her."

Jesse stood and placed Matteo in Sam's arms. "Here. It's hard to be sad holding him."

Sam settled the baby on his shoulder and rubbed circles on his tiny back. Jesse was right. The tension eased. "Sophie and I talked about having kids." He huffed out a breath. "Pip's not the only one who wants one of these."

"Have you seen Sophie?" Jesse asked. "Has she moved on?"

"She talks to me when she drops Piper off after a day at the lake." He smiled a little. "I'm pretty sure Pip tells Sophie how much I miss her, because she always tells *me* how much Sophie misses me."

"Finding out she'd been engaged when she eloped was an enormous chunk of news. Emotions must have been running high." Jesse sighed. "You should talk to her. She's had a chance to think about what you said." He stood. "You want a beer?"

Sam shook his head.

"Mind if I have one?" Jesse asked.

"Fuck no. I'm taking a step back but watching you down a brew will not bother me." Sam moved Matteo down to his lap and played with his fingers. "Is his middle name really for me? There's not some other Sam in your life?"

"It's for you." Jesse smiled. "You're the first person I connected with up here. My best friend."

"That means a lot. The best thing that's happened in a while." His smile was genuine this time. "Thank you."

Chapter Twenty-Four

The Backpack Program

Sam

"I'VE GOT A SURPRISE for you," Sam said as Piper hopped into the car. "We're going to Cara's to celebrate Friday and your first week in second grade."

Piper clapped her hands. "I love Cara's!"

The coffee shop was full, leaving Sam and Piper to settle for a small table in the back. He took a bite of his maple-frosted donut and followed it with a long swallow of iced coffee.

Piper had taken a sip of her mocha smoothie when her eyes widened. "Daddy! There's Sophie and her mother. Sophie! Sophie!" Piper waved her hand to get Sophie's attention.

Her mother? What is Pip talking about? Sam turned to face the door and saw Sophie standing between two teenage girls and a middle-aged woman. All four of them bore an uncanny resemblance to one another, starting with their auburn hair. Sophie said something to the other women then walked toward Sam's table.

My God, that's her mother and her half-sisters. But how? And why does Piper know?

"Hi, Sam. Hi, Pip." Sophie leaned in to hug Piper. "You've got a whipped-cream mustache." She picked up a napkin to wipe Pip's mouth. "Just like this summer."

"I told Daddy it was your mother with you! Can they sit with us, Daddy?"

Sam was stunned.

Before he could reply, Sophie said, "This is a tiny table. It doesn't have room for us."

"We could sit in the park. At one of the picnic tables." Piper smiled at Sophie and Sam. "Pleeease."

Sophie ducked her head to look at Sam. "Are you okay with that?" Her voice was soft, and Sam's heart fluttered.

"Sure," he managed. "We'll meet you over there."

As they walked across the street to the town green, Sam asked, "Piper, how did you know that was Sophie's mother?"

"We had an assembly this afternoon, and Sophie was there with her mother. The school is going to give backpacks to kids who don't have enough food, like Sophie didn't when she was little. Remember when Sophie was upset about the cookies?" She took a bite of her donut. "Sophie talked about it today."

The four red-haired women approached the table, clutching iced coffees and donuts.

Sophie smiled. "Sam and Piper, this is my mother, Lydia Palmer, and my sisters, Destiny and Grace. Mom, Des, Gracie—this is Sam Carpenter and his daughter, Piper."

Sam stood and extended his hand. "It's nice to meet you." *Holy fuck, I feel like I'm in an alternate universe.*

Piper started talking, breaking the awkward silence. "Sophie used to live with us, but then she found a house to move into, and she'd never had a house of her own, so she left us. We still want her to come back. Right, Daddy?" Without giving Sam a chance to answer, Piper continued. "Have you been to her house? She took me there after we'd been to the lake. We go to the lake every Friday..."

Sam laid his hand on Piper's arm. "Sweetie, take a breath. Let Sophie's mom answer."

Lydia smiled. "We stayed with Sophie last night. Did you draw the pictures she has on the walls?"

Piper nodded.

"I like them," Lydia confided. "Could you draw something for me?"

Piper's eyes sparkled. "Yes!"

"We saw pictures of you and your dad there too," Lydia continued.

Sophie put up the pictures of us, of me. I wonder if that includes the kiss photo.

As if she'd read his mind, one of the twins—Sam did not know which one—looked at him with a grin. "Yes, we saw the one of you kissing her."

Sam could feel his face redden. "Actually, that's Sophie kissing me." He smiled at Sophie, and when she smiled back, his stomach flipped over. *This is the most surreal experience of my life.*

He turned to Lydia. "Have you been up here before?"

"This is our first time. It's lovely."

"I told Sophie when she was living with us that we could find room if her family wanted to visit."

"She was mad and not talking to us," said the other twin. She smirked at Sophie.

"Des!" Sophie frowned.

Piper looked up. "My daddy was mad when my mommy moved out, and he didn't talk to her."

"Piper," Sam said in a warning tone.

"Well, you didn't."

Sam wrestled her under his arm playfully.

Lydia laughed. "Families are full of complications."

As Sam tried to muffle her, Piper called out, "Daddy said that, too, when I told him I wanted Sophie to live with us forever."

Sam brought Piper out from under his arm and embraced her in a bear hug. "As you can see, I have no secrets," he joked.

The group joined in with his laughter. Sam studied Lydia. She had the same lilting voice as Sophie, and after living with Norah, he understood enough about clothes to know that her outfit was expensive. It was hard to picture this woman living on the streets and scraping by.

"Can we go see the ducks?" Piper waved her hand toward the small pond at the edge of the park.

Destiny and Grace jumped up. "Come on, we'll take you," Grace said.

Destiny looked toward Sam. "If it's okay."

He nodded, and Lydia stood too. "I'll go with them."

Sam's eyes met Sophie's. "What's going on?"

"Oh, nothing special." She flashed him an embarrassed grin.

Sam cocked his head at her in response.

"I've had a lot of time to think," she said. "I'm trying to make things right."

"Your mother's beautiful. Like her daughters."

Sophie blushed. "How are you?"

"Surviving. I drank too much right after you left. My father staged an intervention." Sam rolled his eyes. "I've had nothing to drink since then. Oh, and Caitlin had the baby."

Sophie clapped her hands. "Boy or girl?"

"Boy. Matteo Samuel."

"Oh, Sam."

"Yeah." His eyes stung. "That's special. Piper said something about an assembly..."

Before he could finish, Piper came running back, with the others trailing behind.

Sophie murmured, "You'll hear about it."

When they had all finished their coffees, Sophie stood. "Ali invited us for dinner, so we need to get over there."

On Saturday morning, as Sam flipped through the pages of the weekly Thetford newspaper, a headline caught his eye.

Local School Establishes Food Shelf. Chelford Elementary to Offer Food and Backpacks.

Sam read the article, which described the food shelf and backpacks filled with staples that would be available to students for the weekend. His heart seized at what he read next.

The program has been established with a generous contribution by speech-language pathologist Sophie Palmer, who received an enthusiastic reception when she addressed the assembled students.

"As a child, there were times when my mother and I didn't have enough food, and we didn't always have a secure place to sleep. If you don't have enough to eat, if you don't have a safe place to live, please let someone know. All of us are here to help you."

After the assembly, Palmer shared that she had funded the program in honor of her mother, Lydia Palmer, and adoptive father, Charlie Palmer. "I only recently gave my mother and Charlie the proper credit for the life they've given me, and I want to acknowledge that as well as help kids who are struggling to survive."

Sam was trying to make sense of it all when a car pulled into his driveway. Piper had drawn a picture for Lydia, and he had a feeling this was her coming to pick it up before heading home.

Piper hopped off the couch and dragged Sam to the door, where they watched Sophie and Lydia climb out of the car. "Where's Des and Gracie?" Piper called.

"Still getting dressed." Lydia came inside and smiled, reaching for the pictures Piper held out to her.

"I made pictures for them too. Do you want to see my room?" Piper stretched her hand out to take Lydia's. They walked down the hall, leaving Sam and Sophie in the kitchen.

Sam looked at Sophie. "I read the article in the paper."

Sophie cocked her head but said nothing.

"It sounds like something that could make a big difference," he added.

"I hope so."

"You're not the same woman who moved out."

She shook her head.

He took a breath. "We should talk."

"I'd like to do that."

"How about dinner on Friday? My week's crazy. Pip's here until Tuesday, and then I have some business things on Wednesday and Thursday."

Sophie gazed into his eyes. "Won't you be having pizza at Norah's?"

"No, she and Piper are going to her parents' house in Connecticut for the weekend."

"Okay." Sophie nodded. "Friday works."

"I'll make a reservation at that restaurant in Norwich." Sam reached out to brush a piece of hair off Sophie's forehead. "I know where Ali's house is. I can pick you up."

Chapter Twenty-Five

The Collapse

Sam

FRIDAY FINALLY ARRIVED, AND as Sam drove to a construction site, he thought about his upcoming date with Sophie. *I could have had her come to the house. We could have cooked together.* He'd considered that all week, but he feared passion would overwhelm them. Every disagreement with Norah had ended with them having sex, and he wanted more with Sophie.

Those thoughts were still swirling when he arrived at the site and climbed the scaffolding. The supervisor pointed out the problem area, and as Sam walked over to get a closer look, he caught sight of his newest co-worker approaching the structure. "Andy, you need a hard hat."

"Come on, boss man. I've been higher than that bareheaded." Andy was young and brash, always pushing boundaries.

"No hard hat, no climb." Sam hoped that would help corral Andy's raw talent. "I'm serious."

Andy grumbled as he walked back to his car, and Sam watched with satisfaction as he returned wearing the hard hat and started to climb. Just as Andy was about to step onto the staging, Sam heard a loud crack, and to his horror, the floor collapsed before his eyes.

He had only a second to register that Andy had plummeted to the ground before he felt himself falling as well.

Sam opened his eyes in the bright, unforgiving lights of an emergency department cubicle. He was being moved. Muddled thoughts filled his mind. He remembered trying to get up, but something pinned his ankle to the ground. Andy had been lying unconscious nearby, and Michael, the supervisor, lay a few feet farther away. Sam could hear him groaning.

Someone had said paramedics were there, and they started an IV and gave him painkillers. Relief had flooded over Sam, and everything else was fuzzy until just now, opening his eyes in this bright room.

Sam couldn't hold back a groan as hands shifted him from an ambulance gurney to the ED bed.

The paramedic started talking. "Thirty-two-year-old male fell twenty feet when the structure he was on collapsed. Landed on his right side, and a steel beam landed on his left ankle. He is conscious and alert, with no loss of consciousness reported. He complains of pain in his right wrist, right chest, and left ankle. There's deformity and swelling to the right wrist, diminished breath sounds on the right, and an obvious open fracture to the left ankle. The left foot is pale and cool to touch with absent distal pulses. Breathing is shallow and labored."

Sam groaned again when the doctor touched his foot.

He heard the paramedic say, "There's two others, Doc, in worse shape than this."

God. Andy and Michael. Worse than this?

The doctor swore softly. "Mr. Carpenter, we're going to take care of you. We need to get some X-rays and a CT scan, but you're going to be okay." The doctor was partway to the door when he said, "Get a Doppler on that left foot."

Someone grasped his left hand. "Sam, it's me. Quinn."

"Quinn? How'd you get here? Never mind, your hospital." He grimaced. "Fuck, my foot is on fire, and it hurts to breathe."

"I was here in the ED when they brought you in," she said. "I know you're hurting. You'll be okay. They need to run some tests, and then they'll be able to make you more comfortable. Can I call someone?"

He closed his eyes. After a minute, he said, "Work has Joe's number—he's my emergency contact." He groaned again. "Will you stay with me?"

Quinn squeezed his uninjured hand again. "I'll stay until your family arrives."

Sophie

Sophie's morning was going well. She was looking forward to having dinner with Sam and having the chance to share all that she'd learned and processed since she left his house.

She was on her way to the break room when an aide from the office stopped her. "There's a phone call for you. The guy said it was urgent."

Sophie's heart pounded as she turned toward the office. The only men who would call her would be Sam or Charlie. *What could be wrong?* The secretary handed her the phone.

She swallowed. "Hello?"

"Sophie, this is Joe, Sam's brother. Sam's been in an accident."

"Oh my God! A car accident?"

"No. He was on a job site, and some scaffolding collapsed. He's in the emergency department at Dartmouth. It's going to take me a couple of hours to get there and probably almost as long for Mom and Dad." He paused. "I know you aren't together, but can you go over until we can get there?" His voice broke. "I don't want him to be alone."

"Of course," she said, her voice shaking. "I'll leave right away. How bad is it?"

"Bad. Broken ribs, collapsed lung, broken wrist, smashed foot. The person who called said he'll be okay, but I'm shook. I told the hospital you'd be coming, so they'll let you in. I'm sorry—I know I was assuming a lot."

"It's fine. I'll head right over." She took a deep breath. "And Joe, thanks for calling me."

Sophie barely held herself together on the drive, and when a staff member directed her to a cubicle that was empty except for a nurse sitting in the corner, her threatening tears spilled out.

Brushing the tears away, she studied the nurse, realizing she looked familiar—she'd seen her in pictures. "Quinn?" When the woman nodded, Sophie introduced herself. "Joe called me."

Quinn stood and seemed to hesitate for a moment before stepping forward to put her arms around Sophie. "He's going to be okay."

I'm sure she knows we're not together. Did she get over the doctor while she was in Honduras and decide she wanted to be with Sam?

No. He wouldn't have asked me to dinner if he was seeing Quinn.

Quinn pulled back. "I was down here when they brought him in, and I told him I'd stay until his family arrived. He's at radiology."

When Sam returned to the room, Sophie reached out for his hand. He opened his eyes, and tears flowed freely from them when he saw her. She wiped his tears away.

He groaned. "I'm really hurting."

"I know, but they're going to take care of you." Sophie looked at Quinn. "Can't they give him something for the pain?"

"He got something in the field, but it's probably wearing off. As soon as they determine what they need to do, they'll get more meds on board."

Sophie continued to grip Sam's hand. "Joe called me," she told him. "I hope you don't mind."

Sam shook his head and moaned as he tried to take a deep breath.

The doctor came in. "Mr. Carpenter, you have a right wrist fracture and several broken ribs. You have a punctured lung, too, and we're going to insert a chest tube to inflate it. You'll feel better when we get that done. The worst of your injuries is your ankle, which will need surgery. After we get the lung tended to, you'll be seeing an orthopedist. Do you understand what I'm telling you?"

Sam nodded.

"Is there anyone here with you?" the doctor asked.

Sam motioned to Sophie with his good hand.

"I'm Sophie Palmer, a friend of Sam's." She stepped forward. "His brother asked me to stay until he could get here. Can you give him something for the pain?"

"We're going to do that before we inflate his lung." The doctor looked at Sophie and Quinn. "You'll need to leave while we do this." Apparently noticing Quinn's scrubs, he asked, "Do you work here?"

She nodded, "But not here in the ED. I'm on the fifth floor east. Come on, Sophie—we should go. This is going to hurt him. We don't want to be anywhere nearby."

She led Sophie outside, where they stood awkwardly together, neither of them knowing what to say until Sophie saw Sam's parents hurrying toward the hospital from the parking lot.

"Trent," she called. "Laura."

When they reached Sophie, Laura gathered her into a hug. "Thank God you're here. But why are you outside?"

Trent's gaze traveled to Quinn. He looked at her quizzically. "Quinn? What are you doing here?"

She explained then filled them in on what they were doing for his lung. "That will be painful for him, so I thought we'd be better waiting out here." She looked at Sophie. "I'm going to head back to my floor. I'll check on him later." She pulled a pen and paper out of her pocket, jotted something down, and said, "Here's my number if you need anything."

Trent still looked confused as Quinn walked away. "Do you know who she is?"

Sophie managed a small smile. "Yes, I know she was once Sam's girlfriend. It's a long story, but they're friends now."

246

Laura put her hand on Trent's arm. "That's not important. How is Sam? You've seen him?"

Sophie described his injuries and added, "He's in bad shape. Let's go back in. Maybe they are done."

A nurse showed them to Sam's cubicle, and they met the doctor as he was leaving.

Laura spoke first. "I'm Sam's mother. How is he?"

"We've inflated his lung," the doctor said. "You can go in, but he's heavily sedated. I'll be back in a bit and give you more details. An orthopedic doctor will come in to look at his ankle."

Sam opened his eyes when they entered and tried to speak, but nothing he said made sense.

Joe arrived and hugged first his mom and then Sophie. He moved to the bed. "Sam. Hey, Sam."

When Sam opened his eyes, Joe shook his head. "You'll do anything for attention."

As Sam raised the middle finger of his left hand, Joe looked at his parents and nodded. "He'll be okay."

The orthopedist came in shortly afterward and outlined what he would do to Sam's ankle. They waited with Sam until he went to the operating room, then a nurse directed them to the waiting area.

As they walked, Joe heaved one sigh then another. "I never want to get a call like that again." He looked at Sophie. "Thank you for coming."

Sophie nodded but felt awkward intruding on a family moment. "I should probably leave."

Joe shook his head. "No, stay. Please."

They arrived at the waiting area, and as they sat down, Trent looked at Joe. "Did you know Sam had been in touch with Quinn?"

"Yeah, it's a long story. It's not a big deal, Dad."

"I know but seeing her surprised me." He gave Joe a look. "We got nothing but time for you to tell me what I've missed out on."

Joe and Sophie together told them how the friendship had developed between Sam and Quinn over the past year. When they finished, Joe invited Sophie to join him in getting some coffee for all of them. It was the first time he had seen her since she moved out of Sam's house.

"How are you?" he asked. "Really?"

"I'm a wreck after seeing him like that, but I know you're talking about our relationship." She drew in a shuddering breath. "We were supposed to go out to dinner tonight. He wanted to talk, and I've worked a lot of things out since I left. Stuff I want to share with him." She wiped a tear away.

Several hours later, the surgeon came to speak to them. "The ankle required pins and plates, but the surgery went well. I expect it to heal completely, although it will be a long road. His right wrist fracture is a clean break, and we have a splint on it for the time being. He has several broken ribs and is being moved to the ICU—"

Laura drew in a sharp breath.

"It's for observation. I expect him to make a full recovery, but we want to keep a close eye on him for the next couple of days. You can go there and see him, but he is highly sedated and will be while he's in the ICU." He took Laura's hand. "He's young and healthy. I assure you, he *will* recover."

They all thanked him and walked to the ICU, where the nurses said only two of them could go in at one time. Sophie and Joe both urged his parents to go first. When Trent and Laura came out a few minutes later, she and Joe entered.

Sophie took Sam's left hand, and his eyes fluttered open.

"We talked to your doctor," Joe said. "You're going to be fine."

Sam squeezed Sophie's hand in response.

Chapter Twenty-Six
Sam's A Bad Patient

Sophie

SOPHIE OPENED HER EYES the next morning to the sound of someone softly calling her name. She sat up and saw Quinn standing nearby in the waiting room. The night before flooded over her as she remembered taking turns with Joe to sit with Sam and calling Norah to let her know about the accident. Norah asked if she should bring Piper to see him, and after conferring with Joe, Sophie told her to wait until Sam was out of intensive care.

"Did you both sleep here all night?" Quinn gestured toward Joe, asleep in a recliner.

"Yes, neither of us wanted to leave. Joe sent his parents home."

"I'm on the way to my ward, but I wanted to see how Sam was. The nurses said he had a good night."

Joe's eyes fluttered open, and he blinked at seeing Quinn then scrambled out of the recliner to his feet. "Quinn. It's been a long time."

"It has." She repeated what she'd told Sophie. "I can't stay. Wish these were better circumstances, but Sam's going to be okay." She reached out to squeeze Joe's hand before she left.

Trent and Laura arrived a couple of hours later, accompanied by Matt.

"I should have come yesterday, but Jilly was sick, and I didn't want to leave her alone with the baby." Matt ran a hand through his hair. "I can't believe this. The Carpenter boys are invincible."

Joe grimaced. "Not so much as we thought when we were teenagers."

Matt went in to see Sam with Laura, and when they came back, a social worker was waiting. She introduced herself and said she wanted to discuss the plan for Sam's discharge.

"He'll need to go to a rehab center for at least a few weeks," the social worker said. "I have information here on several that we recommend. You can look it over and—"

"Rehab center!" Joe glared. "You're talking about a nursing home. He's not going to a fucking nursing home!" When Laura frowned at him, he shook his head. "Excuse my language, but no. Just no. Sam would hate that."

"No need for apology," the social worker said. "I understand emotions are running high. But you've said that Sam lives alone, except for when his seven-year-old daughter is with him. He won't be able to care for himself or her. The rib injuries will severely limit his mobility until they heal. He'll be in a wheelchair for a while—he'll need help bathing, dressing. Every single task of daily life will be a challenge for the next several weeks."

Trent spoke up. "What if one of us stays with him? That could work, couldn't it?"

"Yes, our physical-therapy department can work with the caregiver to show them how to do bed-to-chair transfers, how to bathe him, and everything else." The social worker paused. "But I had the impression you all worked."

"We do." Joe sighed. "Can we have a few minutes to brainstorm?"

"Of course. I have some other patients to see, then I'll come back here."

Sophie watched as Sam's parents and his brothers looked at one another. *I should leave. This is a family thing. Unless...*

Joe spoke first. "Which one of us is it going to be? I'm in the middle of an extensive project, but if none of you can be there, I will be. There's no way he's going to a fucking rehab center."

"I've got the baby during the day," Laura said helplessly. "If I'm down here, either Matt or Jilly will need to take time off from work."

Trent shook his head. "The plant's right out straight. It'll be tough for them to let either Matt or me go."

"I can do it." Sophie's voice was soft and tentative, and they all turned to look at her. "I can take leave. Sam and I didn't part on bad terms. I'd like to do this for him."

The lengthy silence made Sophie worry she had overstepped, and she spoke again. "We were supposed to have dinner together yesterday—to talk. We're not enemies. And Joe's right. Sam would hate being in a rehab center."

Joe looked at Sophie then at Trent and Laura. "Sophie's is the best idea I've heard." His gaze went back to her. "If you're sure?"

"I am."

When the social worker came back, she agreed with their plan.

"Sophie, I can take you down to PT now to set up a schedule for you to work with them," she said. "Sam will be in the ICU for a day or two more then in a regular room for a few days. He's not in any shape to hear about this now, but when he is, someone will have to explain it to him."

Sam

Sam looked around at his new hospital room. *At least there's a window.*

253

The days in the ICU were a blur. He knew his parents and his brothers had visited and that Quinn had stopped by every day on her way to her floor, but he had no memory of anything they said during any of those visits.

What he remembered most was Sophie holding his hand. When the drugs wore off, the pain often overwhelmed him, but the feel of Sophie's hand holding his brought him a sense of peace.

He took stock of his body. Moving from the ICU to this room had hurt like a mother. The movement of the bed over the doorways jostled his body, and the pain caused him to gasp for breath.

Broken ribs, collapsed lung, broken wrist, and the foot. No one has told me what's going on or how long it will all take to heal. Does Piper know what happened to me? He didn't remember her visiting him in the ICU. He hoped she hadn't. *I don't want her to see me like this.*

A nurse came in to administer his painkillers, and he dozed off.

When Sam awoke again, Joe was sitting in a chair, watching him.

"Hey," Sam said, glad to see Joe and happy he was in what he'd come to regard as the golden hour of his new normal—when he wasn't drowsy from the drugs, but the pain was tolerable.

"Hey," Joe said. "You're looking a little better."

"'Little' being the operative word." Sam snorted a laugh. "Whooo, that hurt. No laughing, I guess. Does Norah know what happened? This should be my night with Piper."

"Sophie called her on Friday, and she's updated her every day. We all agreed Pip shouldn't come here, at least until you were in a regular room."

Sam nodded.

"I've got something to talk to you about." Joe tented his hands in front of his mouth. "You're badly banged up."

"No shit."

Joe leaned forward. "You won't be able to take care of yourself when you get sprung from here. A hospital social worker met with us and suggested a rehab center."

Sam's face crumpled. "Fuck. No."

"That's what I said. I advocated for you, bro. But you are going to need help. A lot of it." Joe paused as that sank in for Sam. "We were all there to meet with the social worker—Mom, Dad, Matt, me, and Sophie." He stopped there. "I hope you don't mind that I called her. I wanted someone who could get here quickly. It killed me to think of you injured and alone."

"Don't mind." Sam took a breath and shuddered. "Glad she was there."

"So anyway, we talked about who could move in with you and do all that you're going to need. Sophie volunteered."

Sam took another breath and winced. "Not sure I like that idea. Holding my hand in the ICU was one thing, but moving back into my house…" He grimaced—the golden hour was ending.

"All of us had logistics issues—you know, with our jobs. I mean, any of us would work those out to help you, but it would take some juggling. And while we were trying to figure it out, Sophie said she could take leave, and she wanted to do it."

Sam shook his head. "Like, what will she have to do?"

"Get you out of bed, wash you, dress you—"

"Wait, wait, wait. *Wash me?*"

"Dude, you're going to have a cast on your wrist and your foot. Do you see yourself taking a shower? Your ribs are broken! You're wincing every time you take a breath. Do you really think you're going to move around on your own?"

"Fuck."

"I know it sucks. But think about it. Do you want me or Mom to wash your junk? Or even worse, Dad?" Joe rolled his eyes. "Sophie's seen it all. She'll be fine." Joe smirked at him.

"How long?"

"I'm not sure. The surgeon hasn't given us a timeline. So, is that okay with you? She's already working with physical therapy to learn the best ways to help you."

"I don't like it." Sam gritted his teeth. "I want to work things out with her, and I'm not sure her being my nurse is the best way to do that. But I guess I don't have a choice." Those were the most words Sam had said, and he struggled to catch his breath when he finished.

After some meds, Sam dozed again, and when he awoke, Sophie was sitting where Joe had been.

A nurse came in. "Mr. Carpenter, how are you feeling? We need to get you drinking." She held a cup with a straw up to his mouth, and he took a swallow. "That's a start. I want this all gone when I come back in. Are you in any pain?"

Sam shrugged, and the nurse handed Sophie the cup on her way out.

Sophie pulled her chair close to the bed and placed the cup on the bedside table. She took Sam's hand and grasped it lightly. He closed his eyes and opened them only when she urged him to drink.

The cup was empty when the nurse returned with another one.

Sam stared at her. "I can't even move. You're making me drink so much. What happens when I need to pee?"

"You don't need to worry about that right now."

Sam squirmed on the bed, groaning as pain stabbed his chest. "What do you mean? I don't need to worry about going to the bathroom?"

"You have a catheter," she explained. "Hopefully, we'll get rid of that later today."

Sam recoiled. "A catheter! Jesus!" When Sophie took his hand, he snatched it away. "My God, I'm helpless."

"Sam, it's temporary," Sophie said. "You're going to get stronger every day."

He glared at her, his breathing heavy with agitation.

The nurse moved in front of Sophie. "She's right. For a little while, you are going to need some help. You had a very serious accident, but you'll make strides to get back to normal every day. You need to calm down."

He turned his head away from both women.

When his lunch arrived, he still hadn't looked back at Sophie.

"Sam, you need to eat," she said. "It's chicken. I've cut it up so you can manage it on your own." When he didn't respond, she spoke again. "Sam, eat. It's how you'll heal. Please let me help."

"I don't want your help." His voice reflected his bitterness.

"I'm not going anywhere. You can let me help you, or a nurse will feed you. It's your choice." She left no room for discussion, putting the plate in front of him.

He struggled to feed himself, using his left hand before finally shoving the plate away and closing his eyes.

The afternoon passed in silence until his parents arrived.

Laura leaned in to kiss his cheek. "You gave us a real scare. How do you feel?"

Sam shook his head. "Peachy. I can hardly move, and I can't even pee on my own. Do you know how long I'll be here?"

"Sophie probably knows more than us," Trent said. "She's been here every day."

Sam glared at them before turning away.

Trent tried again. "Buddy, I know it seems bad now, but the doctors assured us you'll make a full recovery."

"I'm not your buddy," Sam muttered.

Trent and Laura looked at Sophie in bewilderment, and she shrugged before motioning for them to follow her outside.

Sam watched them outside his door. He saw a nurse talking to them before he let his suddenly heavy eyes close, hoping he would wake up to find it was all a bad dream.

The next thing he knew, the room was full of people. His parents were still there, along with Sophie, and the surgeon had entered to examine his ankle and wrist.

"You're doing well, Sam," the surgeon said. "We'll put a hard cast on the wrist tomorrow and do the ankle before we release you."

"When will that be?"

"By the end of the week. I'm going to leave orders to discontinue the IV and remove the catheter tonight. When you're eating and drinking and able to pee on your own, we'll talk about your discharge. At least for tonight and tomorrow, you'll be using a bedpan. I don't want that ankle moved."

Sam groaned. "A bedpan? And what do you mean, be able to pee? Why wouldn't I be able to?"

"Sometimes the plumbing doesn't start working right away, but don't worry about it. We can cath you again if we need to."

Sam was quiet for several minutes while the doctor listened to his breathing and his heart.

"Do you have questions?" the doctor asked.

"Yeah, how long am I going to be in the casts? My wrist and my ankle?"

"The wrist was a clean break and should heal in six weeks. I don't even think you'll need physical therapy for that. The ankle is more complex. It was crushed, meaning a lot had to be repaired. I don't want any weight on it for twelve weeks." He paused. "At that point, we'll reevaluate and hopefully get you into a walking boot."

"Twelve weeks! Are you kidding me? I have a seven-year-old daughter. How am I supposed to take care of her?"

"I'm very serious. I expect you to make a full recovery if you follow what I tell you to do. If you don't, that ankle will probably give you trouble for the rest of your life. Twelve weeks of inactivity is a small price to pay." He nodded at Sam and the others. "I'll be back tomorrow."

As he walked out the door, Laura took Sam's hand. "We'll all help you. The time will go by quickly."

Sam snatched his hand away. "I don't want your help. I'm tired. Just leave, please." He closed his eyes and turned away from them.

Chapter Twenty-Seven

Twelve Weeks

Sam

SAM AWOKE THE NEXT morning after a restless night, feeling more clear-headed than the day before as he stared at his ankle.

Twelve weeks without being able to walk! How the fuck am I supposed to live? I don't want to depend on Sophie or my parents. And the bedpan... That is so humiliating. This all sucks.

He closed his eyes but didn't fall back to sleep.

A few minutes later, he heard a voice say, "Sam, it's Quinn. How are you?"

He opened his eyes as she took his hand. "Quinn, I'm all fucked up! I have to pee in a bedpan. I can't even feed myself!" Tears flooded his eyes.

"You have a ton of people to help you," she said gently. "Sophie's been here every day. Your parents and your brothers will help. You'll get through this."

"I don't want Sophie to see me like this."

"Let people help you, Sam." She studied the monitors before looking back at him. "I know it's not exactly the same, but don't be like Caden was and pull away from the person who loves you most." She kissed his forehead. "My shift is about to start, so I need to head out. I'll stop in again later."

He thought about what she said, but it didn't change his feelings. His breakfast arrived, and he struggled to eat with his left hand. A nurse's aide came to his rescue, helping him eat, and told him he would probably be able to use his right hand better after they put the cast on.

Sophie arrived midmorning to find him watching television with a hard cast on his wrist. "Look at you. Awake enough to watch TV, and finally, a cast on your wrist. Has the surgeon been in this morning?"

Sam punched the remote to kill the television. "No." He closed his eyes and turned his head away. *God, why am I being such a jerk to her?*

Sophie settled into a chair and pulled out a book. "Not my usual cozy mystery today. I found a book in the hospital gift store about how to help a friend when he's hurt and acting like an idiot. Fascinating reading."

He didn't respond. At lunchtime, the same nurse's aide came to help Sam and suggested Sophie take a break.

In the afternoon, Sam heard Sophie talking to someone.

"His eyes are closed, but I don't think he's asleep. Maybe he'll be glad to see you, because he's not at all happy that I'm here."

There was a pause, but Sam heard nothing else until Sophie said, "Go on in. I'll take a walk."

"Hey, Sam. It's Caden. Quinn told me what happened."

Sam opened his eyes. "Here to see the cripple, huh?" His voice was flat.

Caden studied him. "Actually, I'm here to visit someone I consider very lucky. Has Quinn told you about my grandfather?"

"No." Sam sounded petulant even to his own ears.

"He was killed in a similar accident when I was in college."

That jolted Sam out of his mood. "Jesus! I'm such an ass."

Caden raised his eyebrows.

"It's stupid, but I hate being this helpless," Sam said. "It's humiliating." He winced as he took a breath.

"Quinn said you broke some ribs."

"Yeah, they hurt like a mother. Everything hurts."

Caden nodded. "I broke some ribs playing hockey a few years ago. It hurt like hell, and you can't do much but rest. They'll take several weeks to heal."

"Well, I'm going to have plenty of time. Twelve weeks before I can put any weight on my ankle. I don't know what I'm going to do."

Caden smiled. "Quinn tells me you have a family who will help. Let them in. They need it as much as you do."

"Daddy!"

Sam shifted his gaze from Caden to the door as Piper and Norah walked in. Norah tried to hold her back, but Piper had none of it as she ran to the bed.

"I've missed you! When are you going home?" Then Piper noticed Caden. "Dr. Brady! What are you doing here? Can I sign your cast, Daddy? That's what we do at school if someone has a cast."

Sam smiled for the first time since the accident. "Caden, this is Norah Taylor, Piper's mom, and maybe you remember the chatterbox. Norah, this is Caden Brady."

Caden reached out to shake Norah's hand.

"We met him the first time we went skiing," Piper said. "Remember Mommy, I told you about it? You were mad. Why do you have your foot propped up, Daddy?"

Norah smiled as she looked at Sam. "She's missed you. And it's nice to meet you, Caden."

"Nice to meet you too. I need to head out. Remember what I said, Sam. You're lucky to be here."

"Can I sit on your bed, Daddy?"

Sam nodded, and Norah lifted her onto the bed, where she snuggled under his good arm. Piper turned toward the window then saw the remote. She stretched to pick it up, and Sam winced with every movement she made.

Norah lifted her away. "You know what? Daddy will feel better if you get down. You can walk around, and perhaps he'll let you adjust the bed."

Sam mouthed, "Thank you," when Piper wasn't looking.

"When are you coming home, Daddy?" Piper asked.

"Maybe this weekend," he said.

Sophie walked in as he said that, and Piper launched herself into her arms.

"It's been forever since I saw you." Piper looked at her mother. "If Daddy comes home this weekend, will I get to be there?"

Sophie looked at Sam with her eyebrows raised.

"I'm having a hard time moving around, so I think you should stay with Mommy for the weekend," he said. "We'll talk on Sunday night after I figure out what it's like being home. I miss you, too, baby girl."

Piper's face settled into a pout until Norah pulled a marker out of her bag and told her to sign Sam's cast.

Sam looked at Sophie. "How about if you take Pip to the cafeteria for ice cream?"

Once they left, Norah asked, "How are you really?"

"Terrible. Everything hurts. I can't take care of myself, and I can't put any weight on my foot for twelve weeks. Twelve weeks,

Norah! How the hell am I going to do that? And I miss Pip. I don't like not having her with me."

"Sophie's called, letting me know how you are, and she's talked to Piper. When you get home, you'll be able to talk to Pip every day, and I bet you'll do better at home than you expect."

"Yeah, whatever."

"You are in a mood, aren't you? Since you don't seem to want company, I'll go find them." And with that, she walked out the door.

I'm such an asshole. At least she understood the message and left me alone.

Sophie had returned to the room when the surgeon entered.

"How are you doing today?" he asked. "Are you finding it a little easier to move that arm now that we've put the cast on?"

"I guess, but I'm still uncomfortable, and the ribs hurt with the slightest movement. The ankle pain is constant."

"Regretfully, that's all to be expected. It's going to be a few weeks before you're comfortable moving around." He listened to Sam's heart and lungs before continuing. "Here's the plan. You'll get a hard cast on the ankle in the morning. They'll take X-rays before they start and then after to ensure they haven't messed up any of my artwork. You'll stay here tomorrow, and if you have no issues, you'll go home the day after that."

He turned his attention to Sophie. "You've worked with physical therapy?"

She nodded. "I've gone down every day, and they've shown me how to help him in and out of bed or a chair. They were helpful and kind, and they seemed to know what I'd need."

"We're lucky to have them. How about getting him into his house? You mentioned stairs."

"His brothers will be there to help."

Sam grimaced at this news.

The surgeon looked back at Sam. "You should stay as quiet as possible for the next couple of weeks. I know you're tired of lying in bed, but you must limit your movement. Don't be a superhero. Sleep when you are tired. That will do as much for your healing as anything else. You'll need a shower chair, and I recommend a wheelchair."

Sam rolled his eyes. "A wheelchair?"

"Unless you want to rely on this lovely lady every time you want to move from point A to point B. Physical therapy can probably fix you up with one."

"It's all taken care of," Sophie said softly, "and the shower chair as well."

The surgeon smiled. "She's going to take good care of you. I'm off for the next couple of days, so my chief resident will check on you, and she'll write your discharge papers. I'll see you in two weeks at my office."

He extended his fist to Sam, who reluctantly bumped it with his left hand. "I know you don't think so now, but you're going to be fine. You're lucky the injuries aren't any worse."

After the surgeon left, Sam looked at Sophie. "You've been busy."

"I want to make things as easy on you as possible."

"Even when I'm being a jerk?"

"Even then."

Chapter Twenty-Eight

Sophie As Nurse

Sam

AS SHE MADE THE turn onto the dirt road to his house, Sam was grateful when Sophie slowed down, because pain tore through him every time they hit a bump. She headed down his driveway to where Matt and Joe were waiting.

Sam spoke for the first time since they left the hospital. "Damn, they're going to bust my chops about being an invalid."

Sophie turned the car off and raised her hand, signaling Joe to give them a minute. She reached for Sam's hand. "I don't think so. They were terrified for you. Joe said he never wants to get a phone call like that again. And neither do I."

Sam put his head back, closed his eyes, and sighed, but he held onto her hand. "You never think when you fill out emergency contact paperwork that it might actually get used—and what the effect will be on the person getting the call." After a moment, he looked at Sophie again. "Well, let's get this show on the road."

Sophie had parked close to the steps, and as Sam opened his door, Joe and Matt approached. Sam swung his good leg out of the car but struggled to maneuver the unwieldy cast. Joe reached in to help him, and he and Matt finally slid their arms around him.

Matt didn't utter a word.

"I'm sorry," Joe said. "This is probably going to hurt."

Sam took a deep breath. "It's okay. Just get me inside." He exhaled loudly as they entered the house and lowered him into the wheelchair. He took a couple of deep breaths before he said anything, willing the pain to stop. "Who knew three steps could be such an issue?"

His parents arrived a few minutes later.

His mother leaned down to kiss his cheek. "I brought chicken pot pie for lunch. It was always your favorite, and I thought you might be ready for something other than hospital food."

Sophie suggested they set up in the kitchen, where everyone could fill their plate, and she wheeled Sam to the table. "I'll get your food." She broke the biscuits into bite-sized pieces to make it easier for him to manage with his left hand, then buttered a roll for him.

Sam looked around the table. "This won't be pretty. I'm not ambidextrous." He concentrated on moving the fork from the plate to his mouth while the conversation swirled around him. He knew they were purposely not making a big deal of it all, and he appreciated that.

After they finished eating, they moved to the living room to watch a football game. After half an hour, Sam was struggling to stay awake, and he knew Sophie and his mother could tell.

Laura stood, and Trent followed suit. "You need to rest, so we're going to head home, but we'll be down midweek or sooner if you need something," his mother said. "Sophie, you know you can call anytime."

Sophie nodded as Joe and Matt took the hint and got up to leave as well. Matt walked over to Sam and clapped him on the shoulder. "Anytime you need help with those stairs, let me know." He hugged Sophie briefly and headed for the door.

Joe looked at Sam, his eyes bright, and swallowed hard before he spoke. "Take it easy." His voice broke, and Sam felt the emotion emanating from him. Then Joe turned, gathered Sophie into a hug, and whispered something in her ear.

She nodded. "I know."

Joe kissed the top of her head and followed Matt out the door.

Sam closed his eyes for several minutes.

Sophie said, "I know you're tired, and that chair's not made for napping. Do you want to lie down on your bed?"

"Yeah, but..." When Sophie looked at him questioningly, he sighed. "I need to go to the bathroom. Do you think we can maneuver me onto the toilet?" He rolled his eyes.

She smiled. "I'm sure we can do that." Their first two tries were failures, but on the third attempt, they figured out how to work together, and as Sophie closed the bathroom door to give him some privacy, she said, "Give a yell when you're done. I'll be right here."

After a few minutes, Sam said, "I'm going to become talented at balancing on one foot."

"What? You aren't standing up, are you?"

Sam heard the alarm in her voice, and he chuckled slightly. "No, I'm not done yet. Don't worry. I'll let you know." A few minutes went by. "Hey, Sophie... thanks." He knew he needed to apologize for his behavior since the accident, and it was easier when he wasn't looking at her. "I'm sorry I was such a jerk at the hospital." He paused, then said, "I'm all done."

Sophie helped him up and supported him the short distance to the bed. She lowered him onto the pillow gently, knowing that every movement hurt his ribs.

While she was arranging his ankle on a pillow, he sighed and said, "We were supposed to be running a half marathon this weekend."

"There'll be another one next year."

When he awoke, Sophie was there. "Do you want something to eat? There was food left over from lunch."

"That sounds good. I don't have the energy to go back out there, though. Can you bring me something? I hate asking that. I feel like I'm making you my slave, and I'd never want to do that."

Sophie frowned at him. "Don't be stupid. You and I both know this is temporary." She helped him sit up and turned the television on, then she brought in two trays and sat in a chair to eat hers while he fought to make his left hand do what he wanted it to.

When they finished, Sam lay back. "My family today... I really felt the love. A year ago, I was barely talking to them. I never thought we'd get here." His voice was thick with emotion.

Sophie helped him to the bathroom again before getting him back to bed.

"I can't sleep in all these clothes," Sam said. "Will you help me get them off?"

Sophie gently pulled his T-shirt off first and gasped when she saw the bruises covering his torso.

Sam tried to laugh it off. "You should see the other guy."

She frowned again and removed his sweatpants. The bruises on his legs were not as bad, but they still seemed to shock her.

He tried joking again. "You probably should leave my boxers on—I know you won't be able to control yourself otherwise."

"Actually..." Sophie pulled out a plastic-wrapped package. "PT recommended you sleep in these."

"Adult diapers? Are you kidding me?" Sam shook his head, grimacing at the movement. "No!"

"If you wake up in the night, needing to go..." She paused. "We've seen how long it takes to move you."

"No." He refused to be that pathetic. "I'm not putting those on."

Sophie rolled her eyes. "Suit yourself. Call if you need me."

The need to pee woke Sam up several hours later, and he called for Sophie. Before she could get to him, his bladder let go, soaking his boxers and the bed sheets.

Fuck. Tears flooded his eyes. *I can't do this.*

Sophie

Sophie scrambled off the couch when she heard Sam call. He was lying in the same position she'd left him in, and she could tell he was crying. He'd told her he was going to stick to over-the-counter meds now that he was home.

"Sam, do you need pain meds?"

She stepped closer to the bed and saw the sheets were wet. *Oh, no.* Kneeling near the head of the bed, she stroked his cheek. "You're okay."

Sam wiped his hand over his eyes. "No, I'm not. Look at this. I should have listened to you." The tears continued to flow, and Sophie could tell he was struggling to breathe. "I'm a fool."

Sophie took his hand. "Maybe." Her mouth quirked. "You're stubborn, that's for sure. Let's get this cleaned up." She helped him to a sitting position. "Give me a minute."

Going to the bathroom, she returned with a towel she spread on the wheelchair. "Now, let's get those boxers off." She grinned at him.

Sam's breath was still shaky. "I can't believe you're not pissed at me."

Sophie's grin grew wider. "Double entendre intended?"

Sam sighed. "I don't know. I know nothing right now."

Sophie slid the boxers off and moved him to the wheelchair. "I'll change the bed and then wash you up." She put a blanket over him.

"I probably ruined the mattress." Sam shook his head, looking disgusted with himself.

"The waterproof mattress pad should have saved it." Sophie pulled everything off the bed and took it to the laundry.

"What?" Sam asked, almost sounding normal. He seemed to get his emotions under control. "What mattress pad?"

"Joe bought it. He said you'd never agree to the Pull-Ups." Sophie finished putting on fresh sheets and turned to face Sam.

"I'm that transparent?"

"Joe knows you well." She wheeled him to the bathroom and washed him gently. "I'll confess, I don't know how we're going to make the shower work."

"There's not a doubt in my mind that you'll figure it out." Sam rolled his eyes. "Get the damn Pull-Ups." After Sophie had him settled on the bed, Sam reached for her arm. "Lay with me for a bit?"

Sophie climbed slowly onto the bed, trying not to jostle him.

Sam extended his arm, saying, "Come close to me, please," and she stretched out next to him.

"I've been an ass," he said. "First at the hospital and then tonight. I don't know why you haven't run out the door. This may be the hardest thing I've ever been through. My body hurts, and my emotions are all over the place." He paused, and Sophie could tell he was trying to keep himself under control despite the tears in his voice. "Please forgive me. I'll try to do better."

Sophie slowly rose on her elbow, not wanting to move the bed and hurt him. She kissed his cheek. "The things you said to me when we split made me think, and they led me to some important changes. I want to help you."

"We were going to go out to dinner. To talk."

"I know. I have a lot I want to share with you, but not tonight. You need to sleep."

276

"Will you stay? Here, in my bed?"

In response, Sophie pulled a blanket over both of them.

Sam murmured, "I wish you were in your birthday suit."

Chapter Twenty-Nine

Sophie Drops The Whole Truth On Sam

Sam

THE NEXT TWO WEEKS went by quickly, more so than Sam dreamed they could. He had frequent visitors, and Piper stayed overnight with them on Saturday night so they could resume their movie-night tradition.

Sam slept more than he thought possible, and he and Sophie became proficient at working together to allow him to regain mobility. By the end of the second week, his ribs were feeling a little better.

One night, they had finished dinner when he said, "I think I need to take a shower tonight—you know, since I'm going to see the doctor tomorrow."

Sophie smiled. "The one you took this morning isn't good enough? I don't think you've gotten very dirty moving from your bed to the table and back."

Sam pulled a pouty face. "I enjoy seeing you in your bathing suit." The first time she helped him shower, she'd worn a T-shirt and shorts that had gotten soaked. She started wearing a bathing suit after that, and he began experiencing stirrings he'd been afraid might never come back.

Most nights, she lay with him until he fell asleep, then stumbled out to the couch in the living room, so she would be close by if he needed her.

His appointment was scheduled for early afternoon, and they started getting ready midmorning. Sam had not been out of the house since Matt and Joe helped him in on the day he left the hospital. He'd been practicing balancing on his good leg with Sophie's help, and he was confident he could handle the steps with her—but by the time they reached the ground, he was sweating heavily. Settling into the car was a relief. Sophie said nothing, but he knew what she was thinking.

He sighed. "We're never going to get me back into the house."

"I know." She blew out her breath. "I wanted to surprise you, but Joe and Emma are coming up tonight for the weekend. We'll have to wait until they get here to go back inside." She looked at him. "You're frustrated, aren't you?"

"Yeah. I felt so good last night, and now I feel almost as bad as I did two weeks ago."

Sophie drove to the hospital in silence and helped him into the wheelchair. They were an hour early, so they went to the food court for lunch. Sam watched as she sent a text. He raised his eyebrows in a silent question, but she just smiled.

Sam had started eating when Quinn tapped him on the shoulder. He whirled his head around, saw her, and broke into a smile.

Quinn sat in the extra chair at the table. "Sophie let me know you were here. I wasn't sure I'd ever see that smile again. How are you?"

He shrugged in response, and Quinn looked toward Sophie.

"Getting out of the house today was more of a challenge than either of us expected," Sophie said. "He's a little discouraged."

"I thought I'd made significant progress, but those three steps took everything I had," Sam told Quinn. "It's very frustrating."

"It's only been two weeks," Quinn reminded him. "You look much better than the last time I saw you."

Sophie remained quiet, but Sam caught her pointed look. He sighed. "I am doing better. My ribs hurt less, and I can move around more. Sophie and I have learned to work together. And... both guys who were with me are still here in the hospital. I need to remember all of that."

After going to radiology for x-rays, they made their way to the surgeon's office. When the surgeon finally arrived, he fist-bumped Sam's left hand and sat on a stool in front of him. "Sorry for the wait. It took a little longer to get your x-rays than I expected. They look good. The wrist and the ribs have made progress, and the ankle doesn't look bad either. How do you think you're doing?"

"The pain has decreased, and we're working well together." Sam nodded toward Sophie.

"I knew you would. I want to listen to your lungs, so let's get you out of that chair." He stood and helped Sam out of the wheelchair. "I don't want to make you get on the table. Are you okay with balancing on one leg? Put your hands against the table. That'll help you."

Once Sam had his balance, the surgeon continued. "That's good. Take some deep breaths." He listened to Sam's lungs and heart, then helped him back into the wheelchair. "Everything sounds good. How are you sleeping?"

"That's one thing I'm excelling at," Sam snorted. "I'm sleeping more than I can ever remember doing."

"It's what your body needs. Don't fight it. Here's the plan. I want you to come in for x-rays in five weeks. I'm hopeful we'll be able to take the cast off your wrist at that point. Your ribs should be relatively pain free by then. We'll have you do one session with physical therapy so they can give you some exercises to strengthen and loosen up the wrist. Are you familiar with knee scooters?"

Sam nodded.

"You can start experimenting with one of those. It'll give you a bit more mobility, but don't overdo it." He looked at Sophie. "PT can set you up with one."

"I already took care of it," she said.

Sam snickered. "Of course you did. I never knew how much she enjoyed being in charge, Doc."

The doctor laughed. "It's good to have someone like that around. I'll see you in five weeks, and then five weeks after that. Hopefully, we'll have you in a boot by Christmas. Questions?"

Sam glanced at Sophie. "Just one. Can we have sex?" He grinned as Sophie blushed and turned away.

The surgeon laughed. "You can do whatever you feel like as long as you stay off that foot. I'd probably give those ribs a couple more weeks before getting too hot and heavy."

Sam smiled. "Thanks."

Sophie wheeled him out of the office. "I can't believe you asked that! Did we get back together when I wasn't looking?"

"I want to be ready." He raised his eyebrows. "What are we going to do now?"

"Joe said they'd be here around five, so we have some time. Do you want to visit Michael and Andy?"

He felt a pang of remorse, thinking of the other two men injured in the accident. "I'd like that, although I feel guilty that I'm home and they're still in the hospital."

"It's not like you came out unscathed. You're just able to recover at home."

They went to Michael's room first and found him sitting in a chair, his broken leg propped on a stool. His face lit up when he saw Sam. "Dude, you look a little better than I do. At least you have clothes on."

Sam chuckled. "The best part of being discharged was getting out of that damn johnny. How are you?"

"Better than I was. I had some internal injuries and complications, but things have turned around now. They're supposed to discharge me tomorrow." Michael shook his head. "This has really sucked."

"It sure has. How long are you going to have the cast?"

"Eight weeks. You?"

"Twelve. I'm going nuts." They chatted a little, then talked about their office, which they knew was severely understaffed with them out.

"We're going to stop and see Andy," Sam said. "Have you heard how he is?"

"He's going to be okay. I guess it was touch and go for a while." He smiled at Sam. "Take it easy, and I'll see you back on the job at some point."

Andy had recently been moved from the ICU to a transitional room. He had a head injury that had left him unconscious for ten days, plus a broken pelvis. He was lying flat on the bed when Sophie and Sam arrived.

Sam reached up to take his hand. "Andy, my man, how are you?"

"I'm going to live, so that's a good thing." He looked up at Sam. "We fucked up."

"Pretty sure it wasn't our fault, although that doesn't make it hurt any less. How long are you going to be here?"

"Not sure. They're talking about rehab. How about you?"

"Crushed my left ankle and broke my right wrist. I'm helpless. No weight on the foot for twelve weeks."

"Bet the office is missing us."

"I imagine they are."

They talked for a few minutes until Andy started to fall asleep.

"I'm sorry," Andy said drowsily. "I'm on some painkillers that knock me out. It's not you."

"I get it," Sam said. "We'll take off. Hopefully, we'll all be back to work by New Year's."

"Hey, boss man. You saved my life by insisting on that hard hat. Thanks."

As Sophie wheeled him toward the exit, she asked, "What do you want to do now?"

"I'd like to spend some time outside. Can we go to a park somewhere and sit for a little while?"

"How about down by the river? We can watch the rowers."

Sam nodded and when they reached the riverside park, she wheeled him to a bench.

"Can you help me onto the bench? I'd like to be out of this chair, to feel normal." When he was settled, Sam put his left arm on the top of the bench. "Come here. Let's just be a couple enjoying the day for a while."

She sat down next to him, and he heaved a sigh of pleasure.

Sophie

Sophie enjoyed the feeling of being close to Sam for a few minutes before she shifted position so she could look at his face. She took his left hand in hers. "When I moved out, I spent a lot of time thinking about what else I had to 'drop' on you."

Sam winced. "I'm sorry. I probably didn't word that the best."

"You worded it perfectly." Sophie stroked his cheek. "I had every aspect of my life so locked down, and when I took the time to think about it, I realized there are other things I hadn't shared with you. I haven't totally figured out why I did that, other than my mother's fierce resolve that Charlie not find out how we had lived."

She clasped his hand again. "So buckle up. I'm about to drop a lot on you. When Corey died, I received a significant amount of money through insurance and savings he had. My therapist suggested I invest it. I was so guilty about having money when Corey was gone that I tried to ignore it. I've never touched it, and it's over half a million now."

Sam whistled.

"I know. When I met you about the room, I acted like I couldn't afford the hotel, which was ridiculous." She laughed ruefully. "When I came back to New England last year, I stayed in a campground until the fall air became too cold, because I was as reluctant to spend money as Corey had been. My therapist and I have had some heavy talks about that since I left you."

She shook her head. "I also never told you that Charlie adopted me. I referred to Destiny and Grace as my half-sisters and that was so misleading." She sighed. "They're as much my sisters as Joe and Matt are your brothers. I am Charlie Palmer's daughter through and through."

Sam nodded. "More?"

"I went to see Richard, to apologize for the shitty way I treated him. And then I went to Rhode Island to see if I could salvage things with my family. They welcomed me back with open arms." She paused for a minute. "Well, maybe not Des and Gracie. They were hurt and angry, but Charlie and my mom were so kind and loving and forgiving."

Her eyes overflowed with tears, and Sam pulled his hand out of hers to wipe them away. "It turned out that after the blowup my mother and I had, she told Charlie everything. But he already knew." She relayed what Charlie had told her. "He's starting a new restaurant named My Four Redheads. They never gave up on me, even after not hearing from me for over three years."

Sam remained quiet, so Sophie continued. "I used some of Corey's money to start the food shelf and backpack program at the school. And as you learned from the newspaper article, I spoke at the assembly. I came out of the shadows, so kids who are hungry or without a safe place to live will remember that one of their teachers went through the same thing and survived."

"You've done more than survive." He stroked her hair. "Thank you."

"I'm not even sure if that's everything, Sam. But it's what bubbled up when I took the time to be still and think about my life." She looked up at him with damp eyes. "I love you. Do we have a chance?"

"I hope so, because I love you too."

Chapter Thirty

The Scooter Scoots

Sam

When Sophie turned into the driveway, Joe and Emma were already waiting.

Joe opened the car door and helped Sam out. "How'd it go this morning, getting down the steps?"

Sam grimaced. "Not well. Let's wait for Sophie to get on my other side."

Norah arrived with Piper as they were going into the house, and chaos ensued as Piper hugged first Joe, then Emma, whom she had met when Sam took her to the Tall Ships festival.

Emma introduced herself to Norah. "We brought Italian takeout. It just needs to be warmed up. And we have wine. Do you want to join us, Norah? There's plenty of food."

Norah looked hesitantly at Sam.

"Stay," he said. "We haven't had Friday pizza or Sunday dinner in weeks."

Sophie wheeled him to the table and went to the kitchen to help Emma with the food.

Sam heard glasses clinking and knew that wine was being poured. He wanted to ask for a beer, but he was still taking steady doses of over-the-counter painkillers and wasn't sure how they would mix. He sighed. *I haven't had a drink since that night Dad was here.* While he was thinking, a commotion broke out in the kitchen.

He heard Sophie gasp and watched as she grabbed Emma's hand. "Emma! Is that an engagement ring?"

Emma blushed and nodded as Joe looked at Sam with a grin.

Piper ran into the kitchen. "I want to see! Let me see! Are you and Uncle Joe going to get married?"

Emma smiled. "Yes, we are. Can you help us carry the glasses to the table?"

When everyone had something to drink, Joe raised his glass. "Sophie's eagle eye let the cat out of the bag, and I'm happy to confirm that Emma and I are engaged."

Sam raised his glass of soda. "Congratulations! I think I speak for all of us, when I say we're so happy for you. To Emma and

Joe!" To Piper, he whispered, "Touch your glass to mine. That's a toast, and it's how you celebrate a big deal."

"Do I get to come to the wedding?" Piper asked, touching her glass to her father's. "When will it be? Will it be in Boston?" She had loved the city.

Joe laughed. "Let's sit down to eat, and we'll answer all your questions." Everyone filled their plates and settled down. "We wouldn't get married without you there, Pip. The details aren't all worked out yet, but it will be soon. We're thinking about New Year's Eve, but we haven't decided on the location."

Sophie smiled. "No long engagement for you."

"No, and it won't be a big thing, either," Emma said. "Small and intimate, with family." She looked at Sophie and Norah and said in a lower voice, "We're trying for a baby, so we don't want to wait."

Sophie reached over to hug her. "I'm so happy for you."

"You're celebrating your big news with us," Sam said. "I'm touched. You could have gone anywhere, but you came to the wilds of backwoods Vermont."

"I have an ulterior motive," Joe said. "I'm building you a ramp tomorrow."

"You're what? I don't need a ramp. God!" Sam shook his head in exasperation.

"Sam, you still have ten weeks before you can walk on that ankle. It'll be a temporary thing that will come down as soon as you don't need it."

290

"Did you know about this?" Sam looked at Sophie.

"We talked about it. And after our struggle this morning—"

"It was my idea, Sam," Joe cut in. "It's about your quality of life."

Sam sighed. "Okay, I know you're right." He didn't like it, but it wouldn't be forever.

When they finished eating, Norah pushed her chair back from the table. "Thanks for including me in your celebration. And congratulations!"

"Hey, Pip," Sam said. "Can you wheel me over to the door so I can say goodbye to your mom?"

Piper eagerly pushed the chair and gave Norah a hug.

"This was fun," Norah said. "I never knew Joe—he seems nice, and Pip obviously loves both of them."

"She does. So you'll pick her up Sunday night?" They had agreed that Piper would spend the weekends with him and the weekdays with Norah.

"Yes, I'll see you then. It's good seeing you more like your old self."

As she walked out the door, Sam sighed. The company was nice, but he was exhausted.

Sophie walked over and kneeled beside him. "You're tired, aren't you? They understand. Pip challenged Joe to a chess match. I'll help you get ready for bed and then get her into bed. Joe and Emma will sleep in my room."

"You mean the guest room? Your room is with me."

She put her arms around him. "Are you sure?"

Sam nodded. "No more sleeping on the couch."

Joe had brought the materials for the ramp, and the next day, Sam watched as Emma, Sophie, and even Piper helped him put it together.

When they finished, Joe said, "It's not to code, but it'll let you get in and out of the house."

"Daddy, can I wheel you back into the house so we can see how it works?" Piper asked.

Sam nodded, and she pushed him up the slight incline then back outside, where Joe was putting away his tools. "This is so cool, Uncle Joe!" She ran back up the ramp and into the house. A minute later, she came out on the knee scooter and sailed down the ramp. "This is fun, Daddy! Are we going to have it here all the time?" He shook his head. "No, we are definitely not keeping it when my foot is better."

"Please, please! It's so much fun!"

"I appreciate this, Joe, but it's coming down when I can walk again. I don't want any reminders." Sam's reply was firm.

Piper pouted, and Joe ruffled her hair. "Maybe next summer, your dad and I can build you something even more fun, like a playhouse with a slide."

She looked at Sam. "Will you really?"

Sam laughed. "This is the first I've heard of it, but yes, it sounds like an excellent project for Carpenter Brothers Carpentry. But what are we going to do now?"

"Let's go for a ride and look at the foliage," Joe suggested. "Emma's only been up here twice when we went to the cabin. We can stop and have dinner somewhere. You've gotten better at feeding yourself, so I think we can take you out in public."

Sam rolled his eyes but was happy to be helped into Emma's SUV to get away from the house again.

They drove around for an hour with Sophie and Emma both oohing and aahing over the reds and oranges of the vibrant fall trees. Sam suggested a restaurant, and as they approached, he said, "Pull close to the door to let Sophie and me out. If you help, I can get in without the wheelchair. And I can sit at a table like a normal person."

"Well, I don't know if you've ever qualified as normal," Joe said, but he did what Sam asked, and the five of them sat at the table with little trouble. After they ordered, Joe looked at Sam. "We're pretty sure we'll be getting married on New Year's Eve, and we're thinking about doing it at the cabin."

"You don't think it'll be rented?"

"No one's rented it yet, and I've asked Mom and Dad to block it off from Christmas Eve through New Year's Day. I thought maybe you'd like to stay there for a few days around Christmas."

Sam looked thoughtfully at Sophie. "I like that idea. Hopefully, I'll have this cast off by then. Is Mom going to decorate for Christmas?" Their mother adored decorating for the holidays.

"Yes, I think she and Jilly have it all planned out." Joe paused. "One more thing. Will you be my best man?"

Sam's heart jumped. When Joe had married the first time, Sam had already exiled himself from his family. This would make up for that in spades. "I'd love to do that. How many people will you have?"

"Strictly immediate family. Emma's parents will come, and her sister will stand up for her. I did the whole dog-and-pony show with Tina, so I'm not interested in doing that again."

Emma spoke up. "And I'm good with that. I'd be fine with eloping to city hall, but Joe wants family there. It'll be an intimate, elegant affair."

Joe's eyes twinkled, and he said softly, "Hopefully, by then we'll be expecting a baby. We're trying really hard." He took Emma's hand as she blushed.

Piper reminded them all that it was movie night when they got home. She and Sophie made popcorn, and they settled in the living room, around the TV. Sam was asleep before the movie was half over but awoke at the end when Joe carried Piper to her bed.

After breakfast the next day, Joe and Emma packed their car to leave.

"Thanks for the ramp," Sam said. "It'll make things much easier. And asking me to be your best man..." His eyes filled with tears. "It means a lot to me." He chuckled and brushed the tears away. "This damn accident has made me so emotional."

Joe gave him a quick hug. "I get it. Talk to you soon."

Sophie stayed home with Sam for one more week before they decided he would be okay on his own, so she could return to work. On several days, he took part in virtual meetings for his job, and his mother came to visit at least twice each week. He was still sleeping a great deal, taking a nap every afternoon.

Sam avoided the wheelchair as much as possible, using the knee scooter to move around the house. Despite it getting easier, he still struggled to move from the scooter to the couch or his bed, but he hid that from Sophie.

They had talked a lot about the future and their relationship, but nothing physical had happened between them. Sam longed to touch her and to feel her touch, but he fell asleep every night while she was doing schoolwork, and Piper kept them busy on the weekends.

The day before his next appointment, Sam had a Zoom meeting with his office. After Sophie left, he wheeled over to the table on his knee scooter. He had become more adept at transferring from the scooter to the chair, although he'd had a couple of falls that Sophie didn't know about.

He was thinking about how much he wanted her as he moved from the scooter to a chair. Then the scooter slid out from under his knee, and he landed hard on his hip.

"Fuck! What the hell happened?" Sam looked at the scooter, now mocking him from halfway across the room. "Dammit, I didn't set the brake!"

He struggled to get into the chair and fell again, coming down on his hip a second time. By the time he settled into the chair and logged onto his computer, the meeting was half over, but he was distracted and contributed nothing.

When the Zoom session ended, Sam eyed the scooter, trying to figure out what to do. He finally decided to lie down on the couch. He hopped over, sank onto the cushions, and turned on the television, selecting a sports talk show before stretching his legs out on the length of the couch.

I'm so tired of this. I'm going to have to get up before Sophie gets home, so she doesn't see the scooter way over there and figure out that I fell. He sighed and ran his hand over his jaw before he closed his eyes and fell asleep.

When Sophie walked in, he was in the kitchen, working on dinner.

She kissed his cheek. "This is a surprise."

"I thought I'd get it started. Why don't you do your schoolwork until it's ready? Then we could go to bed together?" He looked at her with a hopeful smile. He'd dreamed of making love to her during his nap and woke up determined to have her come to bed with him.

"That would be nice. I don't have a lot of work to do tonight, since I'm taking tomorrow off to go to your appointment with you." Sophie worked until dinner was ready.

Sam had wine chilling in the fridge for Sophie, and they enjoyed a leisurely meal for the first time in weeks. When they finished, he said, "Come to bed now. I want to be with you."

She nodded, her cheeks a little pink, and followed him into the bedroom.

Sam came out of the bathroom in his boxers and lay on the bed. When Sophie came out, she sat beside him and leaned down to kiss him. He opened his mouth, inviting her tongue to explore, and put his arms around her.

At the taste of her lips and the feel of her body, he hardened and shifted his hips against her. His voice was husky with desire when he murmured, "The ribs are healed. No pain. I want you."

Sophie nodded and reached for his cock, then she slid his boxers off and caught sight of the bruise on his hip. She recoiled. "What the hell is that? What did you do?"

Sam groaned. "It's nothing. Come back here."

"It's not nothing. That's a nasty bruise. Did you fall?"

"Don't use that tone with me. You're not my mother!"

"What?" She looked hurt and pissed. "I'm concerned!"

"Christ, I'm a big boy. I don't need to tell you everything that happens. We're living like we're brother and sister, and now you're acting like my mother." His voice was angrier than he'd ever used toward her, he realized belatedly, and she turned to walk out of the room.

Lying there, staring blankly at the ceiling, Sam could hear her taking care of the dishes that they had left on the table and loading the dishwasher. It was several minutes before she returned, sitting on the bed and taking his hand.

He raised his head, seeking her eyes, and blinked back tears. "I'm sorry. I don't know what I'm doing. I miss you. I miss us. Hell, I miss me!" He sighed.

"Was today the first time you fell?"

"No, there were a couple of other times, but today was worse. I forgot to set the brake on the scooter, and it scooted away from me." He laughed wryly. "Is that a double entendre?"

Sophie's mouth quirked. "I'm not sure." She leaned down and kissed his lips. "Does it hurt? The bruise?"

"Like a mother." He chuckled again.

Sophie kissed his lips once more, and after raising one finger, she walked out of the room. A few minutes later, she returned with an ice pack that she placed gently on the bruise.

She ran her fingers through his hair. "I miss us too. I'm trying to get caught up on work."

"How's that coming?"

"I'm almost there and should be able to finish this weekend. Then I'll start coming to bed with you."

He nodded. "When I don't have this cast anymore, I'll be able to do more in the kitchen. The scooter will be easier to handle when both hands are fully available."

Sophie took the ice pack back to the kitchen, and when she returned, she undressed and lay next to him. Sam hardened at the sight of her, and she reached over to stroke him. He groaned at her touch and thrust against her hand. "This won't take long," he moaned, his voice thick with desire.

"I know. I've missed watching you explode." Her voice was soft as she increased her grip and stroked him faster.

His hips rose off the bed, and he came with a shout. "Oh my God, my God... Sophie." His breath was fast and shallow, his heart pounding like a jackhammer.

When his breathing slowed down, Sophie leaned over him and kissed him. "I love you so much." She went to the bathroom and came back with a warm washcloth. As she gently wiped him, he started to harden again. She smiled at him. "That was quick. Double entendre intended."

Sam grinned. "There's a lot of pent-up desire there. Thank you for that." He gazed at her. "I love you, and I've missed your touch so much. When I'm fully functional, I'm going to make love to you so often you won't even be able to walk."

Chapter Thirty-One

Baby Talk

Sam

THE X-RAYS THE NEXT day showed Sam's wrist had healed completely, and the cast was removed. Sam expected some loss of strength, but the weakness shocked him. During a session with physical therapy, they gave him exercises to regain strength and mobility. He also scheduled an appointment for December twenty-third to see if his ankle was ready for the cast to be removed.

Sam was diligent about the exercises, and within a couple of weeks, he felt like his wrist was back to normal. He started using crutches, which made it easier to get around.

To celebrate, his mother came down to take him Christmas shopping. While they were out, he was measured for his tuxedo for Joe and Emma's wedding. It surprised him when Joe said he needed to wear a tux, but Joe told him it was going to be a small but very elegant affair. He selected Christmas gifts for Sophie and Piper and talked with his mother about a favor he needed when they went to the cabin on Christmas Eve.

Two weeks before Christmas, Sophie drove him and Piper to a tree farm to cut a Christmas tree as light snow fell.

"Are we going to get two like we did last year, Daddy?" Piper asked. "I want one in my room again."

Sam turned in his seat to look at her. "Yes, we'll get two, but I may not be able to help you pick them out. These crutches won't work well in the snow."

"It's okay," she said. "Sophie and I will pick out good ones."

As they walked into the tree lot, Sam leaned against the car. *I can't believe how different everything is from last year. I was so angry at Norah and so alone.*

He smiled as he saw Sophie and Piper coming back on a wagon, hauling the two trees they had selected. As it stopped next to the car, they jumped off, and Piper tried to help the young man tie the trees on the roof.

Sophie put her arms around Sam and kissed him before snuggling her head into his chest.

Balancing on his good foot, he put his arms around her. "You're cold. Let's go inside the shop and have hot chocolate."

Sophie nodded, and Piper ran ahead of them into the store that sold decorations along with hot drinks and snacks. They ordered hot chocolate and cookies before they sat at a table.

Sam slid his hand over Sophie's and leaned over to kiss her neck. "I'm glad you're here with us."

She smiled. "Me too. I've never gone to a tree lot like this."

"Really?"

She shook her head. "Anytime I've had a tree, it's come from some guy selling them on a corner." She chuckled. "They probably came from Vermont. I've watched the trucks loaded with trees the last few weeks, wondering where they were going."

Sam brushed a stray lock of hair away from her face. "We'll have a tree every year, and we'll pick it out together." He kissed her cheek. "Hey, Pip, I think we need more ornaments. You look around and pick some out."

As she jumped up from the table, Sam grinned at Sophie. "Last year was very basic. Some might say minimalist." When she smiled back, he knew she understood his reference to the day she'd moved in all those months ago. "I want to make this year a little more special."

When they got home, Sophie and Piper carried the trees inside, and Sam directed them to the decorations. Together, the three of them worked to fill the house with Christmas cheer. Afterward, they watched a holiday movie, and Piper insisted on sleeping with the tree lights on.

Sam drew Sophie to him as they headed to bed. "This was a superb day. One of the best since the accident. Was it for you too?"

"It was." She sighed, a happy sound. "I love being part of this life with you and Pip."

Several days before Christmas, Joe drove to Vermont to take care of the final details of the wedding and stopped in Thetford to pick up Sam so they could go to lunch. As they waited for their sandwiches, Joe leaned back in his chair and ran his hand through his hair. "I can't believe how much it takes to plan a 'small, intimate' wedding. There'll be twelve guests. Twelve! But we've talked about nothing else for the last two months." He grinned at Sam, who knew his brother was only pretending to be upset.

"Does that mean the baby-making has been put on the back burner?"

Joe's grin widened, his entire face lighting up. "I didn't say that."

Sam studied him for a minute. "She's already pregnant, isn't she?"

Joe nodded, his face still glowing.

"You're gonna be a dad!" Sam whooped. "That's outstanding! How far along is she?"

"Turns out she was pregnant when we came to build the ramp." He chuckled. "We think it happened the night I proposed. She'll be through her first trimester at the wedding."

"I'm happy for you. Three Carpenter cousins."

"Hopefully it doesn't stop at three." Joe paused. "Can you keep this on the down-low? We want to tell everyone after the ceremony. You dragged it out of me."

Sam threw his head back and guffawed. "Oh sure. You couldn't wait to tell me."

Joe looked chagrined. "You're right. I had to tell someone. I'm gonna be a dad!"

Sam recognized the joy and wonder in Joe's voice.

When they finished eating, their first stop was to pick up the tuxes. They tried them on first, and the shop owner took a picture of them together. He handed the photo to Sam, who turned to Joe.

"We didn't turn out too bad," Sam said. "You should give this to Mom when you get to the house. She'll appreciate it."

They made one more stop, where Sam picked up his last gift for Sophie.

As they were driving back to Thetford, Joe asked, "Is everything all set up?"

"Yup." Sam smiled. "Mom and Jilly are getting the cabin ready for me. And this cast better come off on Friday. That's going to be the best Christmas gift ever."

Sophie walked into the house that afternoon and stored her tote bag in the corner. "I'm not touching that again until after New Year's!"

Sam turned away from the counter and handed her a glass of wine. He tapped his soda can against her glass and said, "To vacation." When she smiled and drank, Sam continued, "I can't wait to go back to work. I can't believe I haven't been to the office in twelve weeks!"

"You're pretty sure that cast is coming off this week, huh? What if—"

"Don't even utter those words. I refuse to consider anything else."

Sophie smiled. "I know how much you want it off. Do you want me to bring in some wood to start a fire?"

"Yeah, and then dinner should be ready."

While she was building the fire, he lit candles on the table and poured a glass of wine for Sophie and himself. She came back to the kitchen after the fire was going and carried the plates Sam had filled to the table.

Sam dimmed the lights slightly, and they sat down across from each other. "I love how the candlelight makes you glow. We need to do this more often."

"I think the glow is left over from my workout."

"Well, you are beautiful. How far did you run tonight?" He saw her hesitate. "That's not a hard question, is it?"

"No. I ran ten."

His face lit up, and he reached across the table to give her a high five. "Why didn't you want to tell me?"

She grimaced. "I'm afraid I'll make you feel bad because you can't run."

"We're not doing that, remember? No downplaying something to protect the other's feelings. I am mad that I can't run with you, but I love seeing what you are accomplishing. And I'll get back to where you are. It's just going to take some time."

When they finished, Sam suggested they sit in the living room. Sophie refilled her wineglass, but Sam declined her offer of more. One glass of wine with dinner had relaxed him, and he was determined not to go any further. He put on some jazzy Christmas music that he knew she liked and stretched his legs in front of him. As Sophie sat down, he pulled her legs across his lap, and she settled against his shoulder. They basked in the warmth from the fireplace and the glow of the Christmas tree.

He smiled at a sudden thought. "I bet when you rented that room that you didn't realize you'd be learning how to build a wood fire."

"That's for sure. I've learned a whole new set of skills while living here with you."

"You're a quick learner." He stroked her hair. "Joe and I picked up our tuxes today."

"I didn't know he was coming up."

"He called after you left for school. We went to lunch before going to the store, then he headed north to complete last-minute details for the wedding." Sam leaned forward so he could see her face. "Emma's pregnant." He grinned, enjoying the way her face burst into a joyful smile.

"So awesome!" she exclaimed. "I bet he's excited."

"That's an understatement. He said they're going to tell everyone after the ceremony, but he was itching to tell someone. So only you and I know, and we're sworn to secrecy."

"We can do that. How far along is she?"

"Almost through the first trimester, according to Joe. She was pregnant when they were here to tell us they were engaged."

"They'll be great parents. I'm so happy for them." She leaned contentedly against Sam.

"I am too." He kissed her hair. "Hey, Sophie, scooch over a little so I can look at you." She slid away, and Sam turned so they were facing each other. "I want our kids to grow up with Joe's and Matt's. Piper will be the older cousin, but I hope we'll have ours in a similar time frame as my brothers." He looked at her with the expectant eyes of a child on Christmas morning.

A slow smile lit up her face. "Kids, huh? More than one?"

He shrugged then nodded.

"I like that idea," she mused. "I mean, we've talked about kids but always in general terms. We've never really gotten specific."

"I know. I'm ready to talk specifics. That's why we're out here and not in the bedroom. I don't want to confuse a life decision with good sex. You know what I mean?"

"I do." She laughed. "You don't want us to decide we should make a baby because we had mind-shattering orgasms."

"Exactly." Sam leaned back and grinned. "Mind-shattering, eh? Tell me more."

Sophie gently punched his arm. "I thought you wanted to talk about life decisions, not discuss your sexual prowess."

"I do." He clasped her hands. "I want to have a baby with you. I hope it'll happen easily, like it did for Joe and Emma, but who knows? We could be like Matt and Jilly, and it might take more time. Either way, I'd like to start trying. Will you think about having the IUD removed? Maybe after the holidays? I realize it's a big step."

"It is, but I feel the same. I want to make a baby with you."

Sam hugged her tightly and lowered his lips to hers.

After a moment, Sophie pulled back a little and asked, "Want to practice tonight?"

He nodded, grinning, and she stood, taking his hand to help him up.

Chapter Thirty-Two

Forever

Sam

ON CHRISTMAS EVE, SAM stood at the top of the ramp, looking down at his left foot, now encased in a boot instead of the hated cast. With the crutches under his arm, he gingerly put his booted foot down on the ramp and raised his right foot slightly. It hurt, and he knew he wasn't ready to run a marathon, but nothing could wipe the wide smile off his face.

This was a major step. His first physical therapy appointment would be three days after Christmas, and he was excited about getting his strength back.

Sophie smiled as she shut the door to the house. "It feels good, huh?"

He nodded. "You can't imagine."

It had snowed that morning, and plows were still cleaning the roads as Sophie drove north. The sky was a bright, glacial blue, and the sun glinted off the snow-covered fir trees. "The fall foliage was pretty," she said, "but today I feel like I'm driving through a fairyland."

"It's always pretty right after a storm. How often have you driven on snow?"

"Not a lot. Can't you tell by how slowly I'm going?"

Sam gripped the armrest a little more tightly. "You're doing fine. No offense, but I can't wait until I can drive again. I'm glad the weather is going to be clear for the next few days, especially since we have to drive back this way to pick up Pip."

Soon after the accident, Norah had let Sam know she was dating Tom, one of her co-workers. Sam was happy for her and not surprised—they'd been friends for a while.

Piper was at Norah's house and would celebrate Christmas Eve and Christmas morning there. Sam would pick her up at noon and keep her until after New Year's so Norah and Tom could go on a cruise. After his first PT appointment, Sam and Sophie would take Piper to Rhode Island for a couple of days.

"You're really okay with not seeing her until tomorrow?"

"It'll be hard not seeing her excitement tonight and tomorrow morning, but I'm happy to have her for such an extended period. Last year was so awkward." He shook his head at the memory of sharing the bed with Norah. "And this works out perfectly with Joe and Emma coming up after her newscast, plus Matt and Jilly spending the morning with her family. I can't wait for a private celebration with you."

Sophie smiled. "I'm looking forward to that. You'll be able to join me in the hot tub."

"You better believe it!" Sam relaxed his hold on the armrest. "Piper is so excited about going to Charlie and Lydia's house. She can't wait to see Des and Gracie again. I think they've become honorary big sisters to her."

It was late afternoon and already dark when Sophie turned into the driveway, and she drew in an audible breath as the cabin came into view. Sam smiled too. White lights encased the bare branches of the maple trees, and every window had a candle with a red bulb. A lit tree was visible through the large windows in the upstairs bedroom.

"Oh, Sam, it's lovely—the lights, the snow, and the candles. It must have taken your mom forever."

"My dad and Matt did the outside lights. Another example of how much he's changed. We never had lights like this."

Sophie parked the car, and they walked into the cabin together. A large Christmas tree stood in the far corner, decorated with white lights, pearl garlands, and frosted silver balls. The fireplace mantle featured evergreen garland and woodland creatures. Everywhere they looked held treasures. The fireplace had the wood laid out, waiting to be lit.

Sam gathered Sophie in his arms. "Merry Christmas."

"This is so warm and welcoming. I love it. And you. Merry Christmas." They embraced for several minutes in the light of the Christmas tree before she pulled away. "The car needs to be unpacked." She took a step toward the door.

"I wish I could help you, but I'd probably make it take longer." Sam leaned on the crutches. "But I can start the fire while you're emptying the car."

By the time she was done, Sam had a robust fire going. He helped her put the presents under the tree, and Sophie asked, "Can we sit here for a little while?"

"Of course." Sam dimmed the lights, and they settled onto the couch. The fire cast a warm glow across the room, and he gazed contentedly at her. "You glow even more in the firelight than you do in candlelight—and I know it's not from your workout this time."

Sophie leaned back against the cushions. "That drive was a little harrowing. I know I scared you a couple of times. It's good to relax."

Sam leaned over and feathered kisses along her neck. "There were a couple of little skids that made me tense, but you did okay." He kissed his way up to her lips and gently touched his lips to hers. She opened her mouth to him, and Sam explored slowly, feeling like he had the first time they kissed. He wanted her but was enjoying the leisurely caresses. He pulled her closer, reveling in not having the heavy cast on his ankle.

Sophie pressed her body against him, relaxing into his embrace for a moment before pulling back to smile at him. "I have a surprise for you." Her voice was soft. "I went to the doctor's the day before yesterday and had the IUD removed." Her smile was both an affirmation and a challenge.

Sam's cock leaped to attention at her words, and he smiled so widely it nearly hurt his cheeks. "Seriously?"

Her smile glowed as she nodded in response.

He pulled her in tight and kissed her with ravenous hunger. "Let's go upstairs now. I have a surprise for you too."

When he let her go, she stood, and as he struggled to get to his feet, she held out her hand. "Let me help you get up."

Sam grinned. "Double entendre intended? I'll take assistance for standing, but I don't need any help to get up." He leaned against her as they slowly climbed the stairs.

Sophie stopped abruptly in the doorway to the bedroom, which had a Christmas tree draped in white lights and gold ribbon. Sam watched her eyes widen as she spied the ice bucket in the corner that held a bottle of champagne, plus the small table for two set with a charcuterie board. The lights were dim, and candlelight glowed.

"What is all this?" she asked. "Where did it come from?"

"My mom and Jilly took care of it before we arrived."

"Are we celebrating getting the cast off?"

"Among other things." He led her to the table and pulled out a chair for her. As she sat, he plucked a strawberry off the tray, held it to her mouth, and watched her take a bite. He braced one hand on the table and one on her chair while he leaned down to kiss her.

"You need to sit down more than I do." Sophie motioned toward the other chair.

Sam pulled it around so that they were facing each other.

Mimicking his actions, Sophie picked up a shrimp, dipped it in cocktail sauce, and fed it to him. "This is so special. It's all our favorites."

He folded one hand over hers. "You really had the IUD removed?" When she smiled and nodded, he let out a big breath. "So we're really doing this? Making a baby?"

"I want your child more than I ever could have imagined." She bit into a shrimp, and some of the cocktail sauce stained her upper lip. Sam leaned forward and licked it off. She shivered then picked up a cracker with cheese to feed him. "I thought that's what we came upstairs for."

"We did, and we will. You upended my plans a bit with that announcement." He fed her another shrimp. "This is so hot. How come we never did it before?"

She shrugged and offered him a strawberry. They continued until the tray was nearly empty. Once Sam gave Sophie the last chocolate-dipped strawberry, she groaned with pleasure, and he slid off his chair to kneel in front of her.

Sophie looked at him and tilted her head, a question in those green eyes that Sam loved.

Sam took her hand. "Do you remember the night I told Norah I didn't want to get back together, and you asked me what I wanted? I told you I want to be so overwhelmingly in love with someone that I couldn't keep it hidden. That I want to have babies with that person. That's you, Sophie. I love you more than I ever thought I could love anyone. I want to have children together and spend the rest of my life with you. Will you marry me?" He looked expectantly at her.

She put her other hand on top of his. "I love you, Sam. I want to shout it from the rooftops—yes, I'll marry you! Yes, yes, yes!"

Sam reached into his pocket and retrieved the ring he'd stashed earlier then slid the one-carat emerald-cut ring onto her finger. "If you want something fancier, we can change it."

Sophie leaned toward him. "It's perfect." She slid off her chair to join him on the floor, where she wrapped her arms around him and joined her mouth with his. Pent-up desire burned between them.

Sam pulled her sweater over her head, lowered his mouth to her breast, and aggressively pushed the lacy bra aside to take her nipple between his teeth.

She moaned and leaned into him, then whispered, "Bed?"

Sam nodded, and she pushed up from the floor. He grasped her hand and pulled himself to a standing position. They embraced and then moved toward the bed as Sam ran his hands up and down Sophie's back. When they reached it, she stopped and unzipped his jeans, fumbling with the button.

Sam gently pushed her down onto the edge of the bed, unbuttoned his jeans, and shoved them to the floor as she grasped his throbbing erection.

Sam stumbled onto the bed, his legs tangled in his pants and the boot encasing his rebuilt ankle.

Sophie smiled. "Let me help." She slid off the bed, unstrapped the boot, and pulled it off along with his jeans.

Sam's breath came fast as Sophie stood up, and he reached for her leggings and slid them to the floor. She kicked them away and climbed back onto the bed. He gazed at her, lying there in only the lacy bra and a thong, and shook his head in wonder. His mouth sought her breasts again, and her hand made its way back to his cock.

They went after each other until Sophie caught sight of the ice bucket. "What about the bubbly?"

"After."

She grinned. "Top or bottom?"

"Bottom."

She pushed him to the pillows and straddled him, his erection coming up against her thong. Sophie slid up and down as Sam removed her bra. He fondled her breasts and rose to push against her then hooked a finger into the thong. "This has to go." His voice was a low growl, and she rolled away to take it off.

He reached for her clit, relishing how wet she was, stroking her as she moaned.

Eventually, Sam guided her back on top of him, and his hips rose to put his cock in position.

Sophie slid down the length of him and stopped. "You feel so good. Can we stay like this all night?"

Sam took her nipple in his mouth, biting and sucking and making her squirm despite her best efforts to stay still.

"Okay, not all night," she moaned. "Make me come."

He continued to suck her breast as he thrust into her. Their frenzied pairing continued until Sophie cried out with her orgasm, and Sam followed right behind, emptying himself into her.

They were both breathless, and Sam put his arms around her and pulled her down on top of him.

When her breathing returned to normal, she raised her head to look at him. "How'd I get so lucky to have a life with a guy like you?" Her eyes were bright with tears.

"I'm thinking the same thing. It's been a long journey, and I didn't believe I'd ever be here. We're going to have a wonderful life." They moved and pushed up to sitting positions together. "Now it's time for the champagne. Will you help me?"

"Of course." She picked up the flutes as Sam balanced carefully on his feet. The cork popped with a resounding burst, and champagne splashed Sophie and the flutes.

They both laughed, and she snatched a napkin from the table to wipe it off. Sam leaned forward, leering at her. "I can clean that up."

She handed him a glass, and he opened his arms to embrace her before they sat together on the edge of the bed.

"I've waited so long for this," Sam said, his throat tight with emotion. "Someone to share my life, to build a family with." He put his hand on her cheek. "You've made me so happy."

He brought his champagne flute lightly against hers. "To forever."

The End

Epilogue

Sophie's car had barely come to a stop when Piper jumped out of her mother's car. Sam climbed out of the passenger side and braced for his daughter's greeting, which was always the same.

"Daddy!" Piper threw herself at him, and he swooped her into his arms. "Did you ask her?" She whispered in Sam's ear.

"I sure did."

"And I said yes." Sophie got out of the car just in time to hear what Piper had asked. She walked over to join their hug.

Piper struggled to be put down and shouted, "Let me see the ring!"

Sophie extended her left hand. A diamond ring twinkled on her finger.

"Ohhhh," Piper breathed. "It's beautiful." She turned to look at her mother. "Daddy and Sophie are getting married. He asked her last night." She hopped on one foot. "And I kept it a secret! I told you I would, Daddy." Her eyes sparkled.

There was a pause, and then Norah said, "Congratulations." She grinned at Piper then looked back at Sam. "I can't believe she didn't tell me."

"Me either." Sam chuckled. "And she's known for over a week."

Norah's boyfriend, Tom, extended his hand to Sam. "Congratulations. That must have been an epic Christmas Eve."

"It was." There was an awkward silence before Sam said, "We should get going, baby girl. Your mom has a longer drive than we do."

Piper was safely buckled in the back seat, watching a movie with headphones on, when Sophie said, "Do you think our engagement surprised Norah?"

"A little. Did you notice the pause before she congratulated us?"

Sophie nodded. "Do you think it bothers her?"

Sam shrugged. "I hope not. Not only because she made it very clear she did not want to be married, but because our relationship just didn't work. I'm glad she's involved with Tom. I want her to be happy, and I hope she wants the same thing for me."

When they arrived at Sam's parents' house, everyone hurried out, excited to congratulate them and see Sophie's ring. Once inside, Joe popped the cork on a bottle of champagne. His mother poured sparkling cider into flutes for Trent and Piper while Joe filled the rest of the glasses then raised his. "To Sam and Sophie. May you have many years of happiness."

After all the glasses had been clinked, Sam watched as Emma pretended to sip her champagne. He caught Joe's eye and winked, sure that no one but him and Sophie knew Emma had abstained. His stomach was doing happy somersaults, and he realized this was the first holiday on which he had absolutely no qualms about being with his father. As his family moved toward the great room where they would exchange presents, Sam reached for Sophie. "I love you. I'm glad you weren't upset that my family all knew about the proposal."

She kissed him. "Not at all. It would have been hard for you to pull it off by yourself. I love your family. This is perfect."

Two days later, after Sam's first PT appointment, the three of them were driving through Franconia Notch on their way to Charlie and Lydia's house in Rhode Island, when Piper said, "Daddy, look at the skiers! Have you skied here? When will we go again?"

Sam turned to look at her. "I skied here a couple of times in high school. And I've made plans for Matt to take you skiing the day after New Year's. You know I'm not going to be able to go this winter."

"I know," Piper grumbled.

Sam turned back to Sophie. "I'm going to be the best physical therapy patient ever. I can't wait to do all the things I enjoy again."

Sophie raised her eyebrows. "All the things? I think there are some things you enjoy that you still do very well."

His cheeks flushed, and desire for her burned through him. "Only because you're there helping me."

Charlie and Lydia walked out to greet them as Sophie turned into the drive. "Let me help you with the bags. It's good to see you without the cast, Sam." Charlie shook his hand as Lydia greeted Sophie with a hug and then reached for Piper.

They made their way inside, with Piper holding Sam's hand. She stood on tiptoe, and Sam bent so she could reach his ear. "How long 'til you tell them?" She was struggling to contain her excitement.

"Not long. Let us get into the house."

Destiny and Grace came down the stairs and swooped Piper into a hug. "Wait until you see all the presents under the tree for you!" They yanked Piper onto the sun porch, where an enormous tree was surrounded by brightly wrapped gifts.

"We may have gone a little overboard." Lydia smiled. "We were making up for lost time."

Sam and Sophie settled on the love seat while Piper sat on the floor between Destiny and Grace. She turned to her father with wide eyes, begging him to spill the news.

Before he could say anything, Lydia set platters of food in front of them. "You must be hungry after the drive. What would you like to drink?"

Sam snatched a shrimp off the platter and looked at Sophie. Her eyes twinkled, and he wanted to feed her the same way he had on Christmas Eve.

"I think soda will be fine, Mom," Sophie answered for all of them as Sam popped the shrimp into his mouth.

"Pip, there's chocolate-dipped strawberries here." Sam grinned at Piper as she plucked three strawberries off the tray and shared them with Sophie's sisters. Excitement was bubbling out of her, and Sam knew it was for more than just the presents under the tree. He squeezed Sophie's hand, feeling the same eagerness as his daughter.

Charlie handed them drinks before sitting on the couch next to Lydia. "All right, which one of you is going to be Santa's helper?" He looked toward the twins.

"Can we wait a minute on that?" Sophie said. "I want to show you my Christmas gift from Sam." She held out her hand, and the twins squealed as Lydia gasped.

Piper jumped up. "They're getting married! That's an engagement ring!"

Sophie's mother and her sisters crowded around, gripping her hand to get a closer look at the ring. "It's beautiful," Lydia breathed.

Charlie shook Sam's hand, and Sam motioned to the chair next to the love seat, asking him to sit.

"I know it's a tradition to ask the father first and hope you don't mind that I didn't do that. Sophie doesn't need anyone's permission, but we hope you'll give us your blessing. I love your daughter very much."

"And it's obvious how much she loves you. We're happy for you."

Lydia nodded in agreement with Charlie's words.

"When's the wedding?" Destiny asked. "Will it be a big one, like you had planned…"

Sophie raised her hand. "With Richard? No. It will be much smaller and simpler. We don't know when or where, but within the next few months."

"Will we get to be bridesmaids?" Grace voiced the question both she and her sister had. As thirteen-year-olds, they had been thrilled that they were going to be in Sophie's wedding with Richard.

"I'm not sure I'm going to have any bridesmaids, but if I do, it will be you guys." Sophie tilted her head. "I hope you're not too disappointed."

After the presents were unwrapped, Sophie joined her mother in the kitchen. "The one thing I know about the wedding, Mom, is that I want you to stand up with me."

"Are you sure?"

"Absolutely. When I came here in the summer, Charlie pointed out to me how extraordinary it was that you kept us together through all those hard years. It opened my eyes to how amazing you are. I love you, and there's no one else I want by my side when I pledge my heart to Sam."

Tears flowed from Lydia's eyes as Sophie embraced her.

Afterword

DID YOU ENJOY THIS book? If you did, leaving a review on Amazon or Goodreads is a wonderful way to let the author know. Reviews are one of the most powerful tools in an author's arsenal.

Sneak Peak

WHEN THEY WERE BACK on the road, Tom asked, "Are you surprised about their engagement?"

"No." Norah lied. She shook her head. "Maybe a little by the timing. He's only known her for a year. It was June when they became a couple, and then they broke up during the summer. So, it seems a little fast." She sighed. "I bet Sophie's biological clock is a factor. I'm happy for them." It was just a slight white lie. ...

Four hours later Norah pushed the code to open the gate to her parents' estate. She was nervous about introducing Tom to her parents, particularly her mother. She didn't give a flying fig what her father thought, but she knew her mother would latch onto Tom like a barnacle on a boat.

Mitzi Taylor had accepted Sam primarily because he had fathered her granddaughter, but she never failed to let Norah know she expected a better partner for her than a man from rural Vermont who always wore a flannel shirt and jeans when he visited. Norah snuck a glance at Tom. He was wearing khaki pants, a white open-collared shirt and a black sweater that Norah suspected was cashmere. *Oh yeah, Mom is going to fall in love with him.* She took a deep breath. *And then she'll have grand expectations as to where the relationship is going.*

By the time they approached the front door, Norah's mother was waiting to greet them. Norah embraced her lightly, kissing her cheek. "Mother, this is Tom Sindal. Tom, my mother, Mitzi Taylor."

Tom leaned in to kiss her cheek. "It's nice to meet you. I can see where Norah got her beauty." He handed her a decorative wine bag. "Norah said you're a fan of white wine."

Oh God, I should have know how charming he would be. She smiled at her mother's look of approval. ...

When they moved to the dining room, Mitzi questioned Tom. "Where are you from?"

"I grew up in Darien. My dad was the president of Darien Savings. He and my mother moved to Arizona a few years ago. My sister is an artist and lives in New Mexico. It's nice to be included in a family dinner."

"Where did you go to college?"

"I went to Yale."

Norah felt the sidelong glance from her mother.

Mitzi continued the questions. "How did you end up in Vermont? We know Norah went there because she appreciated their progressive environmental positions."

Norah's father interrupted before Tom could respond. "Frankly, we think it's time for her to find another state to save. Her degree from Columbia is being wasted in that podunk location. She could have tremendous impact here or in New York. It's time for her to give up her little social experiment."

Norah's face flushed. This was not a new topic with her father, but she had hoped he'd have enough grace not to bring it up with someone he'd just met and at a holiday dinner. *Should have known better.*

But her father wasn't done. "When she left the Agency of Natural Resources, we thought surely she'd be done with Vermont. It was rather humiliating the way they let her go. But she let them move her to a brand-new agency. A demotion in every's eyes, I'm sure."

"It was a lateral move, Father." Norah spoke through gritted teeth.

"Norah's doing great things in Vermont. She'd be sorely missed. By the agency and by me." Tom's voice was even and firm. "My ex-wife is from Vermont. We were young when our son was born and living near her parents enabled us both to pursue our career goals. I fell in love with the state. I'll never leave."

Norah relished watching her father back off, following Tom's response. And she especially like his mention of his ex-wife's career goals. *I'm glad he doesn't l act like his was the most important job. How long do we have to stay before leaving for the airport hotel? Booking that early morning flight was the smartest thing I ever did.*

Do you wonder why Norah is the way she is? There's more to her than the character you love to hate. Follow her story in Whispers of Humility coming on July 17, 2025.

Acknowledgements

I'm so happy to finally give Sam his happily ever after and I hope you've enjoyed his story along with Sophie's.

This is the final manuscript that I worked on with Sally Walker and Sheryl Soffer. I've made many changes since we worked together but their voices will forever be a part of my writing and I'll always be grateful to them.

Thank you to my line editor, Mary Morris, from Red Adept Editing. Working with her has been a tremendous education for me.

My brother, Jason Meilleur was a paramedic in a former life, and he helped me craft the scene in the emergency department when Sam was injured. Jason's a great sounding board and I'm grateful for his assistance.

Thanks to Emily Hensley of Small Fry Marketing for her continual support.

My ARC team keeps me motivated and I can't wait for them to read this.

My husband, Gordy keeps the house running, giving me time to write and revise and my daughter Katie helps keep my music choices contemporary. They are vital pieces of my life.

And as always, thank you to my readers for taking the time to read my books. I'd love to hear your thoughts, don't hesitate to contact me.

Also by Sue Mills

Whispers of Goodbye
Whispers of Forgiveness
Whispers of Mistletoe
Whispers of Starlight
Whispers of Healing

About the author

SUE IS AN AVID reader who ventured into the writing world during the first year of the Pandemic. Her stories showcase men and women working to become whole and happy. Family plays a prominent role as do the steamy encounters which come with falling in love.

Sue is a lifelong Vermonter who counts books, sunsets, and travel as vital to her being. Mountains, from the slopes of Vermont's Greens to the towering peaks of Colorado's Rockies feed her soul.

Her children are grown and flown and she's living her happily ever after with the boy she met in a college library fifty years ago.

Follow her on Facebook, Sue Mills – Author

Or on her website, suemillsauthor.com

Or on Instagram, suemillsauthor

And TikTok, Sue Mills, Author